The Man in the Disappearing Suit

J.S. Johnston

J.S. Johnston

This is a work of fiction. The characters, organizations, and events portrayed in this novel are either products of the author's imagination or are used fictitiously.

The Man in the Disappearing Suit © 2024
All Rights Reserved

No part of this book may be reproduced, or stored in a retrieval system, or transmitted in any form or by any means, electronic, mechanical, photocopying, recording, or otherwise, without express written permission of the publisher.

Written by J.S. Johnston
http://jsjohnstonauthor.com

Cover art by James, GoOnWrite.com
Editor: Jessica Ryn

First Edition 2024
ISBN-13 979-8-218-43545-5
Library of congress control number 2024909876

Printed in the United States of America

For Vanessa who is my muse and my strength.

Chapter 1

"Tell me you got the fucker," ordered Peppermint as she stormed over to me from across the barroom. She did her storming in high heels, which was impressive.

You'd think she'd look less threatening in her plaid miniskirt and white button-up shirt, tied at the bottom to show off her navel and skin the color of coffee with cream. In reality, she'd probably stab you in the face with one of those high heels, if you pissed her off enough. She's one of the local prostitutes, but don't judge her for that. She's about as trustworthy as you can expect another human to be. I never did ask for her real name. Peppermint is perfectly fine with me.

I just came from the interrogation of this guy I arrested, Randal Jablonski. He had a strange habit of luring prostitutes into his truck, driving them to an abandoned warehouse, and setting them on fire. Then he put their ashes in mason jars to display on the mantle over his fireplace. I thought I'd do Peppermint the courtesy of telling her she can go back to sleeping at night. Or not sleeping. She does work odd hours.

"Hey, Sean. Good to see you. What brings you here today?" I replied in as sarcastic a tone as I could manage. She didn't look amused.

My name is Detective Sean Papadopoulos. I work Homicide for the Tampa police. God help me. I came to visit her at the Hollow Giraffe. It's this blues bar in the basement of a building downtown, just below a consignment store. You can see from one side to the other since they banned smoking. On Fridays and Saturdays, they have live bands and sometimes they're not bad. The rest of the time, they pipe in the standards over the speakers—Lightnin' Hopkins, Howlin' Wolf, John Lee Hooker. There's no sign out front. You just have to know where it is. It's usually full of people, so they don't bother advertising.

Peppermint likes to hang out here to pick up new clients and network a little.

She stood beside me while I sat on my barstool nursing my coffee with enough sugar to rot the teeth of an alligator and wished I could replace it with Bailey's Irish Cream. I've been sober going on three years now and days like today make me wonder why I took all the trouble. Murderous pyromaniacs can do that to you.

"Yeah, I got him," I told her, with a smirk and a wince. "He confessed to everything." I held back what he did to that poor girl and the zeal that oozed out of him when he told the story. (And he liked telling that story.) There are things that you don't say to women. Call me old-fashioned.

"You didn't have to come all the way down here to tell me. You could've called." She smiled at me.

"I know. I came to shake him off. He was…" I trailed off with a shudder.

Peppermint tilted her head and laid her hand on my shoulder. "Oh? How did the interrogation go?"

"I punched him in the mouth and got suspended." And followed it up with a drink of my inconceivably sweet coffee. I'm not sure why I didn't just order a Coke.

She chuckled through her nose. And kept chuckling.

"It's not *that* funny."

"And you got suspended for it?" she asked. "For how long?"

"A month," I said, taking another sip.

"A month?"

I turned to Peppermint and threw up my hands. "What was I supposed to do? He threatened my boss."

More laughter.

"Try not to sound so happy. I have to see the shrink for the precinct now."

She took a seat on the stool beside me. "Well, thank God for you, Sean. He deserved a punch in the mouth. No, he deserves to sit in prison and get anally raped until he dies, for what he did to those girls." I wonder if you can actually die from that.

"Harsh."

"Butterscotch was—" A tear collected in the corner of her eye.

I put a hand on her forearm. "I know. You were close. That's a harsh sentence, though. Isn't it?" I took another sip of my sugar with a little coffee in it.

"You got a better one?" she asked like it was obvious.

I thought about that for a minute. "I do not. That sounds like a good fit."

She accidentally brushed up against me with the silken skin of her bare leg. She does that. Sometimes, I think it's on purpose. She also has a habit of standing in a way that perfectly shows off the curves of a naked river nymph in a renaissance painting. I think that's on purpose, too.

"You know your job isn't safe," I told her, taking another sip of terrible coffee that I wished had been spiked. "This is one guy that I caught. With all the working girls in the city and all the business they do, how many other guys are out there just waiting for the right opportunity? What would it take to set them off and make a dozen more, just like this asshole? You need to get out of the business."

"Why Detective, it almost sounds like you care." She smiled and pecked me on the left cheek. Women.

"I'm serious. At least put some pepper spray or something in your purse. I'll even buy it for you if you need me to."

"Yes, sir," she said with a mock salute and a grin. I had a feeling that I wasn't actually getting anywhere. "Are you going to Gasparilla, on Saturday?" she asked, changing the subject.

Every year, Tampa puts on the Gasparilla festival. A butt-ton of ships sail along the river while a parade of floats runs through downtown with a music festival somewhere at the end. It's like Mardi Gras but with pirates.

"I think it's full this year."

"Sean." She looked at me like she didn't believe me.

"What? I just talked to all the pirates earlier today. They said it's full. I swear." I turned to Mark, behind the bar and pleaded, "Mark. Help me out."

He's been exactly one day past nineteen for as long as I've known him. With a chin that could hammer nails and a face so muscular that he must have been doing face exercises. Not sure if that's really a thing.

"I go every year," he offered, looking up from the cash register. "I have a whole pirate outfit that I wear. It's fun. You should come."

"Thanks, Mark," said Peppermint, giving him a broad smile.

"Yeah, thanks, Mark," said I, only not really meaning it.

"You need to get out and meet people."

I motioned to the whole bar.

"You know what I mean," she said, putting a hand on her hip.

"I don't know. Maybe," I said. "You gonna be there working?"

"Baby, I'm always working."

Then Peppermint's attention darted past me as if someone called her name. I turned around to find the news playing on the giant TV suspended from the top of the wall at the end of the bar. The graphic over Sally Turner's left shoulder read TIME SUIT. Her expression said she didn't believe what she was reporting. The sound was off, and the closed captions were on. At the bottom, the marquis changed too fast to read.

Peppermint leaned toward me on her barstool, her plaid miniskirt showing every inch of the lean muscle in her legs that I absolutely was not checking out. Without taking her eyes off the screen, she asked, "Does that say…" She didn't finish her sentence.

The normal chatter died down when the barflies pointed at the text on the screen, mumbling to each other. Someone said, "That can't be real." Someone else followed up with, "It's a joke. Hasta be." They didn't sound very sure of that.

Peppermint spun around to the bar and raised her voice to ask, "Hey. Mark."

He was entranced with the TV along with everyone else and almost didn't turn around to ask, "Yeah?"

"Turn the sound on."

"Oh, right." He reached under the bar to pull out two remotes. He hit the power button on the first one and Robert Johnson abruptly stopped. Then he hit the volume button on the other one, and Sally Turner's voice overpowered the murmur of the crowd.

"…claims that what they call a 'time suit' will let the wearer walk through time the way one walks through a room." With a face that a whole team of makeup professionals must've collaborated on, her brows raised like she was trying to convince someone that Santa Claus ate their cookies. "The project has been under development for almost a decade, funded by tax dollars from the City of Tampa as well as generous donations from companies such as Johnson & Waller. The University of South Florida expects to be ready for full-scale trials within the month." She looked down at her laptop on the news desk and shook her head. "Taylor has the forecast for Gasparilla this weekend. Taylor?"

Mark turned down the volume, taking his queue. "That can't be real. I mean, time travel is just in the movies. Right?"

"It's not world-shattering news," I told him. "*Scientific American* did a story on it about a year ago."

"Do I look to you like someone who reads *Scientific American*?"

"I never asked what you do in your free time."

He cocked his head and looked at me. The truth is, I don't read it either. I heard about the article and wanted to get a copy to read it for myself. To date, it's the only issue I own.

"Anyway, the City of Tampa says it's real. I read they sunk millions of taxpayer dollars into it."

"Really?" interjected Peppermint.

"Yep. Eventually, detectives will be a thing of the past. No more hunting for clues. No more interviewing suspects. People will just go back in time, find out what happened and that'll be it. We'll be the joke of the young, along with typewriters and 8-tracks."

She put her hand on my shoulder as if I needed it. "What will you do?"

"Retire." I said it jokingly, but I like my job. I don't want to be an 8-track.

Then, as if it were waiting its turn, my phone played Chopin's Funeral March. I'd set that as the ringtone for when my boss called. As soon as I laid it down on the bar, it sprung to life with her picture on the display.

You'd think she'd appreciate my defense of her with a bonus and a day off. Instead, she suspended me and added an appointment with the shrink for the precinct. So much for chivalry. And what is it with people and shrinks? It's like they think that all our problems will be solved just by talking about our feelings and having a good cry. What would make things better is to rid the world of people like that piece of shit that disgraced my interrogation room today. I don't mind talking about *those* feelings. Besides, Dr. Striker must be getting tired of seeing me in his office by now.

"Is that your new girlfriend?" Peppermint asked.

I chuckled at that. "That's my boss. You know there's no one else for me."

"Uh-huh," she said, looking at me from the corner of her eye. "We need to fix that."

"No, we don't. I deal with enough insanity at work."

"Well, aren't you going to answer the phone?" she asked.

"Why? She suspended me. This is my time. I decide who I talk to." I took another sip of unbelievably sweet coffee as the punctuation at the end of the sentence.

The phone stopped playing Chopin's Funeral March, and the screen went dim.

"So there!" I told it.

Mark snorted a laugh and went off to clean something.

Then the phone started playing again and her picture reappeared.

Peppermint giggled and mussed my hair. "Tell your boss I said hi," she said, then walked away.

I accidentally hit the button to turn on the video chat. Sargent Martinez's face beamed back at me from the other side of the phone.

"Sean," she said, looking surprised I answered. "I have a new case for you."

"Sorry about that. I meant to hang up on you. Now, where's that button gone to…"

"Don't hang up. It's important. You'll like this." Her lips curled into a half-smile. Like she had already won the fight and was just waiting for all the pieces to land where they should.

"Can't you call me Detective Papadopoulos, like they would on TV? It would sound so much cooler."

"Your name?"

"You know. Say it like, 'Detective Papadopoulos, I have an important case for you, if you choose to accept it.'" I did my best *Mission Impossible* voice.

J.S. Johnston

"If you had a name I could pronounce, I'd use it." Sargent Martinez almost looked like she was joking.

"I'm hanging up."

"Let me give you this job first. Then you can hang up," she said while looking at something on her desk.

"You suspended me. You can't give me any jobs. Remember? I'm on an involuntary vacation for the next month."

"What did you want me to do? You hit a suspect. They wanted me to fire you. Jablonski is talking to his lawyer right now. We'll be lucky if they don't sue the city for police brutality."

"He set girls on fire! And he's calling *us* brutal?"

"Yeah. He is, Sean." Sargent Martinez creased her brows. "Even murderous serial killing psychopaths have rights." She looked at me like I should know that.

I had a few ideas of things I'd happily give him rights to but kept them to myself.

"But he threatened you. Isn't that—"

"You don't need to protect me. I'm fine." She looked at something on her desk again. Papers shuffled offscreen. "I put my ass on the line for you with the disciplinary committee." She looked back up at me, took a breath, and continued. "I'm—we're—un-suspending you. We need you on this one."

"Because only my twenty-plus years on the job can solve this perplexing puzzle?"

"Because we're short on staff right now. Higgins retired. Jones quit so he could go be a park ranger in Montana. And Gomez—"

"Poor Gomez," I said, leaning forward over the bar and resting my chin on my palm. "They tell you this job is safe when you take it."

Sargent Martinez looked right at the camera of her phone and said, "I need you on this one. Everyone else already has too much on their plate and it won't wait for you to come back."

"That's too bad," I said, pretending to be interested in something else in the bar. "Love to help, but I have a lot on my plate, myself." And added a sip of my inexplicably sweet coffee, which was now cold.

"You're going to love this case," she said like a middle-aged man giving out free candy. She cocked her head, looked down at her desk, then up at me from the corner of her eye.

I wished I'd tapped the right button to hang up on her. If there's anything that I hate about Sarge is that she knows I can't resist a good puzzle. She's the drug dealer who can always get to me just by waving a piece of mental crack under my nose.

So, of course, I had to ask, "Why is that?" and hated myself for it right away. I am such an addict.

Sarge turned a computer monitor towards her, put on her glasses, then read from it. "William Horner. African-American male in his mid-thirties found dead in the kitchen of his residence of an apparent gunshot wound to the base of the skull."

I waited for her to continue, but she just stopped. "And? What's the part that'll make me want to come off suspension?" I peered over the rim of my Styrofoam coffee cup as I took another sip and waited for her response. It was still cold.

She dramatically looked down and then back up at me from the other side of the phone. "The gunshot entry wound is angled as such that the trigger of the murder weapon would've been out of the reach of the victim."

"And?"

"And there was no forensic evidence showing that anyone else was there that day."

I let the statement hang in the air for a moment and asked, "Not just that the killer is unidentifiable. Right?"

"Nope. I mean, there was no evidence that anyone else was in the apartment at all. No DNA or fingerprints, even partial. All the hair found in the house belonged to the victim. No threads of textiles that didn't match the victim's clothes. The murder weapon was registered to the victim. Forensics did find prints on it, but they all matched the victim—" Sarge sounded like she was reading from a list.

"That's enough," I interrupted, holding up a hand that she couldn't see. "Please tell me Forensics didn't go trampling through the place like drunken elephants and left everything the way it was."

"No promises," she said with a full smile. Damn drug dealer. "Interested?"

"Just text me the address of the murder scene," I said in a

J.S. Johnston
defeated tone.

Chapter 2

"You understand we keep a safe place here," said Jimmy in a slight Arkansas accent as he steered the golf cart around the bend of the parking lot. His name was neatly embroidered on his shirt, just under the logo of the apartment complex. He was the maintenance man assigned to let me into the place. "We never have any break-ins or fights. I think this is the first time I've seen the cops here for anything."

"You do have security cameras around, right?" I asked from the passenger seat. The black vinal upholstering was painfully warm.

"Absolutely. I already told the guys that were here before. Just give me a time and I'll pull it for them.

"Did you ever get to meet Mr. Horner?" I asked.

"Sure, lots of times. One day the compressor on his A/C froze, and it stopped the whole thing. In the middle of June, no less. You know it normally gets to the mid-nineties by eight in the morning down here, right? So, I get the call to go out and fix it in the middle of the day, sweating so much that I think I might've lost a good five pounds when he shows up behind me with a cold bottle of Gatorade. The blue kind. Can you believe that?"

"I love the blue kind."

"I know, right? He looks at me and says, 'Thanks. I really appreciate it.' Can't imagine why anyone would want to kill him."

He took another corner with the golf cart, and we pulled up to the apartment building. The victim's car was missing and already sitting in the impound lot as evidence. I was a couple of days late for the party.

Jimmy hopped out and led me up the stairs to the front door. There weren't any scratches around the keyhole, so it was unlikely that someone had picked it. And it was obvious that no one kicked it in or there wouldn't be much use for a key. The door swung open and stale air billowed out, smelling of mildew and unwashed dishes. At least Forensics left that for me.

"Thanks," I told him and put the little paper booties over my shoes as I stepped into the house. "I'll have to ask you to wait out here."

"That's just fine with me. I'm not sure I'd want to go in, anyway." He leaned to the side, looking in the doorway like it was the haunted house ride in a carnival. "Listen, I've got some stuff I need to get done today. Can you just give me a call if you need anything else?"

"No problem at all. Thanks for opening up the apartment," I said and put on rubber gloves that make my skin feel gross. Better than leaving my own prints everywhere.

I could see the bloodstains in the kitchen, from where I stood in the doorway. The spray pattern of the red droplets stood out against the light blue tile above the counter. Buildings have a way of announcing where someone was murdered. It shouts at you and demands your attention as if humans have another sense, specific to death. Maybe it's just a relic from back when you never knew if something just behind that bush over there hid a lion or something else that might equally enjoy munching on you. But it's impossible to ignore. But they usually make you come in and look around before they show it to you. This one didn't hold back.

As if invited, I shut the door and made my way to the kitchen. Blood has a certain smell to it. It's a slight copper aroma, like a penny mixed with musk. Pus smells like watered-down fingernail polish remover. Organ tissue reeks of burnt hair soaked in gasoline. The delightful smells wafted out of the kitchen, just under that of rotting food on dishes that had clearly been sitting in the sink for a few days. Come join the exciting world of homicide detectives, they said.

I took out my phone to take my own pictures. They have professionals on the Forensics team with cameras that cost more than what I get paid in a month, but I like to keep a record of what I see as I see it.

The blood had sprayed in long droplets, over the counter and back wall. The wall caught most of it, along with small bits of what looked like bone and gray matter, concentrated in the direction of the gunshot. I found a bullet hole at the top of the wall, near the ceiling where it should be. There wasn't any blood on the floor. Horner would have to have been standing directly in front of the counter when someone came up behind him.

On the counter, to the left and near the opening to the kitchen, sat two full mugs of coffee. One of them had a quirky message that read, I HAVEN'T HAD ENOUGH COFFEE TO DEAL WITH YOU, YET. The other one was brick red with no message. The red one had cream mixed with the coffee, or what looked to be cream. No sign of another person in the house, my ass. I'll be asking if they ran prints on the coffee mugs. A little blue ceramic jar marked SUGAR in fancy white letters sat against the wall on the counter. I ran my gloved pinky across the counter near the mugs and didn't find any tiny grains of sugar around either cup.

Beside them was the paper marker left by the Forensics team, indicating where they found the murder weapon. I took pictures of all of it with my phone.

I opened the door to his fridge, just for general thoroughness. It was mostly stuff for sandwiches: lunchmeat, cheese, those little flat pickles, and a good shelf's worth of condiments. An almost full quart of whole milk stood on the top shelf. A quick check of the date printed on the lid showed that it was about to go bad. It was evident that he wasn't much of a cook. His freezer was full of frozen pizzas and flavored chicken balls. The whole concept of a chicken ball is a crime against nature. And to cover it with a chipotle honey glaze is just rubbing it in.

As I closed the freezer door, the flap of something on top of the unit caught my attention. It was so thin it could've been a piece of paper. So, I stood on my tiptoes to get a better look. At the front of it, right by where the magnetic gasket of the freezer door meets the main housing, a little butterfly lay dead. It was on its side with its wings closed like it had just stopped and fallen over.

"How long have you been there?" I asked as if it would've told me. "Don't answer. I'll be right back." I peeked around the kitchen and found the stepstool on the floor of the pantry closet. Then slid it out and set it in front of the fridge, with the toe of my shoe. I assumed he had a box of little plastic baggies hidden around somewhere. And a quick search of a few open drawers produced just that.

I climbed onto the stool for a better view. An inch of dust caked the top of the refrigerator. I pulled my t-shirt over my nose so I wouldn't breathe any in. The butterfly, however, didn't have any. He was a new addition. Now, whether he was here when the victim died or flew in when the Forensics team processed the house, was a different thing, entirely.

His wings were closed. And the parts that did show were a very undramatic tan, with bits of dark tan mottled in. I didn't recognize him from any of the butterflies around here. You never know what a bug can tell you. Sometimes they can mark a rough time of death. Sometimes they'll absorb whatever chemical is around. But I had no idea about this guy. He just looked out of place and made my detective sense tingle. So, I took his picture and scooped him into the little plastic baggy to figure it out later.

A look around the living room showed me a lived-in mess. Blankets draped over the couch, instead of being folded up and laid over the back cushion. Pillows were scrunched up by the armrest on one side. An old brown paper Wendy's bag full of crumpled-up silver hamburger wrappers still laid on the coffee table with the tempered glass top, along with a small stack of books. It looked like he appreciated a good Lovecraftian horror.

Front and center on the coffee table were brushes, gun oil, some solvents, and other stuff that you'd use to clean a gun. I don't think I'd ever seen anyone put that much effort into shooting someone before. If you want to do something right, I guess.

A pair of black slacks had been neatly folded and laid over the back of a wooden chair, by the front door and in front of what looked like was supposed to be a matching dining table of the same type of wood. But instead of being topped with a pretty centerpiece candle and placemats, piles of mail and Amazon boxes covered it.

With my gloved hands, I lifted a few envelopes. Most of it was the expected junk mail, fliers for department store sales, and coupons for fast food. There were a few pamphlets from Scientologists. Some horror DVDs, still in the plastic bags from the store he got them from. Some of the mail was from the Tampa city government and not the water bill kind. Without opening the envelopes, they looked like check stubs. I'll verify that later and visit his coworkers. They usually have a few things to say about who someone's enemies were and whether they had it coming.

The TV sat on a bench made of particle board with a black laminate finish, like an entertainment center. One of those deals you buy in a box and put together when you get it home. On its shelves, as if they were children at their school desks, were the cable modem, Wi-Fi router, and PlayStation all covered in a layer of dust, thick enough to write your name in. It was hard not to. It really was.

Cat toys lay scattered around in front of the entertainment center. A stuffed blue fish that looked like a badly drawn cartoon. A little stuffed milkman. (Pretty sure they don't have those anymore.) A pink and purple plastic ball with a bell in it. I bent down to examine the milkman. He looked happy to be gainfully employed. I bet he never has to smell what I have to smell at my job. Lucky guy.

I stood up and turned to make my way to the back bedroom when a small gray tabby cat trotted towards me from the hallway and stopped at the threshold to the living room. It took a seat on the floor and watched me as if it came to see who and what I was. And it sat quietly, apparently not bothered by my presence. It did like to watch me, though.

"Hello. Are you the watch cat?" I asked it, squatting down to get closer to its level. "I don't suppose I could convince you to give a statement. Did you see who did it?"

The cat looked at me and blinked.

"Didn't think so. A lot of people don't like cops these days. We get a bad rap."

It remained sitting and stared at me from the threshold. A tiny, adorable Sphinx. Some thought bubbles over its head would have been very helpful.

"Hey, where were you when the other guys came through? Did you get scared and hide?"

It walked out of the threshold and turned to stretch out on its scratching post and indulge itself.

"Is that a yes, or no?"

It casually walked to a spot on the living room floor and sat. Then it stared at the empty dark brown reclining chair.

"Poor guy. I bet you miss him. Don't worry, I'll find who did this."

The cat remained sitting where he was, then turned to look at me. Just as a normal process of going into detective mode, I studied the chair and the end table beside it. But the cat wasn't staring at the chair at all. It was looking at the bag of treats on top of the endtable, beside the chair. He must've been sitting in the spot that he always sat in when the victim tossed him a few.

I picked up the bag and held it up. The label read CATNIP FLAVOR. How do people know what this stuff tastes like? What if it didn't taste like catnip? It's not like I'd ever try one, to be sure.

The cat perked its ears and licked its lips, like all those TV commercials.

I came to a knee, opened the bag, and put one in front of him. "Here ya go, buddy." He gobbled it up and looked at me, expectantly. "That was fast. Want another?"

He fidgeted like I do when the pizza delivery car pulls up in my driveway. I passed him another. He purred as he gobbled it up, as quickly as the first.

"Does this mean we're friends, now?"

He licked his lips.

"If we're friends, then we're going to need to work on your English." Then after a moment's pause added, "Hey, if you've been alone here for days, how long has it been since someone fed you?" I tossed him another treat.

My pants started playing the Funeral March. I mean, the phone in my pants. Whatever. I flicked on the video chat and Sargent Martinez looked back at me from the other side.

"Well?" she asked, expectantly. "What did you figure out? Was I right?"

"He knew his murderer," I started. "He even made coffee for them. They like theirs with cream and no sugar."

"How do you know that wasn't the victim's coffee?"

"Because they didn't have any cream in their fridge. Just an almost full bottle of milk about to go bad. That means they had a guest who asked for it and all he had was the milk that he never drank. Ergo, we're looking for someone who takes their coffee with cream and no sugar."

"I'll put out a dragnet," she said with a sarcastic smile.

"See that you do," I said jokingly, but it didn't sound that way. The cat rubbed against my hand, redirecting my attention. His black stripes were so perfect, you'd think he had his outfit specially made for him. I set the bag on the floor and used my free hand to pull out another treat.

Sargent Martinez watched the probably erratic movements from the camera on the phone and asked, "Did you find something?"

"It's just the witness," I said, half paying attention.

"There was a witness?" she asked, surprised.

"Yeah, but they're refusing to talk. It's a gray tabby."

"They're good at keeping secrets. Have you already called Animal Control?"

"It's okay," I responded as the little guy rubbed against my hand with his furry cheek. I stroked him along his back, in return. "He can hang out at my place until the victim's family claims him."

"So, was I right?"

"About what?"

"About you wanting to take this case."

"Yes," I said with a little venom. "You're an enabler, you know that."

"If that means, 'a good manager who understands the strengths and priorities of the people on her team,' then yes, I am."

"Yeah, yeah. Semantics. Did Forensics really not find any DNA or textiles, other than Horner's? I'd like to think he didn't let someone in wearing a hazmat suit. Unless that's what the kids are wearing, these days."

"You'll have to check with Ron, but that's what they tell me. The place was clean."

"Maybe we're looking for a coffee-drinking ghost, then," I said.

The cat laid down, leaning his back against my leg. I continued to pet him. He stretched out and got comfortable.

"So, what else did you find out?" Martinez asked.

"Nothing interesting. The victim was single and lived alone. He worked too much to have time to cook. But he liked to take books to work, so he must've had a lot of downtime. He made half-decent money, working for the city. And he splurged on a game console, even though he never played it. I probably would've gotten along with him just fine if I knew him when he was alive."

The cat started making slow drowsy blinks.

"Did anyone check the top of the fridge when they came through here?" I asked, remembering what I found.

"Checked it for what?"

"Anything." I shrugged. "It was a mess up there."

"You'll have to check—"

"With Ron. Right. Doesn't hurt to ask."

"Sure doesn't. Enjoy your case, Sean." Her tone of voice was that of a mother glad that her kid liked their Christmas present. That look from the other side of the phone didn't help. I hate that woman.

Chapter 3

I'm in the passenger seat of my mother's car and she's driving on the interstate. The car is an electric golf cart. The sun is out, and it's too bright. For some reason, there are no other cars on the road. We go over a tall bridge that snakes around, over, and under other snake-like bridges that do the same. And for some reason, the fact that my mother died over twenty years ago doesn't bother me.

"I wouldn't have to take you to school if you'd finished all the classes," she told me. "You're three credits short, Sean. Driving a man your age to high school is an absolute disgrace. This is why you're single. Any woman would have to be out of her mind to date someone like you."

I take my mother's scolding with a forced smile because that's what you do. And because I agree with her. "How could I let that happen?" I ask myself. I should be ashamed to have missed such a huge detail and I am. I'll be the oldest guy there.

My mother takes the exit and gets off the interstate. She drives about a mile down some road, then takes a right. We end up in an unlit, rundown alley. Metal trash cans, full to overflowing, line the brick walls. Somehow, it's darker than it was. But not quite night. More like dusk. A small group of people stand in a rough circle, talking to each other. One of them is a cuttlefish, from the waist up and I don't think it's weird.

"We're here. Get out," my mother told me. I get out of her car, which is an electric golf cart, close the door that it has for some reason, and find myself naked. I try to cover the important bits and look for clothes to change into before anyone sees me. But they do see me, and they aren't bothered. So, I stand with them and wait for whatever we're waiting for.

Then the other people are gone. In front of me is the figure of a man. Not a person, though. Just the figure of one. As if a man once inhabited the space in front of me and then disappeared, leaving behind an absence; a man-shaped void, completely black.

It's like looking into a dark room. But there is nothing there, not even empty space. Empty space would be something. But there is nothing. I want to disappear into it. The void is shaped like me. It is death. Suddenly filled with mortal terror, I take a breath and cannot exhale. I cannot look away from the void.

As I back away, I stumble over my feet and the tiny bumps of the dirt road. The void and I are suddenly at the intersection of a crossroad made of hardened dirt, surrounded by empty fields of more dirt. It's night, and all there is is the void.

It turns a head that isn't there and looks at me with eyes that don't exist. The void has been my companion since birth. It has always watched me. And it has always followed me. I look for something to hide behind, but there is nothing.

The void speaks my name in a voice like the cutting edge of a blade, sliding along the soft skin of my stomach. Fear keeps me from running. It takes a step towards me with legs that it doesn't have.

I fall to the ground and take a face full of mud. The searing pain of fire travels through my limbs. I cry out but don't make any noise.

The void takes another step. I scream louder, desperate for anyone to help me. But nothing comes out of my mouth. The laughter of something that isn't there saturates everything. It keeps laughing. It sounds like cruel children with an unfortunate animal.

Its hands are now three long, angled lines that look more like the branches of a tree. It curls its hands into fists and reaches back, almost in slow motion, then brings them down on me like hammers.

I cannot move to get out of its reach. I am unable to stop it. I watch the death blow come for me and shield myself from the coming assault with all my strength and scream.

* * *

I fell off the couch, still screaming, and somehow knocked into the coffee table which spilled a glass of sweet tea all over me. The blanket that normally lies folded up neatly on the back of the couch came with me and tangled me up like a net, and I tried to swim out before I drowned.

"Damn it!" I shouted to the room, peeling off the soaking wet and probably now tea-stained cotton blanket that my parents bought me for Christmas. I really liked that thing, too.

It was just a nightmare. Another one. They woke me up at least a few times a week. An occupational hazard. You'd have to be a psychopath not to have them, doing what I do for a living. They usually don't end so dramatically, though. Or rather, I usually don't end up having to wash something afterward.

I picked myself up and tossed the soggy blanket in the corner, fully intending to deal with it, later. It landed with an unappetizing splat, and I almost laughed. I righted the coffee table and slid it back over by the couch and took my seat.

I must've fallen asleep, going over the security camera footage from the apartment complex, on my laptop. As it happens, Horner's door wasn't in any of it. I'd hoped that it was as simple as finding out who came to visit him, that day. But I guess if this job were easy, anyone could do it. The view from one camera ends at the building to the right of his and the other ends at half a building to the left. Both have a clear view of the road and parking lot, and I could even read the license plates. That's what I was going through when I must've fallen asleep. I'm not sure why, though. Unless I know who I'm looking for, then they're just cars.

T.J. continued to nap on the back of the couch, completely unmoved by my predicament. Good to see that if the proverbial excrement ever did strike the air-circulating device, he'd be on top of things. That's what I've been calling him. He's only here until I can get one of Horner's friends or family to take him. It just felt weird calling him Hey Cat until then, is all. Well, to be completely honest, I gave him a full name as Thomas Jefferson Hooker. Somehow, I couldn't pass up a good reference to an eighties cop show. Another occupational hazard.

"Don't worry about me. I'm fine," I told him as he ignored me and comfortably shifted his weight on the back of the couch to get even more comfortable. He did look very skilled at that.

I fluffed the pillows on the couch and stuffed them in the corner by the armrest so I could try to attain his mastery of comfort. He was challenging me with his long, full-body stretch.

Chopin's Funeral March interrupted the moment and Sargent Martinez's face displayed on my phone.

"For God's sake, what now?" I said to myself, as I reached for it.

"Sean," she said as soon as I hit the accept button, not even waiting for me to say hello. "I'm sending you something."

The phone's SMS text notification chirped.

"Have you seen this on the news?" she asked.

"What?" I asked, flipping to the feed.

"Just watch it."

It was a YouTube link to a news story on CNN. The bottom of the screen prominently displayed the words TIME SUIT in giant letters.

I paused it and said, "I saw something about this, the other day."

"Just watch it," she said.

I tapped the play button. The young Julia Withers sat bolt upright at the news desk in her pastel green dress, perfect makeup, and dark copper hair that I was certain a team of professionals worked very hard on just moments before. She straightened a stack of paper that I'm sure she intended to convey an image of a finger on the pulse of society, looked at the camera with sparkling eyes, and read from the teleprompter in a voice of authority.

"Have nothing to wear and no time to buy anything? Dr. Khatri of the University of South Florida's Physics department, with partial funding from the City of Tampa and companies like Cougar Technologies and VioTech, has been working on a suit that will let the user walk backward in time." She drew out those last three words for dramatic emphasis. "And no, I didn't misspeak. The garment will actually allow the wearer to travel through time. Our science correspondent Will Beats is with Dr. Khatri now and has the details of the story. Will?"

The video cut to a slender man in his thirties with a perfectly tailored suit, holding a microphone and standing in what looked to be a laboratory. Behind him, a white counter ran continuously along the length of the wall, covered in microscopes, stacks of books with different colored sticky notes shoved in between the pages, and laptops that looked nicer than mine. To his right were two women in long white lab coats.

One was an older Indian woman, with salt and pepper hair, cut short, just over her ears. Her large eyes were the color of black opal. Their outer corners curved upwards when she smiled for the camera. I assumed she was the doctor they mentioned.

Standing beside her was a shorter, and very young-looking girl with bright, almost fluorescent blue hair that was teased into loose curls and ran halfway down her back. I was certain that you couldn't find that color of blue, anywhere in nature. Under her white lab coat, she wore a knee-length poofy skirt that matched the color of her hair, only with an added metallic sparkle. I remember buying the doll version of her for my niece's eleventh birthday. She was very excited about it.

"Thank you, Julia," said Will Beats as he straightened his tie. "I'm here at the University of South Florida in Tampa with Dr. Chetna Khatri, head of the Physics department, and her assistant, Clara Heartwell."

Both of them smiled their practiced smiles to the expertly groomed Mr. Beats. The older one straightened her lab coat. The one with blue hair waved to the camera.

"Doctor, I read the paper you wrote on this invention. I have to admit to our viewing audience that I didn't get half of it. Can you explain to the world what makes a time suit work?" Will Beats moved the hand-held microphone with the station's logo over to Dr. Khatri.

"Well," the doctor started, her eyes lighting up. "The suit is made of a matrix of quantum tunneling tachyons, paired in a repeating asymmetrical lattice. Coupled with—" She had been making hand motions in the air as if pointing to something invisible.

"Doctor, Doctor… I hate to have to cut you off. Is there a way you can rephrase that in more layman's terms? Most of our viewers don't have the level of education to know what all that means," requested Will Beats.

Dr. Khatri frowned and looked like she needed a moment to figure out how to do that. Then her assistant Clara, the girl with the glowing blue hair, leaned into the microphone and said, "I'm sorry. What Dr. Khatri means to say is that we've used our knowledge of quantum physics that scientists have been building since the days of the first atom bomb to develop the suit." She looked at the camera and smiled with pride.

"Thank you, Clara. That was well-spoken," said Dr. Khatri with a lingering Indian accent.

"And it lets the wearer travel through time?" asked Will Beats. "Is that right? Is that in a literal sense?"

Both women leaned into the microphone, at the same time, about to say something.

"Go ahead," said Dr. Khatri to Clara, smiling proudly.

She smiled back and answered the question. "That's a little more complicated. You don't travel through it, like in H.G. Wells. That's impossible, according to our current understanding of physics. You travel within the substance of time." She made a gesture with her arm that looked like a swimming fish.

"I'm sorry, you've lost me there. How do you travel within the substance of time?"

"Well, in practical terms, it doesn't deposit you in a certain time, like a DeLorean. You're not part of it. It's more like walking through a museum of another time. You can see everything, but you can't touch any of it."

"That's really mind-blowing if it works."

Clara quickly nodded her head and didn't hold back any amount of excitement from her voice. "We've already had multiple successful tests with the suit. It works."

I paused the video. "They've done this, already?" I asked, unable to hide my alarm.

Martinez laughed. "Yes. They have." The smile on her face was audible. "I've seen it work."

"Wow…" I couldn't think of anything else to say.

"Keep watching," she said.

I hit play.

"Will it show me next week's winning lottery numbers?" he asked in a very game-show voice.

"So far, we've only been able to use it to go upstream to the past. If we could get the winning lotto numbers, we wouldn't need all that funding."

"So, no future, then."

Clara shook her head. "Sorry. No future."

"Well, there you have it," Will Beats said, turning to the camera with his microphone, prominently displaying the station's logo. "Looks like I still have awhile before I can retire to my own private island. Back to you, Julia."

The video ended there. After that article in *Scientific American*, they'd still have to get interviewed on CNN before I'd believe it. And there they were. Hell of a thing to wake up to.

"So just the past, then. Still. Wow…" I said, imagining what I could do with it. "That bit about walking through a museum and not being able to touch anything sounds wonderful. It sounds exactly like what I wish the Forensics team would do, so I can have something to look at when they're done. You think Columbo ever had that problem?"

She snickered. "Columbo didn't need a forensics team. That's why he was so awesome. He could solve the whole thing just by talking to people."

"I know, right? Anyway, why are you calling? You could've just texted me this."

Her voice slowed the way it does when she's about to tell me something important. Usually, it means explaining to me why I'm not getting a raise. "Sean, the City of Tampa donated a lot of money to the project because we think we can use it."

I brought the now-empty glass of sweet tea into the kitchen for a refill and pulled the jug from the fridge.

"Yeah. That's what I read," I said. "I'd love to be one of the people on that team."

"You will be," she said. "That's what I called to tell you."

"What's that, now?" I took a drink of sweet tea, standing in the middle of the kitchen.

"You're the senior-most detective in the precinct. I'm making you head of the time suit project."

I spat a mouthful of my sweet tea all over the stove, almost choking on the remainder.

"What was that noise?" Sargent Martinez asked.

"Can you say that, again?" I asked, wiping my mouth with the back of my hand.

She laughed, "I said I'm making you lead on the time suit project. Congratulations. You'll assess how useful it is to us and whether we should continue funding or not. Then provide your feedback to the Physics Department at USF so they can design the next version of the suit. Try not to fuck it up."

"I… Now I'm not sure how I feel about that. Does my life insurance cover death by freak time travel accident?" I set my glass on the counter by the sink and walked to the living room where T.J. watched me from the back of the couch.

"You'll be fine," she said.

"So, when do I get to go time-traveling?"

"I'll let you know," Sargent Martinez said, then whispered to someone else. "I have to go. Talk to you at work." She hung up.

I set the phone on the arm of the couch and asked T.J., "What do you think? Sound like fun to you?"

He looked at me for a minute then curled up to go back to sleep with a long, deep sigh.

"You're right. It'll be fun."

Cheeseburger in Paradise played on my phone. T.J. woke up and turned his head toward the music.

"You like this?" I asked, gesturing to the phone. He ignored me. "You are so weird." The way he was still laying on the back of the couch like he was melting onto it made me jealous.

Cheeseburger in Paradise was for Ron. I set the ringtone back when I used to drink, I just can't remember what it has to do with him. That's part of the reason I stopped drinking.

"Hey gorgeous," he said from the other side of the video screen. My detective skills told me he didn't really mean that.

The image of myself on the self-facing camera showed me just what my hair looked like after waking up on the couch and almost drowning in a sweet tea-soaked blanket.

"You're just jealous that my hair looks better than yours."

"You caught me. That's exactly what it is." I didn't think he meant that, either.

I brought the blanket to the washing machine and tossed it in. "So, what's up?" I asked.

"Did you forget about the blood tests? All the forensic stuff is done."

"Oh right!" I started the washer.

"Come and get it," Ron said, nodding to someone offscreen.

"Be right there!"

"Fix your hair, first."

"Whatever, Mom."

I threw on a pair of pants, told T.J. to watch the place, and drove into the station.

Chapter 4

I stood at the entrance to the Forensics room (which strangely looked like my high school chemistry lab) and knocked on the open door.

A long row of stainless-steel tables ran along the length of the wall and another one ran parallel to it in the middle of the floor. Microscopes, small stacks of shelves full of plastic bottles, large beakers of God-knows-what, and random appliances overcrowded their tops. One of those hooded vent things stood against the left-hand wall. Black electrical cords about as big around as my thumb hung from the ceiling and I really didn't want to know what they were for.

A boy who looked like he was made out of pipe cleaners looked up from a stack of books. And by "boy," I mean he looked like he was too young to work here. His skin was almost porcelain and perfectly unmarked by the wrinkles and blemishes that come with age, except for the scattering of freckles on the bridge of his nose. His short red hair made him look like a pop star, waiting to be discovered. If it wasn't for his wireframe glasses, you could easily mistake him for Jimmy Olsen.

"Can I help you?" he asked like I was standing in line at McDonald's. He'd been sitting at his desk, just under the poster of the bald eagle perched on a branch that read FORENSIC INTEGRITY in big, bold letters.

"I'm Detective Papadopoulos. Ron called me about the William Horner case. Is he around?"

"Right." He stood up from his chair and called out into the back room. "Ron. Detective Papa-coppa-something is here, about the Horner case." He sat back down and turned his attention to whatever was on the screen of his desktop computer.

"It's Papadopoulos," I corrected him as politely as I could. "Pappa-dappa…"

He turned his head slightly, still not looking away from the computer screen, then went back to his book.

"Forget it," I said.

He flipped a page and adjusted his glasses.

"Must be a good book. What're you reading?" I stepped inside the room and tried to peek over his shoulder.

He finally turned to meet my eyes. Before he answered, he lifted the cover just enough to show the title of the book. For emphasis, he said it out loud. "Analytical Perspectives on Interpretations of Forensic Sciences. Third Edition." Then he went back to reading it.

After a moment of awkward silence, I asked, "Was the library all out of Harry Potter books?"

He stopped reading, sat bolt upright, and turned his chair to face me in a slow ordered fashion. Then he pushed his wireframe glasses up the bridge of his nose. He didn't say anything. He just stared at me.

"Unless that's not what the kids are reading these days."

More staring.

"Percy Jackson?"

More staring.

"Help me out."

Nothing.

"Ron!" I called to the back room, with some urgency.

The red-headed boy slowly turned back to his fancy pants textbook. There're probably big words in it. Like semi-permeable membrane. And cheiloproclitic.

"One second," ordered a husky voice from the back. In a few moments, he walked out, straining to carry a large cardboard box marked CASE NO. 1225485. His dark, shaggy hair insisted on falling in his face, as he did. The unkempt beard and thick layer of man-hair covering his arms might make him look like a werewolf, but his temperament was more family dog than wolf. Also, he's an evidence tech. So, not a real cop.

"Hey, Ron," I said.

J.S. Johnston

"Hey." He slid an empty pizza box onto a table in the center of the room and put the box down.

"Anything left in that?"

"You're about a couple of hours too late," he said.

He opened the hinged lid of the box as I leaned over the table to ask in a hushed tone, "Is he new?" I edged a thumb in the boy's direction, in case Ron didn't know who I was talking about.

"Yeah. That's Allister. What's wrong?" he answered in an equally hushed tone.

"I don't think he likes me."

Ron chuckled. "He's fine. You're just shit with people."

"It is kind of a superpower." I stood up straight and asked in a normal voice, "So what've you got for me?"

"Nothing you can use. I mean unless you can use the fact that there's nothing." He picked up the pizza box, stacked it on top of another one, and put those by the trash can by the door. Ron was a large man and knew it. It did not stop him from eating whatever he wanted. Sometimes he shared.

"That's a lot of nothing in that box," I said, peering in.

"Oh, I have lots of *stuff*. The blood-stained clothes the victim was wearing at the time. The murder weapon, blood splatter samples, fingerprint transfers… but nothing that would actually help." He took out the plastic evidence bag with the murder weapon and laid it on the table. It was a Smith & Wesson Model 64. Even when they're not covered in blood splatter, those things look mean.

"Those are usually things that I find very helpful," I said.

"The gun was obviously just fired when we found it, laying on the counter. It was practically floured in gunshot residue. And we confirmed the wound on the victim matched the fire pattern of this specific gun when we tested it. There's no doubt it was the murder weapon," Ron said in a matter-of-fact tone.

"However?" I asked.

"However, all the prints belonged to the victim. All of them. Like he reached around and shot himself in the back of the head."

"So, you did find prints on it." I folded my arms and leaned back against the wall.

"Yeah, we did," he said. "They didn't wipe it down, afterward. We pulled clear prints from it and later matched all of them to the victim."

"But he *was* shot in the back of the head, right?"

"You got it. Right in the old brain stem. Unless he's secretly part octopus, there's no way he could've done that to himself." Ron made a hand like a gun and pantomimed the action of shooting.

"And there's no chance you just got the entrance and exit wounds backward."

He looked at me like I asked him if he knew how to tie his shoes.

"Didn't think so." I picked up the gun, still in the evidence bag. "You know, they might've been able to do that by just wearing rubber gloves. But I'm guessing that you didn't find any residue."

"And your guess would be right. We didn't even find DNA on it."

"That doesn't sound that unusual. Right?"

"These new tests can sequence the genetic material from no more than a cell or two in the little droplets of mucus left behind from just breathing on something. And we didn't find a thing." Ron said and took the gun back from me.

"Seriously?"

"Seriously," he said. "You don't know how many times we've found DNA that turned out to be one of the lab techs. I yell at all of them not to open any evidence bags outside the enclosure, but do they listen?"

"I listen to you, Ron."

"No, you don't."

"You're right, I don't," I said. "So do you have anything for me that I can use?"

"Well, I can't make it easy on you," Ron said, smiling.

"You could try."

"But what fun would that be?"

"It would be lots of fun for me," I said.

He chuckled and put the gun back in the evidence box.

"Hey, you didn't happen to see the victim's phone when you were processing the scene, did you?"

"Do you really think I'd keep that from you?" Ron asked.

"I don't know. You might hold it for ransom and trade me for a tuna sub." I said, eyeing the empty pizza box.

"Well… I'm not."

"Didn't think so. What about getting a psychic to look for ghosts?"

"If ghosts could kill people, there wouldn't be much use for the death penalty," Ron said as he pulled the evidence box toward him.

"That," I pointed at him, "Was a very good point. There would not be much use." My pants played the first few bars of Kumbaya.

"Your pants are singing again, Sean."

"Well, someone has to. I don't hear you singing."

"Yeah, they told me to stop doing that."

I pulled my phone out and shut off the alarm. "It's just the reminder for my appointment with Dr. Striker."

Ron chuckled. "What was it this time?"

"I hit a suspect."

He laughed hard. And he kept laughing for a while. "What happened?" he asked as he wiped the laughing tears from his eyes.

"He threatened Sarge. And that was after he just got done telling me how he burned a girl to death. I mean who does that?"

"You really suck at this job."

"Yeah, I know." I pulled the box toward me for a quick rummage, before leaving. "Oh, one thing, before I forget." I pulled out the little butterfly that I had stuffed in the baggie. "You missed this guy at the crime scene. He was lying on top of the fridge, already dead. Can you tell me if it's significant?"

Ron turned around and called, "Allister."

He was already looking over and listening to our conversation. As he put his pen down in the spine of the boring textbook he was reading, he said, "Let me see." I handed him the bag, and he gingerly held it up to get a better look.

"Hello, you," he lovingly said to it and adjusted his glasses. "Can I take him out of the bag?" So now he talks.

"Sure, I guess. It's not like it was a pet," I answered.

Allister turned around and practically skipped over to his desk. He moved a lamp and straightened a stack of folders to make a small platform. Then he opened the bag and slid out the little brown butterfly.

"Don't be shy. I'm a professional." I was about to ask him what he was talking about until I realized that he was talking to the butterfly. He grabbed a pen from somewhere and inserted the point between the wings. When he touched the bottom one with the top of his finger and lifted the pen, the room brightened. The tiny butterfly's open wings were an impossible pure orange, like electrified neon. Allister's eyes swelled as he said, "Dryas iulia," like he was reciting a magic spell.

"So, is that significant?" I asked, standing over his shoulder. "Is it rare?"

"Not really," he said definitively. "But if humans keep spraying pesticides and clearing woodland areas, it could get there. And—"

"Allister," said Ron from across the room.

"Right. Sorry. I mean, it's very common in the sub-tropics. You can find them anywhere from Florida to Brazil. They tend to keep to the forests and swamps, though. There's not much for them, in the city. Where did you find him?" So talkative, now.

"On top of the fridge in the victim's house," I said. "It didn't look like a forest. Can you tell me anything about how it lives? Are they raised by hobbyists?"

"Sometimes hobbyists raise them, sure. A lot of zoos keep them because they're easy and active during the day. Just put out what they need, and they'll be fine." He looked at it for a while and started to trail off. "They drink from mud puddles, like a lot of other butterflies. Oh, and they're lacryphagous."

"Are they contagious?"

His expression dropped from his face. "Lacryphagous means they drink tears. A handful of species do that. They irritate the eyes of alligators; their eyes water and they lap it up."

"I'm sorry. It does what?" I asked.

"Drinks its tears. It's just a little butterfly. It doesn't need much."

"I don't understand. Tears? Are you messing with me?"

"Hey, I'm just the one with the degree in forensic entomology. If you don't want my help, you can go ask someone else." He started to put the butterfly back in the baggie.

"Okay, okay. I'm sorry," I said. "I didn't mean it like that."

Allister was like twelve years old and already had an attitude. Ron must've been rubbing off on him.

He stopped putting the butterfly back.

"I just meant that I didn't think alligators even had tears," I explained. "They don't look like the crying type. Does it wait around for the gator to watch a sad movie? Tell it stories about orphan puppies?"

Ron chimed in with, "If you're done with your box of nothing, I'll put it back. I hate it when he talks about bugs."

"Sure, it's fine. Thanks, Ron. Let me know if you don't find anything else," I said to him.

"Whatever," he said as he disappeared into the back room.

"It uses its proboscis," Allister used his pen to point to a long, curled tongue-like thing on the front of its head. "It'll latch on to the upper eyelid and pull back. That'll cause irritation, making it water." He pantomimed the whole process and made me wish he hadn't.

I blinked a few times and rubbed my eyes to squish the imaginary ants that now crawled all over them. "Yeah, but how? He's just a little guy. My fingernail probably weighs more. And alligators are big. Their eyelids probably weigh *a lot* more than he does."

"Butterflies are strong for their size, though. A lot of insects are. The rhinoceros beetle can lift 850 times its own weight." He sounded so proud that he knew that.

I leaned down to get a better look at it. "How does it even get a good grip on an alligator's eyelid? Wouldn't his uh… thingy—"

"Proboscis," Allister offered.

"Thank you. Wouldn't his proboscis just slip right off?"

"Oh, that's the cool part." The Julia butterfly had been laying on the top folder of a stack of them on Allister's desk. He picked up that top book and brought it just under his eyes to get a closer look at it and added, "It latches onto the alligator's eyelid with these tiny hooks that run along the inside of its proboscis. The hairy little fibers wedge in between microscopic imperfections in the animal's armor and make a perfect grip. And they're curved inward like the teeth of an anaconda, so when Dryas iulia pulls back on the eyelid, it's impossible for it to lose its grip. The genius of nature."

"That's why I hate it when he talks about bugs," Ron shouted from across the room.

"Detective? Are you okay?" Allister asked, concerned. "You look pale."

A million imaginary ants crawled all over my eyes.

"I'm fine," I said.

"Are you sure? You look really pale. Do you need to sit down?"

Ron chuckled and walked into the back room.

"I'm fine. Thanks, Allister."

"Okay."

"I'm going to go dunk my head in some water then go talk about my feelings." And I left with more subject matter for nightmares.

Chapter 5

"Is there something that you *do* want to talk about?" asked Dr. Striker, sitting back in his dark blue, microfiber upholstered chair, curved for lumbar support. He crossed his legs like a loaf of challah bread, instead of like a pretzel. I've never trusted guys who cross their legs like challah bread. A handful of framed certificates hung on the wall, behind his desk at the other end of the room. He wouldn't let me walk over to make sure they actually had his name on them or see if any were for completing all the puzzles on the kid's placemat at Denny's. So, I was unable to verify his credentials.

I shrugged my shoulders. "That's a nice suit. We can talk about that." And it *was* a nice suit. It fit his frame well and the blue-gray material looked expensive.

"This is what? The third time you were ordered to come talk to me?" Dr. Striker asked.

"Forth. If you count the last time."

"Sean, do you know how many people I get ordered to see me?"

"I do not have access to that information."

He shook his head in resignation. "It's not important."

"That's good to know."

His expression told me that he did not appreciate my sense of humor. "This time it was for assaulting a suspect in your interrogation room."

I held up a finger. "We have to call them interview rooms, now," I said. "Interrogations make us sound like Nazis."

He looked at me for a minute, becoming visibly agitated. "Can we talk about that?"

"If you want. I think we should call them 'Tell the nice detective everything he wants to know' rooms. It doesn't have quite the same ring to it. But if they understand what the point is going into it, maybe that'll make our jobs easier. But the name is kind of long. We could use the acronym. Does T-T-N-D-E-H-W-T-K spell anything?"

Dr. Striker looked at me with compressed eyes. I could tell from the way he strangled his unfortunate pen that he was getting more and more frustrated. "Detective… Sean," he began, taking his time so he didn't sound like my high school English teacher and doing a lousy job at it. "Sargent Martinez assigned you to me for one hour a week, for the next month. You could use the hour to jerk me around—again—or you could talk to me, and we could work through some anger management issues."

I nodded my head a few times.

Dr. Striker paused and added, "I think it's important that we find a more acceptable outlet."

I pretended to be interested in what he was saying.

"Either way, I still get paid." He uncrossed and crossed his legs, the other way.

"That is a very reasonable attitude, Doctor." I also sounded reasonable.

He waited for me to continue. "Nothing?"

"Nothing, what?" I asked.

He sighed heavily.

I glanced at my watch, then smiled at him.

"Why don't we start with some baby steps? How about I just ask you a simple question? Would you agree to answer it?" It could've been a trick. I became uneasy.

"Yes," I answered like a question.

"What did he say that triggered you? You had to have been holding yourself back, the whole time. What set you over the edge?"

I shook my head, took a breath, and answered him. "The asshole kidnapped a young girl, young enough to be my daughter, held her in an abandoned warehouse for days, allowing her the privilege of pissing in a bucket if she was a good girl. When he was done with her, he burned her alive, just so he could listen to her scream. Then he threatened my boss. I really think you should give me this one."

Dr. Striker uncrossed his legs. "Did he admit to it?"

"With great relish. He was very happy to tell me all about it in gory detail."

J.S. Johnston

"Wow."

"He described to me what her hair smelled like as it burned."

Dr. Striker looked down at the floor.

"He even offered to retell the story, if I wanted him to," I said.

"Do you want to talk about that?" Dr. Striker asked with wide eyes and a raised brow.

"Sure. When I testify at his trial."

My pants started playing Sixteen Tons by Tennessee Ernie Ford. I stood up from my very expensive chair and started for the door.

Dr. Striker shook his head and made the universal "what the hell" sign.

"Sorry, Doc. Duty calls," I said. "That's my reminder to go to a witness's place."

"You made an appointment for—"

"It could be just what I need to crack the case. You never know." I took two steps toward the door.

"We were in the middle of a session. You don't just walk out of a session," he said like I flipped over the checkerboard.

"Sure, I can."

"It—"

"Don't be sad. We can finish this later. That really is a nice suit. You look good."

As I walked out, he mumbled to himself, "Why do I work here?"

There was a lot at Horner's place that told me about Horner, but not much to tell me who he knew or who might want him dead. However, two minutes and a warrant got me into his Facebook and Instagram accounts. He was thankfully very active and some quick snooping told me he was a Gemini, belonged to Lovecraftian horror groups, and liked to buy stuff from their marketplace. All very interesting and none of it was useful.

I didn't see him being controversial enough to make anyone want to murder him. A murder takes a lot of effort. For the most part, it's a crime of passion and you need to be very passionate to spray someone's gray matter all over the tile backsplash in their kitchen. But Horner? Boring. He wasn't involved with the use or the traffic of any illicit narcotics. The Smith & Wesson Model 64 revolver that provided the bullet that tore through his skull was legally purchased at a gun show. He never talked about his family, never went out with friends, and didn't talk about women. Or men. Well, didn't talk about them past six months ago, that is.

* * *

I knocked on the front door at the home of Jeremy Wahlstrom. His ranch-style house looked old and neglected like something out of a movie about the end of the world. The once dark salmon paint on the exterior was now faded and peeling, showing the gray cinder block underneath. The weeds in the front yard almost reached my knees. Metal awnings hung over windows, covered in just enough rust to make me wish I'd gotten a tetanus shot before coming out.

From looking at Horner's Facebook posts, they'd been in a serious relationship, going back longer than I felt like scrolling. He'd regularly post those smiling-couple pictures that make you want to shut down your computer and drop it off a building. They were not for those with weak stomachs. Then about six months ago, he stopped posting them and started leaving some pretty angry memes about everything wrong with the world. Racism, war, climate change, corporate greed. Maybe I should've called first.

The smell of fresh-cut grass and the constant rumble of lawnmowers pushed by men dripping with sweat at the neighboring houses was an unignorable reminder that I wasn't a secret agent. Everything about me from my short haircut to the Chrysler that I parked in the driveway screamed, "There's a cop at that guy's house!" Most of the mowing people looked up to acknowledge me as I pulled in but kept on mowing.

Jeremy Wahlstrom's lime green Buick sat parked on the unpaved dirt driveway next to mine. The sound of the TV drifted through the door over the lawnmowers. When he didn't answer the door, I knocked again.

The teenage kid in the sweat-stained white tank top at the house directly across the street stopped his mower to wipe his face with a towel. I nodded to him with a half-wave when he looked at me. And he kept looking at me, probably squinting at me from behind his sunglasses. He did not wave back. He did go back to mowing. So much for being friendly.

After a while of not getting an answer at the door, I called, "Mr. Wahlstrom? My name is Detective Sean Papadopoulos with the Tampa Police Department. I need to talk to you about your ex-boyfriend, William Horner."

I waited for a moment. When no one came to the door, I walked around to the side of the house to find a window to look through. It could be that he just didn't want to talk to me. But he could also be hurt. So, I looked.

The tobacco-stained white curtains were only halfway shut, letting me see right in. The TV noise was a Telenovela. I can't tell you which one, because I don't watch them, but it looked very dramatic. The TV sat on a faux-wood entertainment bench on the right-hand wall. A small bookshelf full of DVDs leaned up against the far wall. The dark red armrest of the couch on the left-hand side peeked just inside the curtain. But no person.

I checked the backyard, looking between the rotting wood planks of the privacy fence that blocked off every house in the neighborhood. But no one was back there. Just junk and more weeds that needed to be mowed.

I came around to knock on his door for one last time, just to be sure. Maybe he walked to the store and left the TV on to keep burglars away or something. Worked on me, well enough. As I raised my hand to knock, it swung open and slammed against the inside wall. Before I could jump, Jeremy Wahlstrom barreled out of it screaming like a pissed-off jet engine.

He brandished a kitchen knife with a blade as long as my forearm raised high over his head in a Kung-fu grip. As he came at me, I took an unconscious step back and tripped over a loose plank of wood on the porch then tumbled backward, just missing the swing of his knife.

I scrambled to unstrap my gun from the shoulder holster. While I was in mid-swing to aim it, he sliced my arm and the gun fell to the ground. He kept swinging that thing and I tried to get out of his reach so I could react to him, doing a backward crabwalk somewhere in all of it.

"Dude, what the hell?" I shouted.

He leaped at me, while I was still on the ground, the knife in his hand out. I caught his arm at the wrist with both hands. He half-stood up to put his weight on it, doing his damnedest to drive it into my nose. Blood rushed to his face as he strained and bared his rotten teeth.

With a solid kick, I shifted my weight to get out from under him and he fell to the ground. I came to my feet while still holding his wrist. He tried to launch himself at me, from the ground.

"To hell with this," I said and brought a right cross to his chin. He fell unconscious and dropped back to the grassy earth. And finally loosened his kung-fu grip on that knife.

The teenage kid across the street stopped mowing to watch what was going on with an expression that I couldn't make out.

"What?!" I yelled at him, picking up the knife.

* * *

My witness, Jeremy Wahlstrom, regained consciousness sitting on his ratty old couch. I had cuffed his hands behind his back.

I came over with a handful of ice, wrapped in a dishtowel, and held it to his chin.

"Who the hell are you?" he inquired as he jerked away from me.

"I'm Detective Sean Papadopoulos with the Tampa Police Department. You should let me put this on your chin if you want the swelling to stay down."

He tried to stand up, but I put a hand on his shoulder and pushed him back onto his ratty old couch.

"Why am I handcuffed? I didn't do anything!" he shouted at me.

"Because I want to ask you some questions about your ex-boyfriend William Horner without being stabbed." I held the dishtowel full of ice back to his chin.

He pulled away again. "I knew you cops would think I had something to do with it." He shook his head. "I'm not telling you anything."

"What if I said please?"

He looked at me then turned away.

I sighed and paused for a moment. "Mr. Wahlstrom. I didn't come here to give you a shakedown. Someone has murdered your ex-boyfriend."

"And you don't think I watch the news?"

"I'm trying to track down his killer. I'm looking for information. That's all," I said with raised hands.

He stared at the switched-off TV across the room with a stone-blank expression.

"Mr. Wahlstrom?"

"I know my rights. I don't have to say nothin'."

He continued to stare coldly at the blank TV screen.

"Mr. Wahlstrom, you can either talk to me here, or you can talk to a lawyer after I arrest you for trying to stab me with a kitchen knife. Either way—"

"Then, bring me my shoes," he said, still not looking at me.

"You stubborn—" I turned away from him and grit my teeth. When I did, I happened to spot a little orange prescription bottle of pills on the kitchen counter. He noticed me noticing them.

The bottle looked almost full, so I walked over and checked it out. "You take lithium?" I asked.

"No," he said. "I don't need them."

I picked up the bottle. "It's in your name."

"Don't mean I need them."

"Says Dr. Pachico thinks you need them."

"I don't care what he says," Mr. Wahlstrom spat at me then added matter-of-factly. "I am not manic-depressive. I feel fine."

I came around to stand in front of him and showed him the label on the bottle. "Somewhere in that knife-wielding head of yours, you agree with him, or you wouldn't have filled the prescription."

"Well, I changed my mind." He shifted his arms in the cuffs, obviously uncomfortable.

"Okay. How about this," I looked in a couple of cabinets to find where he kept the glasses and found one with The Little Mermaid on the side. "If you take one of your pills, I'll take those cuffs off." I filled the glass with water from the tap.

He cocked his head and squinted his eyes. "That's not how lithium works."

"It's not?"

He smiled. It was a nice, warm smile. His eyes even twinkled a bit. If you stood beside the guy who tried to kill me earlier, you'd think he was a different person. "It's supposed to take about a month."

"That long? The police academy took less time than that."

He chortled.

"Can you just make me feel better?"

"Fine," he said with an eye roll.

"Here." I held out a pill for him between my thumb and forefinger. He opened his mouth for me, and I dropped it in. I half-expected him to spit the water back out at me, but he gulped it down.

He turned his torso to present his cuffed hands. He rubbed his wrists when I uncuffed him, his skin creased from the metal.

"So, ask," he said.

"Why would anyone want to kill William Horner?"

He chuckled. "Hell if I know," he said, still rubbing his wrists.

"Any idea at all?" I asked.

"Nope," he said, shaking his head. "He was dull."

"Did he have any friends?"

He shook his head some more. "All he ever talked about was work drama. You'd think he was born there."

"What kind of drama? Did he get in any fights?"

"He begged his boss for a raise, but I don't think that's a fight," Wahlstrom said.

My phone started playing the Funeral March.

"Your pants are singing."

"It's just my boss," I said, ignoring it.

"Your boss is in your pants? You have a nice job," he said with a smile.

"No, it's—hang on." I dug out my phone and denied the call. "There."

He took a sip of his water and looked at me from over the rim.

"So, did Mr. Horner get the raise?" I asked.

He shook his head. "I loved him, but he could be… well… Bill." He curled one of his legs underneath him.

"I think I get it. Why didn't he just look for another job?"

Jeremy Wahlstrom shrugged his shoulders. "He tried to. He'd had been trying to for a long time but just never got any interviews."

"None? What was he doing wrong?"

"You know people. They like to hold grudges."

I perked up at that. "Grudges about what?" I asked.

"He worked at the traffic switching room downtown about a hundred years ago or something. One day while he was on duty, one of the traffic lights got stuck on green, both ways."

"Both ways?"

He crossed his arms in the air. "Yeah. This way and that way were both green. It happened to be a busy intersection downtown."

"Oh."

"Yeah. A few cars got into accidents and people died."

"Ouch." I winced at that.

"I know, right? It came out later that it had nothing to do with Bill. There was a glitch in the streetlight. But that didn't stop people from hating him for it," Wahlstrom said.

"So, when he went for another job…"

"That always came up in the background check. At least, I assume."

"Right. It's not like they tell you. You just never hear back," I said.

"Yep."

"That is harsh."

He held up his hands in a that's-life sign.

"And you know all of this how?"

Wahlstrom snorted. "He wouldn't shut up about it. That was his idea of pillow talk."

"Some people…" I took out a business card and handed it to him. "If I have more questions, can I call you?"

"Sure. Sorry about the kitchen knife." He found a pen on the endstand beside him and wrote his phone number on the back of my card then returned it to me.

"I needed the workout." I took the card from him and put it in my breast pocket. "Oh, hey. I have Mr. Horner's cat at my place. Did you want me to drop him off for you?"

"Oh god, no. I'm allergic to cats," he said, scrunching his face.

"Really?"

"Horribly, yeah. It's why I broke up with him. He wouldn't get rid of the damn thing."

"Wait. *You* broke up with *him*?" I asked, surprised at that.

"Damn right, I did. He saw how much I suffered. I begged him to get rid of it. *Begged* him!"

"It was you that… Not…"

"I deserve better than that!" Wahlstrom said, crossing his arms.

"Yes sir, you do," I said. "I'll call you if I need anything else. You have a nice day."

He smiled and wiggled his fingers at me.

* * *

I called Sargent Martinez back as I pulled out of Jeremy Wahlstrom's driveway to head back for the station.

She looked at me from the other side of the video chat.

"Sean," she said.

"What's up, boss? Do I get to go play with the time suit?" I asked.

"Assess," she corrected me like my mother. "Assess the capabilities of the time suit and determine if it's a good fit to be added as one of the forensic tools at the Tampa Police Force. And provide your feedback to USF for the next version of the suit."

"Yes!" I shot my fists in the air, completely forgetting about the phone in the one hand with the video chat with Sarge. I think I punched her into the ceiling. "Sorry about that. When do I get to go play?"

"Assess."

"Whatever. When do I get to go assess?"

"I made you an appointment with Dr. Khatri for 3:00 this afternoon."

"Yes! I mean, I think I can make it. You know, if I'm done here, before that. I'll do my best."

Sargent Martinez smiled. "Right. Don't have too much fun. Remember it's for work."

"Oh, I'll be sure and provide my professional opinion and how it might be a service to the department."

"You're welcome, Sean," she said.

"Thanks, Sarge!"

Chapter 6

I tried to kill the time waiting to go play by getting lunch at one of the little spots downtown. A place called Thai Won On makes a pretty mean shrimp Pad Thai. But it didn't help. I still showed up at the University of South Florida's campus a full half-hour early.

"You must be Detective Papa…," said Dr. Khatri with a light Indian accent as she opened the door to her office for me. I recognized her from the news story on TV. It also helped that she wore the typical long white lab coat with her name embroidered on the pocket. In a certain light, she reminded me of my sixth-grade science teacher. Her short graying hair somehow suited her large dark eyes and the gentle curves of her face. She smiled so gently and warmly that I couldn't help smiling back at her.

"It's Papadopoulos, but that's okay. No one ever gets it right. Just call me Sean."

"Okay, Sean." She grinned at me and after a long pause added. "You're a little early."

I couldn't help looking at her office past the door that she stood in. It looked like it used to be a neat and orderly librarian's office until an unfortunate incident involving a family of drunken ferrets. Waist-high stacks of books stood by what I assumed must be a desk under all the mounds of paper. Floating shelves ran across the left wall, haphazardly filled with thick three-ring binders, the occasional book, and more mounds of loose paper. The right wall had a whiteboard that had more handprints in dry-erase marker than words or anything useful.

"Yeah, sorry about that. I couldn't wait," I said, clasping my hands in front of me like a schoolkid. "I can come back if it's a bad time."

"No, no. It's a good thing, actually. I had some errands to do later and if I get you done now, I'll have more time for them." She grabbed a tablet from somewhere inside the room and hit the button to turn it off. "Walk with me down to the lab. Come."

"Sure. Hey, can I ask you a completely unrelated question?"

"What's up?" she asked in a lighthearted voice.

I motioned to the beaver dam that she used as an office. "How… How do you find anything?"

"What do you mean?"

"It… Well, the state of your office…"

"What's wrong with it?" Dr. Khatri asked like she had no idea what I was referring to.

"Does it always look like that?"

"Look like what?" She turned toward me and cocked her head. "What's wrong with it?"

"Absolutely nothing. It looks like a nice place to get some work done. I'm ready to go when you are."

She smiled, shook her head, and closed the door.

I guess I expected the long hallway to look like the inside of a star destroyer with storm troopers marching past us and little mouse droids zipping around. It was not. Dr. Khatri caught me looking into every open door along the way and pausing to see what was in there.

"It's in here," she said, stopping at the door to the Physics lab. I expected armed guards, a retinal scanner, and a blood test before an armored steel door would open for us. There probably should've been. But all she did was stop, grab a handle, and open a door that wasn't even locked.

I wanted to find the suit hanging on a mannequin, in the brightly lit center of a dark room with steam in the background like a superhero costume. So, I could walk up to it as if destiny had brought me to it, touch it, and give it my best Keanu Reeves "Whoa."

When Dr. Khatri opened the door, it was not waiting for me. Much to my disappointment. Nothing but desks with computers with shelves of blade servers along the far wall, all busily whirring away. Boring stuff. I'd speak with her later about her obvious lack of theatrical presentation. She probably knows everything about temporal mechanics and quantum physics, but she don't know Jack about theatricality.

Out of politeness, I resisted the urge to just blurt out, "Where is it?" No, wait. I did blurt it out. I didn't resist very well.

Dr. Khatri laughed in a way that was more like singing. "This is just the monitoring room. It's in there." She motioned to a plain-looking, white-painted side door, right by a shiny metal set of shelves filled with electrical doodads.

I shifted on my feet like a dog that had to go out to pee.

"Dr. Khatri," said the young girl at one of the computers with hair a color of blue that is not found anywhere in nature. I recognized her from the news story on TV. She turned around in her desk chair and stood up. Under her white lab coat, she wore a blue t-shirt with a white line diagram of an insect, drawn as if it were the schematic of a machine. "The computer finally compiled the results from earlier, if you want to see them."

"Thanks, Clara," Dr. Khatri said. "I'll review them later. This is Detective… Sean from the Tampa police."

"I didn't do it," said Clara.

"Do what?" I asked.

"I don't know. Are you a detective-detective or just the rank of Detective?"

"I'm actually a detective-detective," I said. "I work in Homicide. You didn't kill anyone, did you?"

She shook her head. "Not today. Unless you count the burrito that I had for lunch."

"Sadly, killing a burrito is still not a crime."

A stack of paperbacks sat on her desk, obviously well-read from the condition of the spines. *The Silence of the Lambs* lay on the top of the pile.

"I see you like detective stories. Am I everything you expected?"

She squinted her eyes at me. "Actually, I expected you to be taller. And wearing a trench coat."

I smiled. "I usually leave it at home. We *are* in Tampa."

"True. It only gets cold enough to wear a coat, for maybe three days in January."

"Those days are so nice."

"Clara, Sean is here to look at the time suit." Dr. Khatri put a thin hand on my shoulder.

"Right," Clara exclaimed, widening her eyes. "I guess someone has to pay for all our fun."

I almost put my hands together and rubbed them like a supervillain.

"This way," said Dr. Khatri, taking my elbow. "It's in the other room."

The unassuming closet-sized door opened into a large bay with what looked like an extra-wide doorway in the middle of it that didn't go to or come from anywhere. It was just a doorway, with two lengths of material on the sides and one on the top, connecting them. Like the front of a barn, before it's attached to the rest of it.

So, my first question was, "What's that?"

"They like to stick to doorways," answered Dr. Khatri. "Having one in the middle of the room gives us more control of where they appear."

I swear my heart stopped, grabbed my rib cage, and demanded that I ask her, "*What* likes to stick to doorways?"

The doctor grinned, knowingly.

"You're going to love this," said Clara, beside me.

"Andrew," called the doctor to a man working at a laptop on a desk facing the empty doorway. "Initiate a portal for me. Set it a month in the past."

"Sure, Doctor," he responded as he tapped a few keys and clicked something with his mouse.

"Now, do you see that philodendron at the other end of the lab?" Dr. Khatri asked me.

"Sure," I responded. The clay pot with the mess of long vines falling out of it sat on top of a wooden stool along the far wall, across from the doorway in the middle of the room.

"See how green and full it is, with all the tendrils hanging down?"

"I do."

"Okay, Andrew. Start up the portal." Dr. Khatri smiled and crossed her arms like a proud mother.

"You got it." Andrew clicked something with his mouse and the opening of the doorway quickly turned an opaque royal purple, as if someone had dropped a curtain. Then it thinned, showing the other side. And streaks of modulated colors waved over it like the surface of a purple soap bubble. It looked like peering through a swirling purple fog or a sheer curtain. Whatever was now in the doorway, was not a solid thing.

"Okay. What happens next?" I asked.

Clara laughed. No, she giggled. She giggled like someone who knew what I didn't.

"Do you see the philodendron?" asked the doctor, patiently.

"I don't get it." I shrugged. "It's sickly looking and the tendrils are a lot shorter. What did you do to it?"

Clara grabbed my elbow and pulled me to the side until I could see the plant without looking through the shimmering purple doorway. It was back to its healthy, green self with vines halfway to the floor. "Christ, almighty."

Dr. Khatri explained with a grin, "I used to keep that plant in my house. But since I'm never home, I couldn't take care of it. A little over a month ago, I brought it in here to nurse it back to health. It looks happy now, don't you think?"

"So, this thing—" I started to say as I walked up to the doorway in the middle of the room.

"Is a portal through time," said the Doctor, barely containing her pride.

"I told you it was cool," said Clara, leaning into me.

I raised my arm, wondering what the portal would show me if I passed my finger through it.

Clara quickly swatted my arm down. "Don't!"

"Why? What'll happen?" I asked.

"The law of conservation of mass? Hello!"

"Okay? Am I going to have to arrest myself?" I shrugged.

"Don't they send detectives to school?" She planted a hand on her hip and her lips curled into a half-smile.

Dr. Khatri curled hers into a full-smile and added a headshake.

"Not that one, apparently. What did I do?" I asked.

"This is the whole point of the suit." Clara looked at me like I'd get it.

I, in fact, did not get it.

"The first commandment of physics is thou shalt not create nor destroy matter or energy. And you cannot break it," she said.

"What'll happen if I do?" I looked to Dr. Khatri, who let Clara respond to that.

"You *cannot* break it," she said in as factual a tone as I've ever heard.

"See, now you lost me."

"Did you ever watch any of the *Back to The Future* movies?" Clara rolled her hands.

"Sure," I responded, shrugging my shoulders. I wanted to make a 1.21 gigawatts reference but kept it to myself.

"Remember how there were two of Christopher Lloyds and Michael J. Foxes at a few points?"

"I do."

"Well, the laws of the universe absolutely prevent that from happening. By two Christopher Lloyds existing at the same time, he effectively duplicated every particle in his body. And that's impossible by any physics that we currently understand." Clara didn't look as smart as she sounded, from the way she dressed. But there she was.

I inspected my hand as if the individual particles were there in front of me. "So, what would've happened to my finger if I'd stuck it through the portal?"

Dr. Khatri chimed in and said slowly, "We've been working on that problem. But we don't want to send anything through without the suit until we solve it."

"So, not to be all Dunning-Kruger about it, but what's stopping you from just chucking a coffee cup through the portal to see what happens?" I asked.

"Because we're not sure if the molecules of the cup will just return to their present time or convert into energy," Dr. Khatri responded in her light Indian accent.

I shook my head. "And why is that a bad thing?"

The doctor responded, "The first option isn't a point of concern. Well, I'm sure the cup wouldn't be happy about it. But converting matter into energy is what atom bombs do. And well—"

Clara looked at me and pantomimed an explosion with her hands.

"The blast would be around thirty kilometers in diameter," said the doctor, unnervingly analytical about it.

"Yeah, okay. Let's not do that, then," I said, trying to change the subject before I had time to change my mind about going through the portal.

Clara laughed. "Yeah, let's not. I'll grab the suit."

Both Dr. Khatri and Clara helped me get dressed, making sure to fasten, engage, and bolt everything that needed it. They explained that it had to be solid enough to be airtight and even the smallest leak would let the matter of the inside and outside the suit mix and that would be bad. I'd very much like not to be blown up or sent back to the present as a stream of disembodied molecules. I'm no scientist, but they both sound painful.

When everything was fitted and put in place, it looked somewhere between a spacesuit and a racing suit. The helmet fully encompassed my head and screwed into a ring on the neck of the garment. A dark face shield covered almost the whole thing like I was one of those DJs in dubstep music videos. The suit itself was lab coat white with a red racing stripe that ran up the legs and arms.

"Now, what do I do?" I asked from inside the helmet. In my head, I was asking *can I go now can I go now can I go now?*

Clara passed a couple of fingers under the helmet by the chin and flipped a hidden switch. After a click, Dr. Khatri's voice came over newly discovered speakers in the helmet.

I turned around and found her leaning into a microphone by Andrew's laptop.

"Now you can talk," she said.

"Thanks. That's better. Do I just walk through the portal, now?" I asked.

"Hold on," said Clara. She walked behind me and turned a valve. Then a high-pitched squeal of strangled airflow quickly became louder before settling into a constant sigh. "There. Now you can breathe." She patted me on the shoulder.

"Seven-year-old me is jumping on the couch in my mind, right now."

"Well, make sure he doesn't fall off and break a leg. Because we only have the one suit prototype. If anything happens to you in there, we can't come and get you."

I nodded. "No jumping off couches. Got it."

She took my hand and led me back over to the freestanding doorway in the middle of the room with the portal still displaying the sickly yellow plant. Then she stepped back and said, "Remember, you'll be giving us feedback on how well the suit works from a detective's perspective. What you need, what you don't. We'll need it before we design the next one."

I nodded inside my helmet. "Right. Work stuff. Ready to assess and all that."

"Go ahead," said Dr. Khatri, motioning an arm to the open portal. "If you see any Morlocks, don't talk to them."

"Any what? What's a Morlock?" I asked.

"H.G. Wells?" asked Clara with indignance. "The scary guys that came out at night. Don't detectives read?"

"Sure. Updated regulations, law, procedural documentation on handling suspects—"

"Sounds boring," Clara said.

"Well, if they made it fun then everyone would want this job. Then they might pay me less and that would make me sad." I stepped up to the portal and looked through it, trying to let my brain catch up to what I was about to do. Breathe, Sean. "Hey, quick question."

Dr. Khatri looked up from the console, behind me. "Now you have questions?"

"Well, I guess. Yeah. Can I ask a question before I… ya know?"

Her voice smiled. "What's your question?"

"Am I the first guy to ever do this?"

"To do what?"

"To walk through—this," I motioned to the portal. "Am I the guinea pig? No one ever told me that part."

Clara chimed in with, "Oh, you're the first one. Dr. Khatri and I wanted to send in a test subject to see if it works before we tried it."

"Really?" I asked, a little terrified.

"No, not really," Clara said.

"We've all been through, at least once," said Dr. Khatri, clearly amused. "We've been sending people in and out for months, now. You'll be okay. Don't worry."

"Isn't that what they say in every horror movie?" I asked.

Clara patted me on the shoulder and went to take her seat at the console with Dr. Khatri and Andrew.

I took a half-step toward the portal and asked, "Wait. What

happens if you lose power? Will the portal close? What happens to me then? I don't want to——"

"Relax," Dr. Khatri said. "The suit can make its own portals. If anything happens, just ask Watson." She tapped a few things on the console.

"Who's Watson?" I asked, standing no more than a foot from the portal.

"The onboard AI," Clara said. "Sean, you'll be fine. You're just going a few feet in past the doorway."

"What the hell," I said under my breath. "It's not like I was doing anything important today, anyway." I put a hand through the doorway. It effortlessly passed right through and didn't look like anything special.

Dr. Khatri said over the speaker in my helmet, "You won't see anything different until you're on the other side. Then I have to warn you, it can be disorienting."

"Disorienting how? Like vertigo?" I asked.

"No, not like that. It's hard to explain. You'll be alright, but I thought I should say something."

"Alright, then. Here goes."

I took a big step and passed through the portal.

* * *

It was like stepping from a pleasant sunny day out into a hailstorm. So much of whatever it was flew past my helmet at a hundred miles an hour and I shielded my body from it. Missiles of color and light without substance blasted me without warning. Some of it registered as an event and some of it was less than an instant. For a moment, I wasn't there and then I was. The sheer terror of non-existence took hold of me and as the god-awful onslaught of time galloped past, I unconsciously screamed into the microphone of the helmet.

"Hey, hey. Sean. You're fine," said Clara through the helmet speakers. "You're okay. Close your eyes and take a breath."

I did as she said. I shut them tight and took a breath, filling my lungs with the canned air of the helmet.

"Now let it out and open your eyes. What you're seeing, you

56

weren't meant to see. And your brain is just going a little crazy trying to make sense of it."

"Yeah. Imagine that." I slowly opened my eyes, as ordered. Suddenly I was looking at the world from inside a moving river. The current flowed past me with a quivering reality through it. I instinctively braced myself, but nothing pushed on me.

"What's all this flowing past me?" I asked. You'd think I was driving through the rain without a windshield. I brought an arm over my face.

"You're looking at the literal flow of time," Clara answered. "The human brain didn't evolve to perceive it. So, it's normal to freak out, at first." You'd think she was watching a puppy. I'm glad she finds this so damn amusing. "Now turn around and look at us at the console."

Dr. Khatri, Andrew, and Clara waved at me through the purple shimmer. I leaned to the side to look at the same place in the room, but not through the gateway, to find them missing. The whole time I'd still been gripping the doorway, afraid that if I let go, the current would sweep me away to God knows where. The lab door opened, and Dr. Khatri and Clara walked in. Their images swirled and waved like a heat mirage.

"You guys just came in," I said. "You're talking about something that I can't quite hear. Can you see me?"

"Well, we in the present can see you through the portal. But us in the past wouldn't be able to see or hear you. We'd have no idea that you were there."

The shimmering past versions of them wandered around the lab and talked to each other. Dr. Khatri walked up and examined her plant, never once looking in my direction.

"It's an artifact of the principles of time travel. The suit creates a bubble of the present time that lets you walk around in their time, like a submarine. But you can't interact with any of it."

My pants started to play the Funeral March, again. "Now? Really?"

"What's now?" asked Clara over the speakers.

"Nothing. It's just my boss calling. If I can't interact with anything, how am I standing on the floor?" I stood like I was bracing myself against a wind that wasn't blowing me over.

"I don't mean you pass through things, like a ghost," she said. "You don't have any effect on the environment, at all."

"What does that—"

"Watch out!"

While I was talking to Present Clara and not paying attention, Past Clara walked right into me. Even standing in heels, she only comes up to my chin. But she still threw me to the floor as if she were a dozen times my size and the blow knocked the wind right out of me.

"I saw Past Me in your helmet camera. Are you okay?" Clara asked in a concerned voice.

"Holy—Do you work out?"

"Sorry, about not telling you sooner," she said. "That's what I meant by not being able to interact with things. Are you going to be okay?"

"I might need a minute. Good lord, woman." My pants started playing the Funeral March, again. "Oh my god, leave a message!"

Chapter 7

A very large backhoe sat parked in the grass, on the shore of the lake at Robles Park. And a very large alligator dangled from a white rope, tied to its hydraulic scoop. It was dead. Someone had slit its belly open from its throat to its cloaca and removed the contents. Still wet and fresh, blood slowly dripped onto the aforementioned pile of stomach contents beneath it that was drying out in the punishing Tampa sun. The thick smell of offal hung like a fog that wouldn't burn off in the heat of the day.

"Holy boiled Jesus in a hammock, it's hot as balls out here!" said Ron, taking off his mirrored sunglasses to wipe the sweat from his brow with his forearm. "There's not much for us to do," he said, putting them back on. "Most of him ended up in Big Al, over there. Now he's—" He pointed down to the body bag at his feet.

I crouched down and unzipped it. I'm not sure why I was surprised about what I found, considering where he had just come from. There was nothing in the bag but a bloody, partially digested mess of loose meat and bone. (Alligators eat the bones, too.) It was obvious something had ripped the meat from other pieces. It looked like pulled pork if it were still raw and smelled like you'd expect if you left it out in the sun all day. Some of the bones were cracked along their length and even snapped off from other pieces.

"How much of this is the victim?" I asked.

"We think all of it. Or most of it, anyway. We'll have to wait for the DNA tests to come back. We're sure that's a human femur, on top."

"Yeah. That foot looks human, too. At least, I think it's a foot. Normally gators are afraid of people. They usually run when you get close. Not this one, I guess," I said, standing up.

"I know," Ron said. "It was probably in the middle of something at the time. Munching on a duck or whatever. Like that time when that idiot jumped off a pier into a school of mating hammerheads."

"I remember the news story. His last mistake."

Allister walked up to Ron and tapped him on the shoulder. "Exactly how are we supposed to do a bloodstain mapping if all the blood is in the water?" he asked. Somehow, he looked skinnier in the sun. I'm going to have to bring that boy some doughnuts.

"Oh, right. That does make things difficult." Ron looked over at the lake and paused for a moment. "Okay, just get a blood pattern from the bank. And get a water sample to determine the amount of blood in it. We can calculate the dispersal rate by the length of time since the incident."

"Sure thing," said Allister as he ran off.

"Like I said, there's not much for us to do, out here," Ron said to me.

"Yeah, I see that," I said, almost sarcastically. "Is there enough left of him for an ID, at least?"

"Ah!" he said, bringing out his tablet and turning it on. "Just so happens the victim's hand was still in the gator's throat when we hauled him in. We'll still have to wait on DNA, but the prints were beautiful." He said the word 'beautiful' as if someone had just pulled a Thanksgiving turkey from the oven.

"And? Don't keep me waiting. You know I hate that, Ron. I'm the worst date ever."

"Yeah, I know." He slid something over on the tablet. "The prints came back as one Mr. Timothy Sween. Forty-seven-year-old Caucasian male. Works for Patriot Insurance as one of their agents. Likes to post pictures of food on Instagram. Want his opinion on the Middle East crisis?"

"That was fast," I said.

"Yep. Living in the future."

"What did he die of, anyway?"

Ron raised his eyebrows as far as they'd go and looked at me.

"I mean, Big Al. It's obvious what Mr. Sween died of."

"Isn't that for the medical examiner?" Ron asked. "I mean, I'm just a lowly evidence tech."

I smirked at him. "He died from taking your shit. I'll write that down."

Ron smiled and went back to his tablet. "You know I love it when you write down the things I say. It makes me feel important. You going to Gasparilla?"

"You're the second person to ask me that. No, I'm not going."

"I have a pirate hat you can wear. It only smells a little like vomit," Ron said. I couldn't tell if he was joking.

"Sounds tempting, but no," I said.

"Why not? It's fun."

"Wearing your gross pirate hat?"

"You know what I mean," Ron said and swiped something on his tablet.

"How is noisy and overcrowded fun?"

"Because it is." He shrugged. "You going?"

"I'm going to go talk to the witness, now," I said, walking away.

"I can hold your hand if you want."

"Bye, Ron."

He nodded with a small wave, then returned his attention to whatever was on his tablet.

"I don't know what more I can say," said Martin Ortega to the uniformed policewoman, taking his statement under the shade of a sprawling live oak tree. The Spanish moss hung down in curly ribbons, making a screen door of the sunlight. "I come here for my walks in the morning. A guy my age doesn't know how many walks he has left. Now if someone like that is running around in these parks—"

She nodded. "I understand your concern, Mr. Ortega. Some of us use this park, too."

He suddenly became aware of his hands shaking and folded his arms to hide it. "I know. It's just… This is *my* park. You know?"

She looked up from her notepad and met his eyes. "We'll find him. Give us time."

He nodded and tightened his folded arms.

I interrupted with my hand up as if waiting my turn and asked, "Mr. Ortega. Sorry to keep asking you to retell what you saw. My name is Detective Sean Papadopoulos. We fully intend to find the person responsible and bring them to justice. Your help will prove invaluable to that. Now, can you tell me everything you just said to Officer O'Neal? I'm sorry if it's an inconvenience. Any detail you can provide could be exactly what we need."

I pulled out my phone and turned on the recording app. I still plan to get what O'Neal got from him, later. A witness will remember a lot of extra details if you ask them to retell their story a dozen times or so. Sometimes they get pissy, but it works.

"I'll let you take it from here," said Officer O'Neal. She threw a friendly smile to Mr. Ortega as she put her notebook back in her shirt pocket and walked away.

"Well, you see… Did you say it was Officer or Detective?" asked Mr. Ortega.

"It's actually Detective, but it doesn't matter. You can call me Sean. Please continue."

"Well, Sean. Like I said to her, I come here for my walks in the morning. I got here around 7:30."

"And you know the time because how?" I asked.

"Oh, right. The clock on the dash. I looked at it when I got here. My wife wanted me to be home and showered by the time *The Price Is Right* came on," said Mr. Ortega.

"I love that show. Go on." I shifted my weight, holding my phone out, still recording him.

"Well, I just pulled in and hadn't stepped out of the car yet when I saw the uh—This poor guy."

"We identified him as Timothy Sween from his fingerprints. I mean if you wanted to know his name," I said in as gentle a voice as I could manage.

"Poor Timothy." He looked over to the hanging alligator and paused for a moment. "Right, well that's when I saw Timothy on the path there, by the lake. He bent down to tie his shoes. Then someone came charging in from over there." Mr. Ortega pointed to a small grove of palm trees, across the parking lot. "It was such a random thing that I didn't know what to think. But they ran at full speed and plowed right into this poor guy. He fell over and rolled down that embankment into the lake where the alligator was. Then, well… That thing just happened to be right there. He screamed. My god, I could hear it from the car. I got out and ran over to him. It started doing that death roll that they do. When I got there, his top half was lying here on the bank. And that thing was trying to tear off a leg from his bottom half." Mr. Ortega had to pull that last part out like it was stuck in his throat.

I put a hand on his shoulder to comfort him. "Take your time. I have all day."

He nodded and glanced over at a white ibis, a few yards away. It walked on bird stilts, searching for food in the tall grass, completely absorbed in the process.

"Mr. Ortega?"

He looked back at me. "Hmm?"

"Did you see what happened to the person who shoved Mr. Sween into the lake?"

"Well, I saw them run back that way, toward the trees." He pointed his chin in the indicated direction. "But my attention was over here. I didn't see where they went after that," said Mr. Ortega, his voice relaxing a little.

"Can you describe what they looked like?"

"Well, I was still in my car, when I saw it. But they looked small, like a teenager. Maybe a little wiry."

"Do you remember anything about what they were wearing? Their hair?" I asked, gesturing to mine.

He sighed and looked at his shoes. "It all happened so fast. I wasn't paying attention. I remember they were wearing a hat, so I couldn't see their hair. And they had on a white t-shirt and khaki shorts."

"Did you notice any designs on them?" I asked.

He shook his head. "I was at the wrong angle. My car was over here, and they came from over there. I mostly saw their back."

"What about their skin color? Were they black, white, Hispanic…?"

He shook his head again. "I dunno. Light skinned? It's hard to remember. It all happened so fast. I'm sorry."

I nodded. "It's okay." I pulled out my card and handed it to him. "Once you calm down and have time to think about it, people can remember all kinds of stuff that didn't come to them right after the event. If you do happen to remember anything, could you let me know?"

"I'm sorry I didn't have more, off—uh, Sean."

"Nonsense," I said. "Without you, we wouldn't have known it was deliberate. You've been a giant help."

He smiled and looked at my card.

As I walked toward Sargent Martinez, I called back to him, "If you remember anything else, let me know."

He called back, "I will!" He did look very happy to help. Hopefully, he remembers that more than what happened to Sween.

"What did you find out from the witness?" asked Sarge after taking a sip of her coffee. I never understood how people could drink something that hot in ninety-degree weather. It did smell good, though.

"They actually saw the killer do it. They even gave me a description."

"And?" she asked, taking a sip.

"We can rule out half of Florida. Maybe less," I said.

"I'll put out a dragnet. What else?" she asked.

"Either someone knew a big damn alligator would be right here when they pushed him in, or they gave zero shits about him screaming for his life while he was being torn in half, by said big damn alligator. Or both. It looks like both."

"Was it a trained big d—was it a trained alligator? Is that something people do?" Martinez asked.

"Have you ever tried to train one? I'm pretty sure you can't make them do anything they don't want to do."

"Well, are you ready for your present?" she asked, taking another confounding sip of coffee.

"I get a present? It's not my birthday."

"I'm just a good manager like that." She motioned with her head for me to follow her.

A few yards down from where Big Al dangled from the scoop of the backhoe, a wooden pier extended into the lake, ending in a wide, rectangular deck. Around the outside of all of it, ran a weathered and cracked wooden rail. At the end where it finished in a deck over the lake, a little butterfly lay, impossibly orange, pinned to the wooden railing. Its wings were neatly spread out as if it were a specimen in a collection. And it practically glowed in the bright Florida sun.

"They made sure it didn't blow away in the wind," I said like I just found my father's porn. "You really are the best boss ever."

"I know."

"This is an actual, deliberately intentional calling card. The first one could've been called a random thing. A wild butterfly that just got in, somehow." I pointed to it like she didn't know what I was talking about. "This is the killer trying to tell us something. Us. Not the victim. Something directed to the living."

"Is that so?" She smiled.

"Yeah. I mean, a message to the victim would've been shoved someplace uncomfortable. But they laid this out neatly, so we can see it for what they want us to see it as. They're talking to us."

"So, what are they saying?" She leaned up against the wooden rail and took a sip of her coffee. No idea how she wasn't drenched in sweat.

"They're saying—I like pretty butterflies."

"Doesn't sound like a murderer."

"It does not. It sounds more like my niece," I said, staring at the insect. Even in death, it was still the brightest thing there.

"Is she a suspect?"

"If only," I said and turned to face Martinez. "You know, the witness, Mr. Ortega, he saw the murder happen from his car. He watched the whole thing."

"Yeah?"

I lined up where his car would've been with where I was standing. It was a clear line of sight, unobstructed by any trees or buildings. "Yeah. But he never mentioned this."

"What's that?" she asked.

"There's no way he could've seen it from the parking lot," I said.

Uniformed officers stood in the space where Mr. Ortega's car would've been and talked to each other.

"He knew what the killer looked like," I added. "Their general description, anyway. Said he saw them run from those trees, over there."

"Okay."

"Well, if he knew what they looked like, wouldn't they remember them standing over here, beforehand?"

"Maybe the killer came back and planted it, afterward," Martinez suggested.

"From the way he was talking, the killer didn't hang around. That just wouldn't fit."

"Before then?"

"Yeah, but how long, before? Alligators don't just live in one spot. They move around," I said, eyeing the grove of trees that Mr. Ortega reported they ran out of. There wasn't much to hide behind. "The killer couldn't have had that much notice."

"So, what're you thinking?"

"I don't know," I said. And I really didn't. "Maybe you're right. Maybe it really was a trained alligator."

"I am right a lot, you know," she said with a smile and a sip of coffee.

"Now, what I'm dying to know, is what happened at the Horner murder," I said, wiping the sweat from my brow with the back of my hand.

"What do you mean?"

"Well, this Julia butterfly is laid out methodically and intentionally. But the one at Horner's was closed up and laying on top of the fridge like it just died there."

"Maybe it did," Martinez said with a shrug. "Sometimes a cigar is just a cigar. Some kid could've left this."

"Yeah, maybe. It just feels important, is all."

Chapter 8

I pull back the thick curtain, hanging in front of the large bay window. The Nothing Man looks at me without eyes. I am in my childhood home. He stands just outside the window, looking back at me and he isn't there. His form is completely black, but not in color. He is negative space and non-existence. He is the culmination of where things are not. He is death.

I quickly slam the window shut and lock it, before he can get in. He pounds his fist on the window and the glass shakes. I pull the curtains over each other to hide from him. There is still a part between them, and he can still see me. No matter how hard I try to pull them closed, he can still see me.

The Nothing Man races around the outside of the house to another window and I run through cluttered rooms to try to beat him there. As I approach the window, he is reaching his arm through an open crack at the bottom. I try to shut the window on him, but he does not recoil in pain. I get a firm grip on the top of the window and put my weight on it to pull it down, but it makes no difference.

The Nothing Man grabs something inside me. The pain of dismemberment wraps around my gut. He tears into my flesh with piercing claws. I cry out but make no sound.

I scream louder and find myself deep underwater. It's dark, but there is a dim light at the surface, filtering through murky amber. My heavy, waterlogged clothes pull me down. I cannot breathe and fight my way to the light, desperate for air.

The Nothing Man is watching me. He is not struggling to reach the top, as I am. He is effortlessly floating in the water column, just a few feet away. A current steadily pulls me closer to him. I frantically scramble to escape, pushing myself through the water. As I near the surface, he reaches up a hand and as I kick, my foot brushes his outstretched finger.

* * *

I screamed and tightly gripped the armrests on each side of the chair that I sat in, while I flashed my eyes open as if they were spring-loaded. Reality came trickling back to me as my vision unblurred. I'd fallen asleep in the waiting area by the reception desk at Patriot Insurance. And by waiting area, I mean the row of connected chairs with chocolate stains on the ripped upholstery of the cheap cushions on the opposite wall from the receptionist's desk in front of Erica Slain's office.

The young man sitting behind the desk, with hair so short that it looked like he used a potholder as a toupee, dropped his smartphone and looked at me with eyes as wide as I-275.

"Sorry. Bad dream," I said, answering the question that he didn't ask.

He looked at me from the corner of his eye and went back to whatever he was doing on his phone. His suit looked tailored; it fit him so well. Is that what people are doing these days?

I started to take my shoe off to check my foot when the receptionist looked up at me with this face of oh-my-God-what-are-you-doing-the-indignity-of-such-a-thing-is-unimaginable-I-shall-summon-a-policeman-at-once, so I smiled friendly at him and pretended to just be fixing my laces. It's probably fine.

I'd already been through Sween's friends list on social media. It worked well enough with William Horner that it was the first thing I went to with Sween. Most of the friends he talked to regularly were here, at his job. Imagine that. His parents had already both died over a decade ago, and his ex-wife said he didn't talk to his family that much since they had a falling out over the inheritance. If it didn't happen so long ago, I'd be talking to them, right now. But since it did, the next step was to come here.

The nice young man with the potholder toupee looked up from his smartphone and said, "Ms. Slain says she'll see you now." No one said anything over the intercom. Maybe he was psychic. No wonder he wore a tailored suit.

"Just open the door and go in?"

He smiled at me like I just asked him which key was the "any key" and went back to whatever was so interesting on his smartphone. I'm guessing they did not hire him for his people skills.

I stood up slowly and my joints snapped and popped like Rice Krispies. Even my knees sounded old. At least I got a nap. I stepped over to the door, waiting for Mr. People-Person to stop me, but he never so much as glanced my way.

"Erica Slain?" I asked, knocking on the door.

The words, "Come in," came from behind the door, along with the sound of shuffling of paper. I opened it to find her looking back at me from behind the most organized cherrywood desk that I've ever seen. A clean white computer monitor sat in one corner angled towards her. At the other corner was a small white two-tiered shelf with papers neatly placed on both levels. In the middle was absolutely nothing. I got a little nervous.

Erica Slain looked up at me with stabbing blue eyes and a practiced expression of concern, normally reserved for celebrity selfies. "Officer," she said, sitting back in her dark leather upholstered office chair. She waved me in and continued, "Close the door." She dyed her long, heat-straightened hair a washed-out lemon blonde with streaks of honey. It was smooth and thick, like a good milkshake. Not a single root showed, and I guessed the hairdresser's appointment probably cost more than my car payment. Priorities, I guess.

"It's Detective Papadopoulos, actually." I shut the door behind me.

She raised her sculpted eyebrows. "Papa…"

"Papadopoulos. It's okay. Everyone has problems with it. Sean is fine."

"Have a seat, please," she said with an artificial emphasis on the 'please.' She indicated one of the stylish cushioned chairs in front of her desk that looked handpicked from a catalog titled 'Things that will make other people think you're trendy' and flashed me a practiced smile of friendliness. She waited for me to sit down and added, "It's a shame about Timothy," as if she was waiting for that. I expected her next words to be something about selling me the car that I've always wanted. And I suppose it doesn't come as a surprise that she was not on his friends list.

"Yes, it is a shame." I pulled out my phone and turned on the voice recording app.

"I'm sorry to keep you waiting. Someone tried to make an insurance claim for a kidney transplant, and we had to deny it. Boy, was she mad. She tried to tell me that she'd die if she didn't get it." Ms. Slain shook her head, opened a drawer in her desk, and rummaged through it. "That's between her and her doctor. She should've thought of that before and got the additional policy that would've covered it." She rolled her eyes and smiled like it was a silly thing to do. "It would've only been another couple hundred bucks a month. But you know how people always try to get something for nothing."

"That's people for ya," I tried not to say sarcastically as I put the phone on her unbelievably organized cherrywood desk. I bet it would smell like cherries if I used it for kindling.

"I mean we're not denying treatment. Just payment. We're not doctors."

"Right."

"Are you recording this?" she asked, literally looking down her nose at it. You'd think it was a dead mouse.

"Oh, I'm sorry. Yes, I am recording. Memory turns to shit as you get older. You understand." I straightened the phone on her unbelievably organized desk.

"I'd—really feel better if you didn't. You understand," she said like I asked to pee on her couch.

This happens a lot. And here's how I deal with it: "I get it," I said, agreeing. Then I picked up the phone, turned it towards me, tapped a few spots on the screen, turned the screen off, and slid it into my shirt pocket, still recording everything. Perfectly legal in the state of Florida. "Okay?"

"Thanks, so much, officer," she said in an irritatingly rehearsed friendly tone.

"Not a problem," I said reassuringly, the phone still recording in my pocket. "You didn't kill him, did you?" I used my play 'gotcha' voice. There was only a little hint of repulsion in it, but I don't think she caught it.

She looked at me with an open mouth.

"Just kidding." I tilted my head and pointed a playful finger at her.

She let out a relieved chuckle and rolled her eyes as if that was a close one.

"So, what can you tell me about Timothy Sween?"

She shrugged. "He was a mediocre employee. Well, he used to be better when he started, or so they tell me. Now, most years he just barely makes his quota. And—"

"I mean, what can you tell me about *him*? As a person," I said. "What were his ambitions? Complaints? What did he talk about when he got going about the things that he likes? And why would someone want to kill him?"

She shook her head as if I'd just spoken to her in Mandarin Chinese.

"Anything?"

She folded her hands, lacing her fingers together, and placed them on her desk as she leaned forward in her chair. "Look, officer."

"It's detective, but that's okay. Go ahead."

"Detective," she said, collecting her words. "I'm probably the last person you want to ask. Health insurance agents cycle in and out of here probably every six months to a year. Not everyone can tell a grieving widow we're not to blame for them being unable to afford their husband's surgery. Normally, as soon as a new hire finds out what the job is, they're looking for a new job or they just quit when they can't handle it anymore." She paused for a moment and continued. "We don't have time to get chummy with them."

"You mentioned something about how Timothy used to be better or so they told you. Does that mean he's been here longer than you?"

She nodded. "When I first took this role, the other managers told me about him. Sort of a 'watch out for this guy' talk. He's the only one on my team that's been here longer than me. Most agents aren't here that long, but a few of them stick around."

"How long has he been here?" I asked, hoping the recording app on my phone was picking her up.

"A while. Years back, there was this multi-car accident in Tampa, and he happened to get the call for a few of the victims. Of course, the doctors tried to make claims that things were medically necessary, and people would die without them, and yadda, yadda, yadda." She rolled her hands. "They always say that. So of course, he had to deny what their policies didn't cover. As was his job, right? Well, he tried to get another job after that, like people tend to do. But he couldn't find anything. They said that no one wanted to hire him, and he's been here ever since."

"I guess that would explain his mediocre performance."

Erica Slain scoffed. "You'd think that if he couldn't get anything else he'd make damn sure he did well at this one. But he just barely makes his quotas, shows up at his desk within a minute of the start of his shift, and takes exactly the number of sick days he has every year," She rolled her eyes. "He makes sure we don't have anything to complain about but nothing more than that."

"Huh. But you have to have at least talked to him, right?"

"Sure," she said. "We have performance reviews twice a year."

"And?"

"And I give him his review, he never has any questions, then that's it. It's like he just shut off," Slain said with a shrug and a blank face.

"Did you ever ask him if he was okay?"

"Well, it's like I said before—"

"You don't get chummy with the help. Right," I said, nodding. "Thanks for speaking with me. I think that's all my questions."

"You're welcome, Officer."

"Det—never mind." I pulled out a business card and handed it to her. "I'll call you if I need anything else," I said in as friendly a voice as I could muster. "Would it be possible to speak with his coworkers, now?"

"If you feel you need to. But most of them have already had their lunches."

"I'm sorry?" I raised my eyebrows at that.

"I mean, they wouldn't be able to speak with you, now. But some of them still have their lunch breaks coming up and I can have them come to the office and—"

"Wait." I cleared my throat. "So, you'd have them give up their lunch hour to talk to the detective investigating their coworker's murder?"

She shook her head and looked at me like I just asked to confirm that people don't really live inside the TV. "Well, yes. Officer, you have no idea how much money we'd lose in sales if we didn't have people answering the calls."

"Ms. Slain," I said slowly to make sure she understood me. "Someone died. Someone on your team. That you saw every day. Someone threw him to a ravenous alligator who ripped him in half while he was still alive."

She looked at me from the other side of her expensive desk like she didn't know how to react.

"Ripped in half while he was still alive! Do you have any idea what that must've been like for him? You don't think finding his murderer is worth a little money?"

She gently shook her head and replied as if reading from the employee manual, "It's the company's money."

I tried to contain a few choice swear words and rubbed my forehead. "Okay, how about you give me the names, addresses, and phone numbers of the rest of the people on his team?"

She looked at me for a moment. I don't think she could tell whether I was kidding or not.

"Don't make me get a subpoena, Ms. Slain." I got up out of the chair and stood up to my full height.

"Give—Give me a moment." She leaned into her computer and started clicking and typing.

I didn't get anything useful out of them, anyway. One of them liked talking to Sween but didn't know him outside of work. One of them thought he was crazy for preferring *Star Wars* to *Star Trek*, and another thought he was cute. All very interesting conversations but none of them produced anything that would lead to why someone would want to push Sween into the jaws of a cantankerous alligator that was bigger than my living room.

Then I got the call from Sargent Martinez and my day got a lot better.

Chapter 9

"You really are the best boss ever," I told Sergeant Martinez as I took the helmet from her.

"I know. Just don't forget to come back. I'd hate to go through all the trouble of training a new guy." She had a spark in her eye, normally reserved for Department Pizza Day.

"Detective Papadopoulos: Lost in the Past. That's not a bad idea for a TV series," I said.

"It'd never work. You're a lot better a detective than you are an actor."

"True. But what if I got Idris Elba to play my part?"

"Just remember to give me a share of the royalties." She made the thumbs up as she walked backward and took her place beside Sargent Williams and Chief Rogers at the front of the crowd, a few yards away under the shade of a live oak tree. They had set up a large monitor to the side of them so they could watch the feed from the camera in my helmet. Nothing like performance anxiety.

Ron stood by the monitor in those mirrored sunglasses that made him look like a henchman in a 1970s cop show. He was probably curious to see how close his forensic efforts came to the actual event. I imagine it's like the magician showing you exactly how they did it, right after the trick. I wouldn't pass up something like that, either. He saw me notice him and nodded. The way he looked at me, you'd think I was headed to orbit. I guess traveling through time is just as good.

With him as always was Allister, standing just to his side with his arms crossed. He swayed back and forth, shifting his weight from one foot to the other. He might've had to pee. Hard to say what goes through that kid's head.

A few yards in front of me stood the doorway from the lab at the

University of South Florida. Its skeleton in the middle of the parking lot drenched in the Florida sun looked even weirder than back at the lab. They blocked off the parking lot to Robles Park to give us some space to do this. But that didn't stop people in the neighborhood from just walking over to see what was going on. One of them had his phone out to take a video.

They set up a trial run for the time suit at the site of the Sween murder. Unlike the Horner murder, thanks to the eyewitness testimony of Mr. Ortega, we know exactly when it happened. And that made this the perfect thing to find out if the suit could show us enough to put someone in jail.

As Clara fastened my helmet to my collar, she felt the need to remind me, "Remember, you can't change anything in the past. You can look but you can't touch."

"I remember. I still have the bruises on my ass," I said through the helmet.

"And whatever you do, don't take the helmet off to try to get a better look at something." She fastened my gloves to my sleeves.

"Yeah, yeah. I know. The second law of thermodynamics or whatever."

"The law of conservation of matter and energy," she said like a scolding.

"Right. $E=MC^2$ and all that."

She put her hands on my shoulders and looked up at me. "Are you okay?"

"I'm about to walk into the past and witness a guy getting ripped apart by an alligator, Clara. I'm as okay as my brain will let me be."

Her smile curled all the way up to her ears.

"I'll be alright. Thanks," I said as reassuringly as I could manage.

"You're cute when you're worried," she said as she walked off to the console, a few yards in the other direction. A bundle of black cables led from the side of it to a van in the parking lot, farther back.

"Can you hear me, Detective Papadopoulos?" asked Dr. Khatri over the helmet's speakers.

I turned to find her at the console, talking into a microphone. I raised my arm for a thumbs up. "Loud and clear, Doctor. Thanks for getting my name right."

J.S. Johnston

She sat on a lawn chair in front of the console and tapped a few buttons. In a moment or two, a low hum started to build from the van. It was so gradual that I didn't notice it start, but it grew so strong that it rattled my heart inside my chest. The people who'd wandered over to the park looked at each other with eyes that said they weren't certain whether to be worried or not.

Someone muttered something to someone else in an anxious tone. Allister leaned into Ron and looked like he asked him if they should run. Captain Paganini said something angrily to Sargent Martinez and pointed at the van. Chief Rogers left the shade of the live oak tree to storm over to Dr. Khatri and Clara at the console.

Then as if the bubble finally burst, the doorway filled with a light-purple translucent membrane that shimmered with streaks of reds and blues. The past lingered just a few feet ahead of me. It waited for me, like the tiny waves that lap the shoreline.

"The portal is set for twenty minutes before the murder took place," said Dr. Khatri over the speakers in my helmet. "That should give you plenty of time to acclimate yourself and still give a margin of error." Her voice reminded me of a flute. Even the word murder was calming.

"Hey, quick thought," I said, again through the helmet. "What happens if I'm—" I waved my hand in the direction of the shimmering doorway. "And the portal shuts down? Am I going to be stuck in there, forever? I mean, stuck back then. Back there. Whatever adverb I'm supposed to be using." All of a sudden, I was the kid who didn't want his parents to shut his bedroom door at night.

"Don't worry," Clara said in as assuring a tone as I'd ever heard her use. "Everything will be fine." She patted me on the shoulder. If anything does happen, the suit's onboard AI can make its own portals in an emergency. Just tell Watson when you want to go, and he'll do the rest. Okay?"

I nodded my head inside the helmet. "Okay."

"Now get your butt in there."

I'd already had the first round in the time suit. But with my boss and the rest of the people who sign my paychecks watching, I channeled the spirits of Neil Armstrong and Buzz Aldrin. I stepped up to the shimmering purple doorway, stopped, turned to them, and raised my arm for a thumbs up. And made a cheesy smile that they probably couldn't see through the glare of my helmet.

My boss returned the thumb. Her boss looked at me like I was wasting his money. No one took my picture. I stepped through the portal.

* * *

The past came rushing at me like the current of a river and my stomach started doing cartwheels. I hated that part. Reflections and shining streams and emptiness ran past me, and I raised an arm to shield my eyes as if they were debris caught in the wind.

My heart pounded and tried its damndest to climb out of my throat. The pain of a boa constrictor wrapped around my chest, squeezing like something out of the Spanish Inquisition. I fell to my knees and grabbed the doorway. You did this before, Sean. Why was it so much harder, this time? Just breathe.

"Sean, your heart rate, and respiration are up. Are you okay?" asked Clara through the helmet speakers.

"Yep. Never better. Just another day at work." I sat on the ground and tried not to throw up in my helmet.

After a pause, she asked, "So, what are you doing, Friday night?"

"What?"

"I've always wanted to date a detective. There's this Italian place, downtown off Westshore Boulevard. And I bet your butt looks cute in jeans."

"Seriously!? Right now?"

"It's okay. No one can hear us. We can talk sexy all we want," Clara said with a slow and sensual voice.

"Clara, I'm old enough to be your father. And *his* father."

"You don't want to date me? Don't you think I'm pretty?"

"You're very pretty. But I don't want to date anyone. And seriously, I probably have a good twenty years on you."

"It'll be okay. I'll be gentle," she said like she was waiting for me to say that.

"Clara!"

She giggled. "Sorry about that. But your heart rate and respiration are below scary levels, now."

She was right. I'd calmed down a little.

"I just had to get your mind off of freaking out for a minute. The second time is the worst," she said with assurance in her voice.

I groaned and wished I could rub my forehead.

The world opened up, reducing from the chaos at the bottom of a waterfall to the constant flow of a river. The walking path lay just ahead of me by the lake and the slash pine trees off to the right, where Mr. Ortega said the murderer came from. They shimmered and waved like a heat mirage.

"I was serious when I said that no one could hear us. The video feed is being recorded but not the audio."

"Thank you for that." I steadied myself on the weird freestanding doorway and slowly stood up to my full height with unneeded care.

She laughed. "So, what did you mean about not wanting to date anyone?"

"You sure ask a lot of questions," I said, steadying myself in the current of time.

"It might be a while before anything happens. We may as well talk."

My stomach was still doing an Irish jig. A bad one, too. "So where did you get that blue hair?"

"The hairdresser gave it to me. What was that you said about not wanting to date?"

"What was that? I think comms are starting to cut out." I walked over to the pier that hung over the water, while I had time to wait for everything to start happening.

"You know, I bet you've questioned a million people, Mister Homicide Detective. Why is one question so hard to answer?"

"Don't worry. If I'm ever called in for questioning, no one will ever ask me why I'm not dating anyone."

"Where are you going?" she asked. I guess she was paying attention to the video feed from my helmet.

"When we were working the crime scene, we found an orange butterfly pinned to the railing of this pier." I kept walking. "I need to see if it was there before or after Mr. Sween was murdered."

"A little butterfly? Did you recognize the species?"

"Well—" I finally came close enough to see it, already pinned to the railing as if it was waiting. "It's that one there."

"Oh wow. It's so pretty," she said in a dreamy voice.

"Even with all this weird time stuff everywhere, yeah. Do you know anything about it?"

"They're all over here."

"They are?" I asked.

"Yep. They range from here, to South America. They're pretty common."

"Allister said the same thing," I said, waiting patiently for the scarry part to happen.

"Who?"

"A guy I work with. He's in Forensics."

"Well, some kid probably left it there. I wouldn't pay too much attention. They're really common," she said, dismissing it.

Then it started happening as if actors in a play came out from behind a curtain. Timothy Sween walked up the path by the lake as casually as if it were any other day. The killer crouched down by the slash pine trees.

"Something's happening. Hold on," I said.

"I can see it on the monitor."

"I'm going to move closer to the trees so I can see who's in there," I said, taking a step.

"No. Move to the path so you can record them coming towards you."

Sween kept walking closer at a good pace, his white Disney World T-shirt dark with sweat, and no idea what was about to happen.

"Good idea. I'll be able to get a better look at their face, that way. Are you recording this?"

"Whoops," she said.

"Clara!"

"I've been recording everything. Relax." She giggled.

Sween trotted to a stop, still on the walking path, and bent down to tie his shoe. The murderer waited crouched in the trees, then stood up, just a few yards away. I hurried through the grass over to Sween.

"Just be careful not to get in anyone's way," she said. I'm a time-traveler now and people are still telling me what to do.

"I know, I know. Any more orders and you're going to have to start paying me."

I stood right beside Sween while he was still kneeling, tying his shoe, and waited. The murderer launched out of the trees and came barreling towards him. Their face emerged from the streamy fog of the time current but still couldn't make it out.

Sween stopped tying his shoes, apparently hearing the murderer running through the grass. Just as he looked up to see what it was, they plowed into him with all their weight like a football player. Sween rolled down the embankment. His feet left the ground and flailed in the air. He made a splash in the water and franticly scrambled to get out.

Big Al came out of nowhere. He effortlessly zipped through the water over to Sween and drove teeth as big as my palm into his leg with almost three thousand pounds of bite force. The sound of the bone cracking invaded my helmet.

The murderer clipped my left side as they ran past me and sent me to the ground. Sween cried out with everything he had as the alligator pulled him into the lake and underwater for a death roll. His cries mixed with watery gurgles, meat tearing and ripping, and bones cracking and then he didn't make noise anymore. The alligator reared its head back to let one of Sween's legs pass down its throat. A small piece of the meat fell into the water and blood billowed out. It reminded me of a tea bag.

Sween's torso lay on the embankment; his intestines trailed behind him. But he wasn't finished, yet. He tried to scream. His eyes scrunched up and his mouth gaped open, but nothing came out. Then he went limp.

Mr. Ortega shut his car door and ran towards the scene. I had to back up to keep from getting run over.

That feeling in my stomach came back to me and I tried not to throw up in my helmet. I always get to the murder scenes after the fact. It's all over and done by the time I show up. I've never watched them actually—happen—before. At least it went the way the witness said.

"Clara, tell me you got that."

The line was silent, except for a low hiss and the occasional crackle.

"Clara?"

Just more hissing.

I knocked on my helmet.

"I really hope you're just ignoring me."

Nothing.

"They invent a time suit and can't get the radio to work," I said to myself.

Big Al swam over and plucked the lifeless torso of Timothy Sween off the embankment and threw his head back to let it slide down his throat. It was so dispassionate that you'd think it was a dog with a treat.

Mr. Ortega ran over to the patch of trees to throw up. He failed to include that in his statement. I would, too.

Someone stood on the shore of the other side of the lake. Or rather the absence of someone. A black person-shaped form. I couldn't tell whether they saw me or not. They might've been looking at me. They were standing out in the sun and looked stark black from head to foot, like the shadow of something.

"Clara, are you seeing this?" I asked through the helmet's mic.

Nothing but hissing.

"Damn."

All of a sudden, the figure ran towards me, out onto the lake, and kept running. The surface of the water rippled in the wind and the figure just ran over the top of it like it was solid ground and came right at me. Holy Christ.

"Clara! For the love of God. Clara!" I shouted into the mic.

The shadow figure kept running at me, getting closer. Then I recognized it as the Nothing Man from my dreams. He zipped across the lake through the current of time that flowed between us.

"No. No, this is impossible. How is—"

The Nothing Man was almost on me, still running across the surface of the lake. I started unconsciously walking backward and my heart tried to beat its way out of my ribcage.

"Clara?"

He was right there and still—he just wasn't. He wasn't a solid form. There wasn't a physical object painted black. There was nothing there! I swear to God, there was nothing there!

"No!" I shouted and stumbled on a rock and fell to the ground.

Still running at full speed, the Nothing Man held up his hand. I could make out that he held an elongated shape, as long as my arm. He held it aloft as he ran like he was showing it to me.

I scrambled to my feet, not bothering to come to my full height before running across the parking lot, back to the portal. He was on me by the time I got there. Jesus, I'm getting old. He took a swipe and just missed me as I passed through and stumbled on the lip.

* * *

"Turn it off!" I screamed as soon as my foot landed on the other side. "Hurry!"

Clara sat at the console. Dr. Khatri sat beside her and bent over to flip a switch. In no longer than a moment, the portal disappeared like a popped soap bubble.

I fumbled at the stupid helmet with my gloved hands, trying to find whatever fastened it to my collar so I could yank it off. You'd think if these geniuses were smart enough to build a time machine, they could design a helmet fastening whateveritscalled that didn't need a college degree to undo, and why the hell are my fingers so damn big?

Clara shot up from her chair and rushed over to me. "What happened? What's wrong?" she asked, shooing my hands away so she could take my helmet off.

As soon as she unlatched it, I grabbed it with both hands, threw it off my head and sucked in a deep breath of fresh air.

"What?" she demanded.

"Seriously?"

Chapter 10

A tiny paw, as soft as goose down touched me on my bare shoulder as I lay in bed. It was as gentle as the brush of angel hair. But it was still enough to shove me out of one world and into another, waking me from a good dream. I forget what it was about, but I know I liked it.

I sluggishly rolled over to address what had reached in and pulled me back into reality and found T.J. sitting on my nightstand, just a few inches away. The little radar dishes that he used for ears were pointed right at me. The light peeking in from between the curtains draped over his face and highlighted his immense jade green eyes as if he were in an old movie. His front paws stood together, at attention.

He looked like he was waiting for me to do something, and I was supposed to know what it was. Maybe cats are telepathic and the reason they stare at us is that they don't understand why we don't answer them. That's probably what it is.

I rolled over to go back to sleep, determined to rejoin the world I left, and pulled the comforter over my shoulder to help get me there.

It wasn't three seconds later when he tapped me on the ear with his paw, with just a little more force. It was like a wet willy with tiny cat hairs, instead of the wet part. I shivered and rubbed my ear.

"Go away," I forced out through the semi-paralysis of a sleepy haze. I didn't know what he wanted, and I wasn't about to get up and feed him. It's not like he has to go to work for a living. He could wait.

Then, he tapped me on the ear again like it was a crosswalk button that didn't actually do anything.

"Stop it!" I waved away an imaginary paw without making the effort to open my eyes.

Just when I'd almost drifted back to sleep, another tap came, followed by a very quiet meow. Like I'd forgotten.

I pulled the covers up over my ear. Easy fix.

He casually stepped over onto the bed next to me like it was his job. And ruffled through my hair as he sniffed at it. The sound invaded the comforter like it wasn't there. I never knew cats breathed that loud. Then he tapped me on the head.

"You're exactly one step from becoming homeless, cat!"

He stepped back to the nightstand and sat down. I took a calming sigh. Then he meowed louder.

I rolled over with righteous fury to face my tormentor and threw off the covers. "I swear to God if you don't—" Then I happened to notice the alarm clock that T.J. sat next to. It was set to wake me up over an hour ago. But it didn't go off. Or maybe it did. I wasn't really sure. "Good cat!" I scratched him behind his ear, kissed his head then jumped out of bed.

I didn't sleep much that night. For some reason when I turned off the lights, every shadow on the walls of the bedroom looked vaguely human; a jury of my shadowy peers, standing in judgment of my sins. I kept telling myself it was just a weird day and to ignore it. But then every time I shut my eyes, I swear I could hear someone walking around. I did my best to not imagine an ax murderer in the kitchen fixing himself a sandwich. So, I must've overslept. Occupational hazard, I guess.

I'm pretty sure I set a world record for the fastest shower ever taken that still included soap and shampoo. I'm not sure if I used either of them in the right place or in the right order, but it happened. Somewhere in the middle of the bedlam I grabbed a bowl from the dishwasher and poured T.J. some of the milk from the fridge for helping me out. He did wake me up so I wouldn't be late, after all. Well, not very late, anyway.

I'd scheduled another appointment with Dr. Striker. The website didn't have an option for "never" or "when I'm free" so I just picked whatever day was furthest out. Sargent Martinez said that since I walked out of the last one, it didn't count. You'd think I'd at least get partial credit.

"You need to talk to him," she said. "He's a valuable resource," she said. Then she said some other stuff about not being Superman that I wasn't listening to. Maybe she isn't the best boss ever.

When I ran out of the house in a blaze of newfound efficiency, I told T.J. to watch the place and not to let anyone in who promises they're totally not a burglar. He didn't look like he was up to the task. But then, who does?

* * *

"You look like you haven't slept in a while," said Dr. Striker. I think that translates to 'You look like shit.' I suddenly couldn't remember if I shaved that morning. He leaned back in his chair and rested his elbows on the armrests. Then he crossed his legs. His pant leg raised, showing off the superior quality of his argyle socks. "Everything okay?" The doctor serves.

"You know how the life of a homicide detective is. We work when we're needed. Most of us don't sleep much." The detective returns the doctor's serve. I passed a hand over my chin to check if I'd shaved, but casually to not make it look like I was trying to. And I verified that I, in fact, did not shave.

"Heard about your experience, the other day. Going back in time and witnessing a murder must be jarring." The doctor returns the return.

"Yeah, it was. But it was in the past so there's nothing I could've done."

"It must've been tough to watch it happen and not help," he said.

I let the dead air hang in the room.

Then he added, "Someone like you, being on the force as long as you have, sworn to protect and defend, being forced to stand by while a brutal murder took place."

I nodded my head like I was expecting him to say more things.

I don't think he bought it. He pulled over the laptop sitting on the rolling stand beside him, clicked the mouse a couple of times, and read something from it. "And then there was… What did you call it?" His face scrunched up like he was sucking on a lemon drop. "A shadow. You put in your report that a shadow person was there with you. What's a shadow person?"

"Morlock," I corrected him.

"I'm sorry?" he asked.

"Morlock is less terrifying."

Damn. The point goes to the mean old doctor.

He raised an eyebrow and looked up at me from his laptop. "Morlock?" He said it like he didn't believe me. Imagine that.

"It's from Jules Verne's *The Time Machine* and—"

He nodded. "I had to do a high school book report on it." He uncrossed and crossed his legs. "I mean tell me about it. What was it like?" Damn open-ended questions.

"I put it all in my report. Is that what you're reading? If not, I could email it to you." Another point for the handsome detective.

"I have it here on the screen, thanks. But I think it'd do you more good if we could talk about it. Things are normally easier to deal with if you don't let them fester." Damn. Another point for Striker. I'm not giving him any more points. Please, detective gods. Have pity on a humble practitioner and show me the way out.

"Well, there's not much to say. It looked like a man. But it was more like the shadow of one." I shrugged my shoulders. "The end." I'm not sure whether that was a point for me or not.

"When you came back out, you screamed to shut off the portal. What happened?"

I didn't realize that was in the report. Damn. I got tired of the game and leaned forward in my chair. "Look. Dr. Striker. You seem like you're a nice guy. But I see a lot of shit in my job. We all do. I once processed a crime scene where a guy was stuffed into an industrial microwave and cooked until he exploded like an egg. I just came from a scene where a guy was ripped in half by an alligator. Sometimes it gets to be too much for us, and we can lash out. We do our best to cope but sometimes the occasional punch to the proboscis can slip out. Now I know you mean well. But unless you can take one of those degrees off the wall and use it to rid the world of horribly broken, murderous people, then there's not much point to this. Is there?" I sat back in my chair. Another point for the dashing young detective. Maybe not so young.

Dr. Striker leaned forward in his chair. "I know." He looked at the floor and nodded. "I absolutely understand everything you just said. I've been here for over ten years, and I've seen guys do a lot more than punching someone in their proboscis when they couldn't take it, anymore."

"Good. You get it, then." I smiled in relief.

"Yeah, I get it. It's a horrible job and you're all just doing your best to cope."

"You got it!"

He settled himself in his chair and said, "Now, if you want to be able to keep it together well enough to do your job and maybe retire one day, I can help with that. I can help you manage and redirect all that rage at the horrible things people do to each other to someplace safe. Maybe have fewer nightmares."

"I never told you about the nightmares."

He sat back and laced his fingers together. "You didn't have to. Everyone in Homicide has them, now and then."

"They do?"

"Did you think you were the only one? You've seen what you do for a living. You'd have to be a psychopath not to be bothered by it."

I paused for a moment with no idea how to respond to that. Damn. Another point to the doctor.

My phone chimed its alert for a text and Dr. Striker watched me fish it out of my pocket with this look on his face like he'd caught me trying to skip school. I pretended not to pick up on it.

The text was from Clara - "We finally downloaded the helmet footage. Come see it." She added two very happy smiley faces at the end.

I held up the phone as if showing him my badge. "Sorry, Doctor. Gotta go!" Touchdown! Or home run. Or goal. I don't know. I hate sports.

* * *

You take your life into your own hands in Tampa midday traffic. All the same, I headed down I-275 to get over to the University of South Florida. Clara could've just posted the time suit camera footage online for me, but I did not want to stay and have my brain opened up by Dr. Striker's psychological scalpel. The door could have been on fire, and I'd still have left. Besides, Clara did ask me to come and

87

view the footage. And I'd hate to let down a young lady.

The blurry face of Sween's murderer, as it was just before he ran me over, displayed on the computer monitor in the lab at the University of South Florida's Physics department. I became the first time-traveling detective, wearing a zillion-dollar specially designed suit that took years to perfect, all so I could watch an event as it happens to bring a murderer to justice. And the picture is blurry.

"Great. The quality is so good that it perfectly resembles about a million people in Tampa," I noted.

"It's not that bad," said Clara scrolling the wheel of her mouse to enlarge the picture, making it pixilated and even more blurry.

"Not that bad? Clara, that could be anybody. Hell, it could be Kim Jong-Un for all you can tell from that." I slid over the small stack of yellow-paged detective novels so I could put an elbow on the console.

"Hey, what do you want from me? We only invented time travel. Not like that means anything."

"The camera has already been invented! Just run down to Best Buy, get a good one, and use it. Hell, I'll even help you duct tape it onto the helmet!" I yelled at her.

She pushed the mouse away and swung her chair around to face me. "Is that seriously what you think we do here? Your bosses sunk millions into this, and you think we just tape stuff together and hope for the best? Screw quantum physics and temporal mechanics! Let's just start duck-taping stuff together! It'll be fine!"

"I'm sorry. I didn't mean for it to come out like that," I said. After a moment, added, "It's just that we went to a lot of trouble to go back in time and get the killer's face. I still don't understand how that's even possible, but there I was, looking right at him. He even knocked me over and this is the most detailed picture we could get. It's just frustrating, is all." I leaned into the monitor and squinted my eyes a little. "It almost looks like my cousin."

"Is he a detective too?" she asked and returned to the image on the monitor to some science thing with numbers and a very colorful pie chart.

"He is gainfully employed in a factory making pants."

She snorted out an unexpected laugh. "I guess everyone needs pants."

"The world would be better off without them if you asked me." I picked up one of her detective novels and examined it. "Why do you read these?"

She took it from me and replaced it on the top of the stack. "I like how everything wraps up so neatly at the end."

"Unlike real life, I guess. Right?"

"So, are we ever going to talk about what you saw?" she asked, redirecting the conversation.

"We were just looking at what I saw." I paused a moment while she eyed me. "You mean the other thing. The Morlock."

She smiled. "What did your Morlock look like?"

"I told you, already. Nothing. It was like going to the movies then all of a sudden, there's a big person-shaped hole in the screen."

She shook her head. "Did they have a color or texture?"

"No, nothing. It looked like outer space without the stars."

Clara shook her head again as if she were waiting for me to finish a sentence.

"I think this job really is getting to me," I said. "I thought it was scary enough in there without me seeing things. Over there. Back then. Whatever."

Dr. Khatri stepped in from the other room and suggested, "It sounds like a time shadow."

I scratched my forehead. "A what-shadow?"

She asked Clara, "Remember? We hypothesized that due to the photons flowing from one temporal medium to the next the resulting images would naturally distort. And the temporal medium itself would also inhibit the photoelectromagnetic spectrum and absorb their quantum charges."

"I feel like I need a doctorate just to talk to you guys," I said.

Clara smiled and put a hand on the doctor's forearm. "That's right. A time shadow." She was happy about it, and I have no idea why. Then she looked at me and translated. "There was another pocket of time where you were. So, what you saw was an optical illusion. The light couldn't bounce off of the object to your eye like it normally does, so it just looked black to you. It was basically a shadow of the fourth dimension."

"So, by another pocket of time, you mean—"

She nodded her head. "I mean that there was another man there in another time suit. Right."

"But I thought you ladies had the only one. Could someone else have invented another suit and followed me back?"

Both women giggled for a minute. Clara even put her hand to her mouth. Maybe I should look into some online quantum physics classes. I waited for someone to fill me in on the joke.

"It's a good thing you're so cute," said Clara.

Dr. Khatri smiled and said, "It's a time suit. It doesn't matter when they got it."

I pinched the bridge of my nose and sat back in my desk chair. "So why didn't the other guy show up on the video feed? And why couldn't you see him through the portal like you could see me and everything else?"

Dr. Khatri started to roll her hands and took a breath.

"I changed my mind," I interjected, putting up a hand to stop her. "I don't want to know. What does a migraine feel like?"

My phone started playing the Funeral March from my pocket. I really need to change it to something else.

I turned on the video chat and Sargent Martinez's shining face beamed back at me. It looked like she was out in the sun.

"What's up, Sarge?"

Clara inched closer to look at the phone screen. "Hey, you. Stick to your detective books."

She made a pouting face, and I caved in. Dr. Khatri smiled at me.

"Who's that with you?" asked Sargent Martinez, craning her head as if it helped.

"Just a concerned citizen. What's up?"

"Have a new case for you," Martinez said.

"I'm already working two. Well, technically, it's the same one."

"You're still only working one," she assured me. "Did you go to the Gasparilla parade, last night?"

"No. Why? What happened?" I asked.

"I'm texting you the address. I'll see you when you get here."

Clara looked up at me like her favorite show was just about to go into a commercial.

"Hell. See you in a bit."

Chapter 11

The body of Sandra Miller leaned against the brick wall, next to the entrance to Renni's Beach and Surf Shop on Ashley Drive. She sat upright but slouched over with her head reaching for her stomach. Her face showed a lifeless expression of melancholy.

She was dressed in a dark green tank top, khaki shorts, and red flip-flops that showed her toenails which were freshly painted a matching shade of red. A large black, three-cornered pirate hat, complete with skull and crossbones on the front, adorned her graying head. A pound and a half of plastic Gasparilla bead necklaces hung around her neck. Her lipstick was the color of deep rust.

Her dark brown skin was clear, with no obvious signs of lacerations or bruising, anywhere. Both of her hands lay on her lap like she was meditating and just fell asleep.

The section of sidewalk and part of the road where the squad cars were parked was taped off, all the way down to the corner of Brorein Street. The typical uniformed police stood along the barrier to keep the locals from ignoring it and just waltzing in. Cars slowed down as they passed us so their drivers could get a good look at the danger lurking in their neighborhood.

"Excuse me, sir," yelled the store manager, walking up to me on the sidewalk. Or rather, stomping up to me, like I worked for him.

"It's Detective Papadopoulos," I told him with my hands in the air and palms toward him to stop his advance. "How can I help you?"

He wore the same clothes he sold in the store: a pair of blue board shorts with an orange hibiscus flower pattern, brown flip-flops with a twine thong, and a matching brown T-shirt with the words SURF OR DIE printed on it. His stringy blonde hair came down to his shoulders, making him look like a talking mop.

"I don't want to be a pain," he said. However, I believe he did wish to be a pain. "You guys have the entranceway blocked off with your yellow tape." The little muscles on his temples pulsed as he ground his teeth.

"That's because this is a crime scene, Mr...."

"Anders. Joseph Anders," he said. "I'm the store manager, here at Renni's Beach and Surf Shop."

"Hey, is it really owned by a guy named Renni? If so, is it short for Regenold?"

"Mr. Diplodocus, as long as—"

"It's Detective Diplodo—I mean, Papadopoulos," I corrected him.

"How long are you guys going to stay out here?" he asked, sounding as impatient as one can sound.

"Until we're done processing the murder scene by the door to your shop. Why do you ask?"

"Because no one can get in and buy anything, is why." He snapped at me with the anger of a Chiwawa. "You've been out here for hours. Do you know how much money we're losing?"

"No. Do you know who killed this woman on your doorstep?"

"What? Of course, I don't."

"Well, then we're going to stay out here until we can figure it out. We might be awhile."

I think he had a stroke. Or an aneurysm. I don't know, I'm not a doctor. "Can I at least be compensated for lost revenue? I called this in because I'm a concerned citizen. I didn't expect to go bankrupt from it," he said.

Before he could yell anything else at me, I stepped close to him and lowered my voice. "Now, we don't usually do this, but if you want, I can talk to the Sarge about that."

"Yeah?" His eyes brightened.

"Yeah. The Sarge and I are pretty close. These things are always negotiable. I mean, you do pay your taxes, right?"

"I do. A hell of a lot of taxes," he said with a chuckle.

"There you are. You're an upstanding part of the community. She's bound to listen."

"Yeah. Yeah, I am."

"Now, if you help me out, I can even put the word in for you about that," I said as sincerely as I could manage.

"Sure. What can I do?" He was positively enthusiastic. Ron stood just a few paces away, trying not to look like he was listening in on the conversation.

I took out my phone and started the voice recording app. "I just have a couple of questions for you, regarding this poor woman, here."

"No problem. Go ahead. Please."

"Now, you were the one to report the body, right?" I asked, holding out my phone.

He energetically nodded his head. "I did. When I came in, this morning."

"And that was when?"

"At 7:43, this morning," he said. "That's when I always get here."

"Punctual. Now, she must've been out here for a while, and no one noticed. But you were the one to see something was wrong. What tipped you off?"

"Well, I thought she was homeless, and I didn't want her to scare off customers, so I told her to get up and leave."

"You thought she was homeless," I said, confirming.

"Well, yeah. I don't have a problem with them, but I have a business to run."

"Those are nice clothes for a homeless person," I motioned to the body sitting on the ground.

"Well, you know how they all are." There was poison in his voice.

"Ah. And then what happened?"

"Well, she wouldn't leave. So, I assumed she just wanted to pass out drunk and picked my door. People give them money and all they do is spend it on booze and drugs." His voice had a sting of annoyance.

"Gasparilla beads around her neck, a pirate hat on her head, and you assumed she was a strung-out homeless person. Go on," I said.

"Yeah, well anyway, I grabbed her shoulder and tried shaking her to wake her up." His face changed to something that looked like accidentally taking a drink of spoiled orange juice. "She was so cold and stiff."

"Is that when you called 9-1-1?"

"Well, I had to finish eating my breakfast burrito first, but yeah," he said with a nod.

"Your breakfast burrito."

"It was from Casa Del Taco. You know what they cost. I wasn't about to let it get cold. Besides, it's not like she was going to get any worse. Right?" He smiled at me like he hoped I'd join in on the joke.

"That is very true. Thank you, Mr. Anders." I shut off the voice recording app and put my phone back in my pocket.

"So, you guys will reimburse us for lost income?"

I smiled. "Of course not. I told you we never do that. But your assistance is invaluable to us, sir." I kept smiling.

"What the hell?" he shouted at me, letting me smell the remains of that burrito on his breath. "You said you'd talk to your boss if I answered your damn questions!"

"Yes. I did. And I will. She is my boss. I talk to her every day. I will tell her that you've been very helpful, just like I said." Still smiling.

"But you're not—?"

I chuckled. "Mr. Anders don't be silly. I told you we never do that."

"What? You're kidding!" He looked like he may have forgotten to keep breathing.

"I'm afraid it's against department policy to kid, Mr. Anders. But I do want to express how appreciative I am of your assistance."

"Fucking cops!" He threw up his hands and stormed back into his shop. On his way in, he mumbled something about "I pay my goddamn taxes!" Or something like that. I wasn't listening.

"You really are shit with people," said Ron as he walked up to me, again with his mirrored sunglasses that made him look like an extra in a bad 1980s cop show.

"What do you mean? I thought I handled that very well."

"Interactions that are handled very well, generally don't end with a citizen screaming 'fucking cops' as they storm away."

"Sometimes they do."

He laughed. "Your new friend left the butterfly on the dashboard of her car, four blocks over,"

"Yeah," I answered, still looking at Sandra Miller's earthly remains. "Confirms they're not picking their victims at random. There is a method to it."

"And you might not even know it was a murder, otherwise. There's not a scratch on her."

"I did notice that," I said with a stroke of my chin.

Ron set down the large forensics tackle box that he'd been carrying and crouched down to open it. "So, how's that cat working out? What did you name it, again?"

"His name is T.J.," I answered. "And he left me a watery glob of diarrhea on the rug in front of the TV. I came home last night and almost stepped in it before I saw it."

He blurted out a big belly laugh. "That's nasty."

"I couldn't figure out what stank so bad. I looked down and there it was. So, I scrubbed it with soap and water for probably an hour, and I still don't think I got it all. Do you think we can get the crime scene cleaners to take care of it?"

Ron kept laughing.

"You wouldn't laugh if you saw it."

"Yes, I would," he said.

"Oh, right."

"You didn't give him any milk, did you?"

"Maybe," I said with a shrug. "Why do you ask?"

"Because cats are lactose intolerant. It gives them the shits." Ron took a spray bottle of something out of his tackle box and applied it to the wall, next to the victim. "So, was that why you didn't go to the Gasparilla, last night?"

"Ron, you know I don't drink, anymore. That's all the Gasparilla is. Drunken people pretending to be pirates."

"It's celebrating the history of Tampa," he said.

I snickered. "By getting drunk and pretending to be a pirate."

"You have a point." He took out his cell phone and started taking pictures of the wall that he'd just sprayed with whatever it was.

"What are you taking pictures of?"

"Evidence," he said. "It's a crime scene. What else would I be taking pictures of? It's like you don't know what I do for a living."

"Apologies, Your Highness. Please forgive my unforgivable ignorance," I said and bowed to him.

"Bring me Subway and we're good."

Several onlookers had begun to gather at the yellow police tape that blocked off the crime scene. They pointed at Sandra Miller's body, sitting against the brick wall, and murmured uneasy words to each other. Some of them had their phones out to take a video of everything like they always do. I'm sure it'll end up on YouTube in an hour. The uniformed cops standing along the yellow tape tried to get them to stop but weren't very convincing.

Allister pushed past all of them as he came up the sidewalk, rolling what looked like airplane luggage behind him. The luggage looked like it must've weighed at least twice what Allister did.

He pulled up beside the victim and mumbled, "Hey Ron. Sean," with a nod to each of us then opened his goodies.

"Did you guys go, last night?" I asked Ron, looking down the street.

"We do every year," he answered. "Sue makes a pretty hot wench."

"Were there a lot of people? I mean, as much as usual?" I asked.

"Seemed like it. There are always thousands of people out for it. Why?"

"Well, doesn't the parade route come right down this road?" I asked, gesturing to it.

"I think so. Where are we?"

I glanced at the street sign at the corner and said, "Ashley Drive."

"It should, then. We should be towards the end of it, actually."

"So, there would've been a million people all up and down here. She's not tucked away in a building or even behind a dumpster. She's right out in the open, facing the street. How did she end up dead with all those people around? And how did no one notice her until this morning?"

"I think I've seen this in a movie, somewhere," said Ron, waving at the medical examiner as they parked their white panel van on the other side of the street. The conspicuous blue lettering on the sliding side door read POLICE CITY OF TAMPA as if one would need confirmation about who it belonged to.

"Me too," I said. "I'll be interested in what the autopsy has to say about the cause of death. Horner was shot in the head. Sween was thrown to an alligator in front of an eyewitness. Those were pretty obvious. But this one—There's not a mark on her. We'd never know she was murdered if it wasn't for that butterfly."

"Isn't that funny?"

"Yeah, isn't it?" I paused to watch the regular pulse of traffic make its way down the road, hoping something important would fall into place, somewhere in my brain. Maybe that only works in the movies.

Allister, lost in his own world, collected the tiny maggots from Sandra Miller's corpse that had already hatched. He carefully grabbed each one with a pair of metal tweezers, about as long as my outstretched hand, and tucked it into plastic evidence bags, as if anyone would want them. The fascinated smile he wore as he performed his ghoulish deed creeped me out, just a little.

"Hey, Allister. Quick question," I said.

He stopped the abduction of his wriggling prey and then gradually—and dramatically—looked up at me. I think he was trying to make a point that I was interrupting him.

"How long does it take to set butterfly wings?"

"What?" asked Allister, not even attempting to hide the irritation in his voice.

"You know. For display. For a specimen. That's something people do, right?"

"Yeah, you can set them," he said.

"How long would it take?"

"Well, it depends." He sealed the evidence bag full of maggots then stood to his full height and wiped his sweaty hands on his khakis. "Usually a week or two, depending on the size of it. You have to immobilize the wings and fix them into position first. How big of a butterfly are you working with?"

"Do you remember the one I brought in the other day? Dry… uh—"

"Dryas iulia."

"Right, right," I said. "The killer left another one in the victim's car, spread out just like at the Sween murder. How long would it take to make them do that?"

"I'd leave it sitting in the freezer for a couple of weeks, to be sure." He wiped the sweat from his brow. "If you take it out too soon, the wings will retract a little and you can't undo it."

"Do you need any special chemicals?"

"No, nothing. I mean you could, but you don't need any. You can just freeze them. Then take them out to set them out the way you want them and let them dry."

"So, whoever did this would've had to have had a few of them set up ahead of time."

Allister nodded his head. "Probably. It's not something you can do for a science fair the next morning."

"That's perfect. Thanks, Allister. Where did you learn all that stuff? Do they have a school for it?"

He shook his head and went back to what he was doing before I rudely interrupted him. He crouched down beside the body of Sandra Miller and continued to abduct the crawling things that wriggled on her earthly remains, baking in the Tampa afternoon sun. The reason for his fascination with them completely eluded me. Maybe he knew something I didn't. And maybe if I knew what that thing was, if there was one thing, I could join him in his fascination. Or maybe he just liked being different.

Ron watched me watching him. He chuckled to himself as he pulled out a long extension cord from his tackle box and dropped it on the ground.

As I walked up to him, I asked, "Is it me?"

Chapter 12

I stopped at Tampa Pizza and Wings for a large pepperoni. Hand-tossed, baked in a hundred-year-old wood fire oven, and kissed by an Italian angel. The word on the street is that they specially hand-pick the tomatoes for the marinara sauce from the west side of Mount Vesuvius.

It rested in the passenger seat of my Chrysler 300 as I drove to the station. I'd brought my flannel comforter from home to lay on top of it and keep it nice and warm on the drive. When I carried it into the building, people would stop in their tracks to get a momentary whiff of the aroma that emanated from it like Cleopatra's own perfume. However, carrying any pizza through an office building without the entire place noticing is a physical impossibility. And this is the best pizza in all of Tampa. Three people asked me about it, just in the parking lot.

I walked it across the building, all the way to the morgue, still wrapped in the flannel comforter, and stopped in front of the M.E.'s desk. Holding the pizza behind my back wasn't exactly hiding it from him.

"Dr. Stevens, I presume," I was trying to make a joke. I knew who he was. He's been working here longer than I have. And I think he had a good ten years of age on me with all the gray hair to prove it. Well, the hair that was left, anyway. He was clean-shaven and mostly bald with a Friar Tuck doughnut ring of the aforementioned gray hair above his ears.

Other than the computer monitor that stood in the center of it, his desk was mainly stacks of paper and manilla folders. As I stood before him, his head was down, studying the printed-out papers that he shuffled back and forth on his desk. He wore a crisp white button-up dress shirt with a whimsical pirate-themed green tie. The tie would be fitting for Gasparilla, which was the day before. So, I wasn't sure if he'd been home to change clothes or if he just liked it. Nothing wrong with a pirate tie, I guess.

"No." He didn't even bother to look up from his papers.

"No, what? I haven't asked anything."

"You were about to. The answer is no," he said, still not looking up.

"How do you know the answer if I haven't asked the question?"

He finally stopped and met my eyes. "Because no one ever comes down here to say hi. Everyone wants me to put their case ahead of everyone else's. Like theirs is somehow immensely more important than the others. I'm a person, you know. I have feelings. I can't be pushed around and coerced by anyone who thinks they're Columbo."

Nodding my head, I said, "You're absolutely right. You are a person and I care about your feelings."

"Good. You understand."

"Yes. I do." I smiled.

"Then you're okay with me getting to your case in the order in which it came in."

"If that's the way you handle things here, then I'll just have to accept it."

"Good...," he said and tapped his desk with his forefinger. "What's that behind your back?"

I pulled out the pizza and removed the flannel comforter. "I was going to give you this to put my case ahead of the others. You're right about it not being more important than anyone else's case. So, I thought I'd offer this to... encourage you to reprioritize your workload."

"I see. You wanted to bribe me. I think there's a law against that."

"Well, if you want to split hairs, you can call it that if you want."

"That smells good," he said, wrinkling his nose to sniff the air.

"It does, doesn't it?"

He studied the box in my hands and licked his lips, just a little. "I love Tampa Pizza and Wings."

I nodded and said, "I noticed. Went there specifically because they're your favorite. But since your resolve is stronger than I expected, I'll go share this with Ron."

"I hate you." He scowled.

"I know." I smiled.

"Come with me and bring the pizza."

"Yes, Doctor."

He badged in to unlock the door behind his desk and led me through it. And I made a full-body shiver as soon as the chilled air hit me. I wrapped my arms around my chest in a self-hug.

"Never been back here before, Sean?" he asked as he grabbed a white lab coat, hanging on the wall beside the door.

"It's been a while."

"We have to keep it cold to keep the bodies from—"

I nodded my head. "Yeah, I know. I just forgot about this part, is all. Caught me off guard." The whole reason I moved to Florida was to get away from the cold. I can't be the only one.

He led me to the autopsy room, or at least that's what I've always referred to it as. I don't know if it has an official name. Three substantial human-sized, shiny aluminum tables stood in the middle of the floor, laid end to end like pencils still in the pack. A raised edge ran the outside of each table that suggested what they were intended to keep from running all over the floor. Each table had a large basin attached to its foot, complete with a faucet that would look completely normal on anyone's kitchen sink. A separate sheet of aluminum full of holes like the bottom of a colander took up most of the middle of it. If the autopsy table were a bed, you could say it was the fitted sheet. There's a thought.

Dr. Stevens found a plastic apron, hanging on the wall beside the people-freezers, behind the tables. He put it on with the dispassion of your average butcher.

"Put the pizza down on the desk, beside you. Yours is the Miller case, right?" he asked, tying the apron strings behind his back.

I nodded.

"Have a seat." He motioned to the rolling chair in front of the desk to the right of me.

"How long will this take?" I asked.

"An hour or two, maybe. Depends on what I find." He opened the lid to the pizza box and removed a slice. It did smell like the food of the gods.

J.S. Johnston

"How can you eat that and—do that?"

He shrugged. "You just get used to it." Then he took a bite, opened Sandra Miller's human refrigerator door, and started his work. Dr. Stevens did his thing for close to two hours, just like he said. He was not in a rush, nor did he take his time about it. Stevens had the concentration and care of a craftsman. He'd make precise and deliberate incisions, remove each organ, weigh it, and move on to the next. Occasionally, he'd break to take off his gloves and have a slice of pizza while he looked at the body and sorted through his thoughts. Then he'd throw on a fresh pair of gloves and continue his work. He stepped through predetermined points in whatever process he had, each one leading him somewhere new. As he worked, he spoke into a microphone that hung down from the ceiling, recording what he found for later transcription.

I'd never taken the time to watch an autopsy before. I was nine years old all over again and my parents took me to a candy store. They stretched what looked like a hundred pounds of creamy white taffy in front of this big glass window for all the kids, then laid it out on this table about the size of the one Sandra Miller now laid on and cut it up into bite-sized pieces. Nine-year-old me could not imagine there was that much taffy in the world. And they did it with this another-day-at-the-office attitude that I never understood. Watching Dr. Stevens was a lot like that but with less candy.

When he finally finished his work, he turned away from Sandra Miller's body and said, "She died of old age." Then he took off a rubber glove.

I creased my brow and glared at him. "She did not." I wanted him to be joking.

"As far as I can tell, that's what happened."

"Come on. I've been here for two hours!" I shouted. "Even I know people don't actually die of old age. It's heart disease or stroke or gunshot or something. People don't just expire like yogurt."

"I'm not a fortune teller, Sean. And bodies don't leave error logs like computers. All I can see here is that she died." He gestured to the body, removed his other glove, and threw it in the trashcan with the red liner.

"Two hours, Dr. Stevens!"

He shrugged and shook his head. "There were no lacerations, punctures, or burns on the body. She had a healthy heart, liver, and kidneys. She did have high blood pressure but in the normal range for an African-American female of her age and not high enough to lead to a health risk. An excess of cholesterol was not present in her arteries. There was no sign of a stroke. Her lungs were absolutely pink." He picked up a slice of pizza and continued. "There is evidence of cardiac arrest, but the typical damage that a heart attack will leave is absent. So, no blockage, but her heart did stop." He took a bite of his pizza.

"You were in that poor woman's chest like you were changing the transmission in an old Chevy, and all you can tell me is that her heart stopped?" I used my special voice for this. "Do you have any idea why?"

He shrugged again as he chewed then said in the most nonchalant tone I can imagine. "It could've been drugs. You'll have to wait on the tox screen to come back for that one."

"She didn't do drugs! Why would you just assume she was strung out on drugs and that must've been what killed her?" I yelled at him.

And people must yell at him a lot because he wasn't even bothered. "I'm not saying she was a bad person, Sean. You know how people are at the Gasparilla. A lot of things seem like a good idea when you're out at night having fun with your friends. Maybe she met a guy. And maybe he made a convincing case about why she should—"

"She didn't do drugs!"

"If you say so," he said. "But the tox screen is the logical next step."

"But that takes weeks to come back."

He swallowed and said, "Which is why it's done after other causes are ruled out." Then he took another bite.

"Two hours I sat here! And that's all you can tell me?"

"Yep." He chewed and continued. "It could only have been a drug overdose or other toxin. The tox screen will have to tell you what it was."

"Weeks! I don't have that kind of time. There's a serial killer on the loose and this is his third victim! The longer it takes to find them, the longer—" I had risen to my feet and was now flailing my arms like a crazy person who got their coffee order wrong at Starbucks. I practically towered over him, and he just looked at me. I wished he'd share whatever medication he was taking.

"What do you want me to do?" he asked. "I've ruled out everything else. I can tell you for a fact that the cause of death was not natural causes or trauma. That only leaves an overdose of a drug or toxin and that's where my job ends. Thank you for the pizza." He took another bite.

I sighed. "Who do I need to buy pizza for, now?" I massaged my forehead.

He chuckled. "I think that's just how long it takes. We send it out to a lab, and it comes back after a few weeks. Sorry, Sean. The pizza is good, though."

"Yeah, no problem. Thanks for going out of your way to get this done for me." I got up from the chair and said, "Take it easy," before heading for the door.

Dr. Stevens held up the remains of his slice of pizza like it was a glass of beer in response.

* * *

I drove across town, back to the Horner residence. With everything that's happened, I still didn't have anything to go on. It wasn't a jigsaw puzzle with no picture on the box. It was a Connect the Dots with no dots to connect. Just a big piece of paper. Three people were dead, and not only did I have no idea who killed them—I also had no idea why. No suspects and no evidence. Sherlock Holmes would've had this figured out while he was still sitting in his drawing room. I was three victims down and I was clueless about what to do next.

So, I fought the rush hour traffic and went back to the Horner residence. That's what you're supposed to do, right? When you get lost, go back to the beginning, and start again. That's what my mother used to say when I was a kid. (I mean, she didn't *verbally* say that, but she might've if I'd have asked.) So, I did. Besides, it had more evidence than the other two scenes, even if it was next to nothing. The other two had completely nothing.

Yellow police tape still covered the door when I got there. The apartment complex maintenance guy, what's-his-name, remembered me and gave me the key. So, I just let myself in. He was supposed to come with me, but I told him I wouldn't tell anyone. Score one point for laziness.

Everything was still where I left it, as far as I could tell. The mess of gun cleaning gear on the coffee table, the bag of cat treats on the endstand, the bloodstain in the kitchen… The crime scene is still locked up, so it should be untouched. I took a breath, cleared my head, pretended like I hadn't been here before, and started over.

It was pointless to map out footprints by that time. Between Ron's forensic team and my own tromping around the first time I was there, you wouldn't be able to tell if actual humans were here or a bunch of drunken chimpanzees. (I had no reason to think chimpanzees were responsible.) I'd already processed the kitchen where Horner died, so I didn't expect much from there, other than confirmation bias. So, I started in the back bedroom and methodically worked my way to the front door, picking up everything and looking at it, just in case it said, "If anyone is reading this, so-and-so must've killed me." I didn't find that. But something had to be in there that I missed the first time.

The place was just a small, one-bedroom/one-bath layout that didn't even have a spot for a washer and dryer. He did have a faux-wood (Actually cheap particle board) computer desk stuffed in a corner of his bedroom with a laptop connected to a sizable computer monitor. The computer chair's cushion was thick and looked like a place you could sit for a few hours. I imagined him sitting there and writing cosmic horror stories, like the books piled on his dining table. Crumpled paper fast food bags and their accompanying soda cups with the straws still in them covered the desk. The bed was unmade, and the sheets were unwashed. Horner's funk was still pretty strong on them.

All the walls in the place were painted the typical hospital-grade sanitized white, that every apartment complex seems to think everyone wants to have. I never understood where they got that Idea. Maybe it's just one of those things they tell each other, and no one bothers to question it. Like how hiring managers think if an applicant asks about their hours, then they must be a clock-watcher or how people only use ten percent of their brain when we actually use all of it and how America is the land of opportunity when we have one of the worst rates of upward mobility in the world and… I forgot what I was talking about. Right! The apartment!

I went through all his medication in the bathroom medicine cabinet, looking for anything prescribed to anyone else. And I looked in all the places where no one thinks anyone would look for things like crack or meth. I didn't find any. I did find globs of dried toothpaste in the sink and matching dried urine covering the toilet and floor around it. Bathrooms are disgusting places. But his was not the worst I've ever had to search.

I went through all the mail and stacks of paperback books on the dining table. Some of the books were still in their plastic bags. (Seriously. Does anyone ever eat there?) You'd think he'd at least keep the bills and throw out the weekly K-Mart fliers and envelopes full of coupons for shit he'll never use. Instead, they were all in one big pile on the dining table. I could probably find out when he moved in, just by digging to the bottom of the pile.

I even went through the garbage in the trash can; it was mostly little baggies of used kitty litter and the box it came in. It made me wish T.J. could talk so he could just tell me who killed Horner. Maybe one day someone will breed talking cats. Or not. It sounds a little scary now that I think about it.

The whole apartment was in the same state of lived-in disarray. It wasn't the bear cave of my college days, but it didn't look like he spent a lot of time on housework, either. By the time I was done combing the place, it was dark.

That meant he didn't have visitors often, if ever. I wouldn't spend long cleaning either if no one ever came over. And that bothered me. In fact, I hated it. People don't kill people they don't know. Or that's the way it's supposed to be. The alternative is someone like Randal Jablonski who killed all the women he could find that fit a template and he could talk into getting into his truck. Or someone like the Zodiac Killer who just murdered for opportunity. Because he liked it. William Horner not being very social, never having anyone come over, and then having the backsplash in his kitchen painted with his gray matter scared the shit out of me. Because that meant it could've been anyone. Even me. I really like not being dead.

So, if I couldn't find anything physical that linked him to his murderer, it had to be who he was. It was all too orderly to be a race hate crime, assuming the murderer was of another race. And murderers of opportunity don't come into your house so you can make them coffee while they shoot you with your own gun. Someone wanted William Horner dead because he was William Horner. And I still didn't know what that meant.

Add to that, something about this scene was different from the other two. They happened outside. This was in his kitchen. The other two could've been written off as any reason someone would have for killing another person. Even accidental, not that it ever happens. But this was very, very intimate. I refused to believe the victim didn't know his killer. He did make them coffee. Which means he knew they were here. Which means he met them at the door and let them in.

And why is this scene the only one where the calling card butterfly wasn't mounted to something with its wings spread out? Why was it hidden on the forgotten top of a refrigerator? What connection does he have with the other victims?

I sat in his chair to watch his TV and let it all congeal in my head. It'd already been dusted for prints, so I didn't have to worry about that. I hit the power button on the remote and the TV came on as it should, but the screen was nothing but solid blue.

"Huh. Cable's out," I said to myself. You have to not pay your bill for a couple of months before they shut it off. And William Horner didn't seem to me like a guy who wouldn't pay it. Just as I was wondering how I was supposed to do my thinking, my pants rang.

I didn't recognize the number. I'd normally assume it was someone calling to inform me that my car's extended warranty had expired and let it go to voice mail, but I wanted someone to yell at, so I answered it.

"Detective Papadopoulos." I used a very authoritative voice. Sometimes it gets a good reaction from solicitors.

"Sean, it's me. Dr. Stevens. You were right," he said on the other end of the phone.

J.S. Johnston

"I was? I mean, of course, I was. What was I right about?"

"I took another look at Sandra Miller's body." His voice echoed like he was walking around and looking at something.

"And? What was I right about? Not that I don't believe you. I am right a lot."

"She wasn't a druggie. Well, I mean, it was probably a drug overdose. But whatever drug killed her, she didn't willingly take it."

I sat forward in William Horner's chair and said, "Really? You can tell that?"

"Well, there's no test for it. But after you left and things around here calmed down, I just wanted to confirm my position to add to my report and take another look at the body. You tend to miss a lot of things when someone bribes you with pizza and stands over your shoulder while you work."

"Yeah, yeah. What did you find?"

He paused for a moment. I assumed it was to look at what he was going to tell me about. "On her left thigh, towards the lateral section and just above where her hand would touch it, there's an injection site."

"And that proves she didn't give it to herself?"

"Well, no, but yeah," he said. "If you give yourself an injection, it'll be in the stomach or in the front of the thigh where you can easily get at it. They teach diabetics how to give themselves insulin that way. And if she sat for an injection, it'd most likely be in the shoulder. An injection site down there would be too awkward for either."

"So, someone came up to her and gave her the injection."

"Looks that way. I still can't tell you what they injected her with, but I can tell you she didn't want it."

"You are a kind, beautiful man, Dr. Stevens," I said, getting up from the chair. "I take back everything I said about you."

"What did you say about me?"

"Nothing. Thanks." I hung up the phone.

I dialed Sargent Martinez. She picked up on the first ring. "Yeah?"

"Sarge. Can you schedule another use of the time suit at the Sandra Miller murder scene?"

Chapter 13

I was surprised it didn't happen sooner. The idea of time travel has fascinated people since probably forever. So, you'd think they'd be camping in the USF parking lot to get even a little news about a time suit, but they just never did.

Maybe the world brushed off the idea of it with the same disregard as the people on the news. The world, being the people that are supposed to know what they're talking about, I mean. The news reported on it, but they didn't believe it, either. They talked about it in the same 'why not' tone of voice they'd use for a psychic Pomeranian winning the lottery. Because time travel isn't supposed to be possible. (And technically, it still isn't.) So, I guess they just brushed it off as yet another attempt to break the laws of nature by a group of well-funded fringe lunatics because they saw a movie once. I'm guessing. I didn't go ask anyone.

Now, however, news anchors with their accompanying camera people crowded the top level of a parking garage on Ashley Drive, just in sight of Sandra Miller's murder scene. They were clamoring like baby birds in the nest, shouting over each other to get their questions heard.

"You called them," I said to Sargent Martinez as she fastened my time suit.

She chortled, looking at whatever she was fastening and not up at me. "Yes, Sean. I called them."

"But why did you call them? Now they're here."

"You haven't been watching the news, have you?"

"No. Why? What's on it?" I asked.

She stopped what she was doing and looked up at me. "They've been reporting on Tampa's serial killer. It's all they've been talking about."

J.S. Johnston

"Oh, that."

"Yes. That. Everyone is scared. The media know we don't have any leads or even an idea of who's being targeted. So now Tampa has a boogeyman," she said and turned to the crowd of reporters.

"That's very sexist of you. What makes you think it's a man?"

She smirked at me. "Boogeyperson. The news is calling them the Butterfly Killer."

"That's the best they could come up with?"

"The point is it leaves the whole city with a sense of dread. I invited the press so they could watch us use the time suit. So, the citizens whose taxes pay our bills might sleep better at night when they see we're doing everything in our power to find the killer."

"I'd say no other police department has ever walked back in time to solve any case. That does put us ahead of the running," I said.

A uniformed cop stood in front of the horde of excited reporters. They looked like they were trying to explain that someone would be there shortly to give their official statement. And they looked about as useless as a fifth leg on a kitchen table. The horde kept shouting their questions, trying to get the cop to comment about anything.

"I'd better go," said Sargent Martinez. "They look like they're about to eat Officer Dunning. Don't get lost coming back."

"You said that before. Is there something I don't know?"

She walked off without answering.

Once she relieved Officer Dunning, Clara walked up to me. Her hair looked even bluer in the afternoon sun. "How long do you think it'll be?" I asked her. "It's hot up here." It really was hot. There's nothing like the black paved top floor of a garage building to make an already hot Tampa day even hotter.

"Good lord, it's hot," she agreed. "Maybe we should've done this on the level below this one."

"I already asked. I was told there isn't enough light down there and to stop whining."

She chuckled and fastened a glove to my sleeve. "So, is that your boss?" she asked, motioning to Sarge with her chin.

"Yeah. She spoils me." I gestured to the time suit.

Clara watched Sarge work her spells on the mob of reporters with the same curiosity I had watching Dr. Stevens work on the remains of Sandra Miller. I couldn't help an adoring smile. Then without looking up at me, Clara mentioned, "She's pretty." Then she paused for a moment and added, "Looks like she's in her element."

"That's her superpower," I said. "Wait 'til she really gets going."

Sarge gave them what looked like a well-rehearsed speech about the three victims, their names, where the bodies were discovered, and how the Tampa Police Department had grief counselors working with the victim's families. She assured them that we had committed all the available resources to find the killer and bring them to justice. It was very skillful. She used her serious voice and made a lot of very impressive arm movements. Then she opened the floor for questions.

The mob erupted into a flurry of them, shouting over each other. Sarge wasn't even perturbed. She had this gentle smile on her face and lifted her chin slightly. She raised her arm to point at someone, like that wizard from Fantasia.

"Do you have any suspects?" asked a reporter lady at the front of the mob with very big hair and in a very tight purple dress.

"We're currently building a list of suspects. I'm sure you'll understand why we won't release that."

As soon as she finished her sentence, the mob erupted again in a very Mount Saint Helens way.

"Easy," said Sargent Martinez with her palms toward the crowd. She pointed at a short man in a white button-up shirt with the sleeves rolled to his elbows. He held a small pad of paper in one hand and a pen in the other.

"Do you know if the murders are related?" asked the man.

"At this point in the investigation, we haven't ruled that out. However, we are exploring several theories."

Sarge looked in the crowd to pick someone else when a man in the back blurted out, "Does this have anything to do with the time suit?" The crowd all looked at him and then back to Sarge like it was the question they were waiting for.

"The timing is coincidental, as far as we've been able to determine. So far, the evidence does not indicate a connection. Again, we are exploring multiple explanations."

Before Sargent Martinez could point at a reporter for their question, someone else shouted, "Could the murders be racially motivated?"

"So far, the evidence does not suggest that." She pointed to someone else.

"Wow," said Clara. "I just got a chill." She fastened my left boot.

"That's called verbal kung-fu," I replied. "I told you it was her superpower."

"Don't worry. We'll give them a show." She put my helmet on my head and fastened it to my collar.

Off to the side, Dr. Khatri sat in front of the console, in the middle of the blacktop. She leaned into the microphone and asked, "Can you hear me?"

"Yes, your earrings look nice."

She cocked her head and smiled at me.

"Yes, I can hear you."

"Mr. Smart Detective," she said.

Sargent Martinez interrupted one of the reporters in the middle of a question that they weren't going to get answered, anyway. "If you'll turn your attention to the empty doorway, oddly placed in the middle of the parking area, they're about to start it up."

Clara put a hand on my shoulder and said, "Don't get lost," as she walked away.

"Why does everyone keep saying that?"

Dr. Khatri flipped a few switches on her console then a purple sheen covered the doorway, standing in the center of the top level of the parking garage. Oohs and aahs burst forth from the crowd of reporters on the far end, along with the sound of a thousand cameras snapping a million pictures each. Probably not that many. But a lot.

I took a breath, trying not to think about the next part. And the Morlock from the last time.

Clara took her seat at the console beside Dr. Khatri and leaned forward to the microphone. She turned her head to look at me and started to say, "Don't worry. The third time is always—"

I raised my finger. "Please don't say it."

* * *

I stepped through and let the current of time wash over me. Within a moment, it was the night of the Gasparilla. The harsh afternoon sun was still behind me, on the other side of the portal. Shouting and music rose up to meet me from the street below. The top parking level where I stood was full of parked cars and grinning stragglers in pirate garb. I took a minute for my brain to adjust to what just happened.

"I'm here," I said into the helmet microphone even though they could see me through the portal.

"Roger that," answered Clara. "Or is it copy that? Do you guys say Roger or copy?"

"We say copy. The military says Roger."

"Got it. I mean, copy that!"

"You're weird, Clara."

"I know."

A young man in his twenties dressed as a discount version of Jack Sparrow (A Jack Sparrow who'd just ripped off his sleeves to escape a shark attack, evidently) walked with an arm sculpted in steel around a young girl about the same age dressed like an expensive version of Morgan Adams (In a skirt just long enough for me to use as a dinner napkin) toward the elevator that took them to street level. The girl was just a slight wisp of a thing and would not have made a scary pirate. The way they were stumbling across the blacktop made me believe they would not have passed a sobriety test.

"How did they manage to drive all the way up here without running anyone over?" asked Clara over the helmet's speakers.

I shook my head. "Maybe I should check the grill of their car, just to be sure."

She giggled. It was a very endearing giggle.

I walked over to the street side of the parking level, to get a look below. I rested both hands on the concrete half-wall and leaned over into a stream of consciousness, running past me. The ever-present current of time made itself known as it rushed through the pavement and buildings. The ground level was just a waving heat mirage, instead of the people on the street and sidewalk; a swirl of almost-shapes and wisps of pseudo-colors, a bit like forgetting your glasses. I couldn't even make out the second level of the parking building. It was just a streak of gray where a building should be. The silent flow had become cathartic. I didn't expect that.

"Well, that's disappointing," said Clara, disappointed. "You can't see anything."

"I figured that's what I'd get when I walked over here, but it never hurts to check."

"I guess. Hey, if you hurry and follow the pirates, you won't have to walk all the way down there."

"That sounds like a good idea." I trotted across the now-darkened parking level and stayed right behind them, all the way into the elevator. Once inside, they stood just in front of the door, unable to wait for another step before getting their hands on each other—and wouldn't move aside so I could squeeze past them. The doors almost closed on me. (I'm still wondering what would've happened to me if they had.) And then they started making out. I mean, they really went at it. So hard that he might've been able to tell what she had for breakfast. He grabbed her ass with one hand and crept a hand up the back of her pirate shirt with the other. I lurked around in the elevator like the invisible man, invading their privacy. And I got the idea they would've still gone at it, even if they knew I was standing right behind them.

"Aww, they're gonna make a beautiful baby pirate," Clara said over the helmet speakers.

"Clara," I started to say like her father until I caught myself. "That's enough for you." I turned my head to the side, so the amorous pirate couple was no longer on camera.

"Hey, I was watching that!"

"I don't know what you're talking about. I'm very interested in the wood grain paneling they used in this elevator. It was a very bold choice. Don't you think?"

"Meanie!" she scolded me.

The elevator ride was quick. We were only three levels up. It came to a stop, and the doors slid open before the couple could get very far, thank God. Sleeveless Jack Sparrow unbolted himself from Sexy Morgan Adams and they both disembarked. I stayed right on their heels, to be sure the doors wouldn't shut behind them and lock me in.

They opened up facing the lit interior of the ground level of the parking garage, full of cars.

The music from the street thumped in my chest. It was a lively beat. I walked out with them, just a little creeped out that my footsteps were absent. Nothing but those of the pirate couple echoing through the cement garage.

There were only the three of us in there, so I couldn't pretend I didn't notice. Their footsteps bounced between the concrete floor, walls, and ceiling, which made a perfect resonance chamber. But mine did not. It was like I wasn't really there. Which I guess I wasn't. Or I was but not. Whatever. It was creepy. I may as well have been a ghost.

"So, how're you going to find her in all those people?" asked Clara.

"I just assumed I'd stick to the wall and walk over to Renni's Beach and Surf Shop where they found her. Or duck and weave between people if I have to, the same as I did in the hallways of my old high school. Why do you ask?" It was a long walk to the side door of the parking garage. I wish someone would've thought of that when they set up the press conference.

"Well, it was really crowded."

"Did you go?" I asked.

"Of course. I think you're the only person in Tampa who doesn't."

"That's not true. I once talked to a seeing-eye dog who said he'd never been," I said as I made my way through the garage.

"A seeing-eye dog. Really?"

"No, not really. He said he went every year. So how many people were—Holy Mary mother of God!"

Sleeveless Jack Sparrow pushed the bar to open the side door for Sexy Morgan Adams, revealing so many people that they looked like a solid wall of human Jell-O. A drunken, rowdy, shouting, dancing, undulating, boisterous, bead-throwing, exuberant, jumping, shouting, (I already said that)—and mobile—solid wall of human Jell-O. It was way worse than high school. The pirate couple walked out and disappeared into the mass of humans like it was just another night out and the door began to shut.

J.S. Johnston

"What're you waiting for?" Clara asked, more than a little pushy. "It's almost shut. Go!"

I did not want to go. I was afraid of being the first time-traveler to be suffocated to death by a crowd of pirates. And not in a fun way. They ran back and forth, really excited about whatever was going on, and barely any space between them. Towards the street, the crowd was packed in so tight, they may as well have been lying on top of each other.

"How are there this many people in Tampa?"

"Have you seen the interstate? The door's almost shut. Hurry!" she shouted.

I flipped sideways to squeeze past, just as it shut with an unsettling bang of finality. All of Tampa existed on the sidewalk of Ashley Drive and was a lot happier to be there than me. I pushed myself up against the concrete wall of the parking garage as if I were on the ledge of a skyrise building. People ran just in front of me with no idea they held my life in their hands.

"I'm showing your pulse and respiration are climbing, Sean. I need you to calm down."

"Do you see this? I should not be calm right now!" A blonde girl with weird-colored streamers in her hair ran past me and almost took me out. I jerked back and accidentally smacked my helmet on the concrete wall behind me. "You go to this every year?"

She laughed and said, "It wouldn't be that bad if they could see you. It's a lot of fun."

"I'm not having fun, Clara."

She laughed for a while.

I took a moment to get my bearings and figure out which way to Renni's Beach and Surf Shop then inched along the wall like a time-traveling cockroach. I made decent progress for a while and soon the sign for Renni's emerged from the swirling fog of time. But just as I was picking up a little speed, a guy rolled over a red cooler and set it along the wall, right where I was walking. Then he opened it, grabbed a can of something, closed it, and sat down on the cooler to watch the excitement.

"Don't we have a law against that?" I asked, now stopped in my tracks, in front of the oblivious drinking man. Green and white stripes ran up and down his face, and I had no idea if he was celebrating pirates or a soccer team that I wasn't aware of.

"Just climb over him."

"What? I can't just—"

"It's not like he'd even notice. This all already happened. You can't change the past, remember?"

I studied him for a moment and considered my ability to successfully scale the man. "Nope. That's not something I can do. I will fall on my ass, break your expensive suit, and probably die." The man kept drinking and looking out into the crowd like I wasn't there. Which I wasn't. "I need to figure out something else."

Where I wanted to be was in sight, but randomly moving immovable objects coursed and flowed over my path to get there; like a game of Frogger made of humans. People still play that, right? I was almost there. All there was between me and Renni's was a driveway and a gravel parking lot. Sounds great but there weren't any side doors to duck into, even if I could open a side door. Which I couldn't.

"Is it possible to stop everything?" I asked.

"Stop what? Time?" Her voice was indignant. It does sound like a silly question now that I think about it.

"I guess that's no?"

She giggled. "It's not a holodeck. This is the real thing."

"That's a no." I waited for a break in the swirling mass of people. Something I could Frogger my way through. Then Sandra Miller walked into my line of sight. I could recognize her even through the heat mirage of the current of time. She looked happy. And completely enveloped in the moment, celebrating whatever the hell Gasparilla celebrates. She looked beautiful with a smile that shined under the lights that ran over and across the street.

"There she is!" shouted Clara in my ear.

"I see her."

And as I looked for a way to get through, someone walked up to her. "There!" I shouted. "Jimmy Buffett! Do you see him?"

"Jimmy who?"

"Buffett. Jimmy Buffett. Cheeseburger in Paradise. Do you see him?" I was still shouting as if I needed to.

"I have no idea who that is."

"Jesus. How old am I?"

"Pretty old."

"Bright orange and red Hawaiian shirt with white captain's hat!" I was pointing at him like she could see. Jimmy Buffett was right up against her like he knew her. And put a hand on the side of her upper thigh.

I found a quick break in the undulating crowd and ran to it, squeezing my way between an overweight man and an older one. Then found another break and ran to it. And another, and another, trying to get close enough to Jimmy Buffett to clearly record his face. Damn the way everything looked in the past. I may as well have had my eyes crossed.

"Sean, you're going to—" Clara tried to warn me.

Sandra Miller looked back at Jimmy Buffett with a scrunched-up face. She winced as he injected her with something and jerked away, putting a hand on him to shove him back as well. Jimmy reached out and grabbed her by the upper arm.

"Sean, look out!"

A college-age man in a white tank top and blue board shorts walked right into me. He wasn't running or even at a brisk pace. It was as casual as if he were walking to the kitchen to make a sandwich. He still crashed into me like a sledgehammer. The force of it knocked the wind out of me as it sent me into someone walking the other way. From there, I hit the ground hard enough to slide along the sidewalk. I lay there for a heartbeat in the fetal position then looked up to find Jimmy Buffett easing Sandra Miller onto the sidewalk. He sat her down and leaned her back against the wall behind her. Sandra Miller looked like she was trying to fight him off with halfhearted slaps to his arms and face like children play-fighting.

Jimmy Buffett didn't take any notice. He put her pirate hat on her graying head and walked away. She watched him, then gently eased her head down, like she was tired and wanted a nap.

I was still lying on the ground when a pair of flip-flops walked toward me. I scrambled out of the way just in time for them to only connect with my shin. That really hurt.

Something like screaming rang through the helmet's speakers. It was distant, just on the edge of my hearing, like a crowd of people. Or someone watching a Godzilla movie in the background with the volume down too low.

"What's that?" I asked.

The screaming got louder.

"Clara? Are you still there?"

"No!" she shouted. Then she got quieter as if she walked away. "No, you don't understand!" She was really upset. It wasn't a movie.

"Don't understand what?" I shouted.

No response.

"Clara?"

Someone was talking in the distance, but I couldn't make out what they were saying over the roar of the Gasparilla music and bustling mob, just a few feet away. They made a speech that I couldn't make out.

"Clara, talk to me! Clara!"

A moment passed. She screamed a drawn-out, "No!" Then she cut out.

"Clara?"

Nothing.

"Clara!"

Nothing.

I ran around the building and up three flights to the top level of the parking garage. The swirling purple doorway in the middle, my way to get back to the safety of present time, was gone.

"Fuck."

Chapter 14

I stared for a while at the place where the time portal used to be. I think somewhere in the back of my brain, I expected it to just show back up. Like it was just behind a cloud or something. Maybe Clara and Dr. Khatri forgot to tell me about some weird temporal mechanic that might cause this because to them it was just common sense and why would you tell people that air is clear, grass is green, and purple swirly time portals sometimes disappear cutting off communication to the present-day and stranding people in the past forever? They should already know that. Or maybe they did say something, and I just wasn't paying attention. I do that, sometimes. One of my ex-girlfriends broke up with me for it. Or I think that's what it was. I wasn't really listening at the time.

At any rate, I stood on the top level of the parking garage on Ashley Drive and stared at the place where the time portal—my way to get home—no longer was. And it did not come back.

Just to be sure, I even went over and stood in the place where it should be. It was a dumb idea. But it was still better than just staring at it. Nothing happened. I was still stuck in the past, surrounded by the waving shimmers of the current of time. There's a sentence I never thought I would say.

So, what do you do when you're stuck somewhere in the river of time, and you can't call a TARDIS to come get you? You'd think I'd be panicking, wondering how long it would take for the suit's air supply to run out, but I wasn't. Not your intrepid hero, Detective Papadopoulos. No sir! What did I do? What method of genius did I use to try to MacGyver my way out of this mess? Nothing, actually. I wandered back down two stories to watch the Gasparilla parade.

I think it was shock. Realizing I was stuck in the past feels like a good time to have been in shock. One minute I told myself it would be best to stay where I was and wait for Clara and Dr. Khatri to fix whatever was broken and reinitialize the portal. The next, I was down on the sidewalk in a tucked away corner, watching giant pirate ships go down the street, lit up in the Tampa night. And I wondered if Ron would feed T.J.

A crowd of smiling Floridians dressed as pirates lingered in the heat mirage of time, itself. They shouted and cheered, just a few feet away from me. One man wore a long black coat with a swirling design of thin rope that traveled down the lapel to his waist. His long facial hair and dark eye shadow made him look like Blackbeard.

A woman with long, brownish-red hair in tight curls walked up to him. She wore a low-cut, billowing white shirt and a three-cornered hat that made me think of someone close to Ann Bonny. She took each of his hands in hers and then stood on her tiptoes to kiss him. A moment later, she stumbled and almost fell over.

Behind them, a pirate ship float full of sexy women pirates throwing colored bead necklaces to the masses drove down the street. (I still don't get why people throw beads, but there you are.) The sides of the thing looked like they were cardboard. But the painted lines across it made it look like wooden planks. Or that was the intent, anyway. Several painted cannons ran along the middle that wouldn't have scared anyone. A string of white LED lights, which were obviously not period correct, connected the three masts that stood along its deck. The ship and krewe (Yes, that's how it's spelled) eased down the road at a walking pace, following other ships that looked more believable. The cheering onlookers didn't seem to mind.

I was so lulled by the scene, like watching fish in an aquarium, that I didn't notice him, at first. Out of the corner of my eye, he was just a person in shadow in a crowd of other people, passing in and out of a field of shadows. He just didn't catch my attention, at first. It was when I was watching the pirate ship float that I noticed he wasn't jumping around, like everyone else around him. He was standing. Then someone in a long blue pirate coat passed in front of him and made it obvious that he shouldn't be in shadow. He should've been lit up as brightly as everyone else around him. And he wasn't watching the parade. He was watching *me*.

I stopped breathing and unconsciously backed up into the wall, behind me. The Morlock took a step then another, easily working his way through the mass of people, like a skilled driver in rush hour traffic. He wasn't in a hurry. His steps were patient, practiced, and calm. He was nothing but a shadow, but I swear it looked like he didn't take his eyes off me. He didn't even move his head.

All of a sudden, I remembered Clara telling me this suit could make its own portals. *That's* when it popped into my head. And not on the top level of the parking garage when I stared at an empty spot on the pavement where the portal used to be. I really suck at this job. Clara never explained how to open one though, which would have been very helpful. She just said the AI could do it. Like buying a new stereo without even an instruction manual to read like stereo instructions. Is that still a thing people say?

The shadow man was still coming for me, so I bolted. Or I tried to, anyway. I took off at full speed, got two steps out, and smacked straight into a skinny high school kid with his face painted in brown, and black stripes. He kept walking like he didn't just send me to the concrete with an elbow to the sternum.

The Morlock didn't even pick up his pace when he saw me lying on the ground. He just kept strolling through the crowd like he had all night. Like Jason god damn Vorhees.

I tried looking around my suit for a panel of buttons like Darth Vader has on his. (They never did explain the point of them. I swear one had to be the radio.) I patted myself down for anything—Arms, chest, hands… But nothing. It was more like a racing suit than a spacesuit. All streamlined and efficient.

The shadow man was almost on me, so I rolled over and ran toward a crowd of people around a stand selling those glowing necklaces.

"Alexa!" I shouted into my helmet. No response came. I weaved my way between some people, putting them between me and the shadow man. He kept coming, not in any hurry. "Siri?" No response. What did she say its name was?

I ducked around the corner of a building. "Hey, Google," I said quietly, even though the Shadow Man couldn't hear me, anyway. "Anyone!"

I peered around the corner and found the Morlock, still making his way to me, passing around a fat guy with a large white plastic cup of something in one hand and a corn dog in the other.

"Damn it, Clara. You could've at least told me how to turn this thing on." If only I could remember what she said its name was.

The body of Sandra Miller leaned up against a wall as if she had just sat down to take a nap in the middle of a pirate parade. And no one was bothering her. They passed by and clearly saw her, but they left her alone. I'm not sure what that says about people.

The shadow man was getting close. I wasn't sure if he knew where I was, so I ducked into a brightly lit surf shop. A rock propped open the glass door, so I let myself in. The inside had barely enough room to walk around. Turnstiles (Is that the right word?) full of clothes cramped the sales floor. Bikinis hung on the walls, alongside pirate-themed Hawaiian shirts.

I couldn't just slide over some clothes to hide inside the turnstiles, so I had to duck low enough to hide between them.

"Wait a second," I said to myself because no one else was listening to me. Clara probably wrote whatever AI assistant was powering this thing, herself. And what would Clara name an AI assistant that she built herself? "Watson," I said firmly into the helmet. Glowing digital displays in greens, reds, and blues splashed across the glass of the helmet made me feel like I was sitting in the cockpit of a jet fighter. "This is so cool," I said in a little more than a whisper as the digital display wrapped around my face.

A British-sounding male voice came over the helmet's speakers and dispassionately recited, "Watson, version 3.21—online. Greetings, Detective Papadopoulos. Checking for system updates. Error: unable to access update server. Attempting to determine cause."

"I can tell you why," I told the computer person. "The portal back home shut down."

"Verifying… Confirmed. No temporal gateway detected."

I poked my head past the turnstile of swimsuits to look toward the door to check for the Morlock. No shadowy figure. Just people badly dressed as pirates wandering in and out.

"Keep your voice down. I'm trying to hide," I said, still crouched down.

"Vibrations in the atmospheric medium of the time suit do not propagate to the surrounding temporal environment."

"Yeah, well make me feel better."

"Lowering volume. Is this an acceptable level?"

"It's fine. Now can you—" Something hard crashed into my ribs, and I went sprawling across the linoleum tile floor. When I took a breath, pain covered my left side like a meat blanket. I tried to howl in agony, but it hurt too much to get anything out. When I turned to see what hit me, I found the Morlock. He stood over me with his legs spread in a prison yard stance. The blackness of his right arm extended into the shape of a baseball bat. So that's what hit me.

"Suit integrity reduced by ten percent. Best practice would be to avoid impacts—"

"I got it!" I barked at Watson.

"A tear in the time suit may prove fatal—"

"I said, I got it!"

The Morlock took his weapon in both hands and raised it over his head like an ax. He paused for just a moment, like he wanted me to fully appreciate what he was about to do, then brought it down.

I jerked out of the way just as the bat-shadow smacked against the linoleum floor with the force of a falling tree and did not make a sound. Then he pulled back to batter up and swung at my head. I threw up both arms in front of my face to block it. It still hurt like hell when it hit.

"Ah!" I screamed.

"Suit integrity reduced by seven percent. Please exercise caution, Detective Papadopoulos," came Watson's helpful computer voice.

"Please stop talking."

The Morlock kept swinging, hitting my raised forearms. Then on one of his swings, I caught the bat in my open palms and tried to take it from him. He just kicked me away like I wasn't anything more than an annoyance. And he kept his bat. I went back to the floor.

"Watson, can you open a portal out of here?"

"I possess the ability to create multiple temporal gateways, limited by battery capacity."

The black figure angrily walked toward me. I crawled backward, to get away from it. A woman strolled between us to browse the swimsuits on the rack, blocking his path.

"Well? Make a portal!"

"Please verbally provide a temporal destination," Watson said.

The Morlock silently ran around the turnstile to get to me only to be cut off by some kid that looked a lot like the lady, browsing through the sodas in the machine against the wall. The Morlock paced back and forth, looking for a way around him like a tiger in a cage.

"It doesn't matter. Anywhere."

He leaned the bat against his shoulder like a street thug and waited for the kid to move.

"Please verbally provide a temporal destination," Watson repeated.

"Oh, come on!" I tried to remember the date of the present. Not an easy thing to do when Death is waiting for you with a baseball bat. "January... something."

The kid finally moved, taking a step toward the soda machine to slide his card through the reader. The Morlock ran at me as soon as he had enough room to slip by. I turned to run to the back of the store but didn't get far before stopping for a passing shopper. The Morlock plowed into me like a linebacker, slamming me into them.

I was back on the floor. This time with the Morlock on top of me. He sat on my chest, straddling me, and raised that damn bat to bring the butt down on the glass of my helmet like a spear.

"Please exercise caution, Detective Papadopoulos. A break in the glass of the helmet may prove—"

"I know! Shut up!"

I caught the Morlock's arms as he tried to strike my helmet; they were thick and firm like steel bars. He had me pinned on the ground, pushing the end of the bat closer to the glass of my helmet. I put everything I had into pushing him away and he still kept inching it closer. Christ, he was strong.

"Watson," I shouted. "Open a portal to the tenth of December 2021!"

"Acknowledged, Detective. Initiating temporal gateway."

Behind the Morlock, a swirling purple membrane covered the doorway. People looked like they magically appeared walking out of it, instead of walking through it.

I pushed the Morlock to the side and let go of his arms. He pounded the floor with his bat, missing me. I scrambled to my feet and ran to the time portal, covering the doorway. I got about twenty feet from it when He snagged my ankle in an inhuman grip which sent me back to the floor. The chin part of the helmet smacked the tile. The sound it made stopped my heart for three seconds.

"Structural integ—"

"Not now!"

"That almost cracked the helmet, detective," Watson said in an inappropriately calm voice.

As the Morlock came to his feet behind me, I kicked him as hard as I could in his kneecap. It hit solid under my boot, like stomping on the ground, but down he went. I scrambled for the portal. On the other side, it was still night, still clear, but any trace of the boisterous crowds of fake pirates was gone.

Behind me, on the other side of the translucent time portal, a black hole in human form picked itself up and came for me.

Chapter 15

"Shut it down! Shut the portal!" I screamed into the helmet as the Morlock barreled at me with the conviction of a freight train, the baseball bat in its hand.

"Acknowledged. Discontinuing temporal gateway."

The purple sheen that covered the doorway to the crowded store disappeared like the membrane of a soap bubble, just as the Morlock was inches away and reaching out for it. It took a moment for my brain to catch up. One minute he was there in the hurried brightly lit space, and the next it was all replaced by a locked door with darkened glass. It was like someone had changed the channel.

"Watson, we need to work on your sense of urgency."

"Shall I set a reminder for work on my sense of urgency?"

"That's okay. Cancel request."

"Acknowledged. Canceling request."

I paused a moment to be sure the Morlock wouldn't come up behind me like in every horror movie, ever. Occupational hazard, I guess. Or maybe just too many movies. It was eerie how quiet the street was, after the commotion of just a minute ago. Nothing but the occasional passing car and the hum of the window air conditioner, the next building over.

For whatever reason, the ever-present current of time wasn't disorienting to the point of nausea, anymore. It had become comforting, like watching the fish swim around in an aquarium. The waves of a heat mirage streaked by me, making the occasional car driving down the street look like they were all about to have a cheesy flashback scene.

A homeless man in a filthy army-green t-shirt and jean shorts wandered down the sidewalk at an aimless pace. His once light Caucasian skin had turned leathery brown from standing out in the sun, collecting spare change from good Samaritans. His overgrown beard was disheveled and gnarly. I could barely tell it was blonde, under all the grease and dirt.

He ran his fingers along his scalp from front to back, through his matted, greasy blonde hair, and looked at me. Or looked at the door of the surf shop that I stood in front of. He was in the past so he couldn't see me. I wasn't really there with him. He was just performing actions that had already happened in a one-way progression of a timeline that neither he nor I had any control over. He still looked like he was looking at me.

"Hey, Watson."

"Yes, Detective Papadopoulos?" he asked, sounding like we didn't just almost get murdered.

"Can you show me a map of the area?"

"Of course." Short pause. "Displaying map."

A line-drawing map of the downtown Tampa streets replaced the jet fighter heads-up display that was projected onto the inside of my helmet. Orange rectangles represented the buildings along the light gray streets of the map. A neon-blue circle on Ashley Drive by the river marked my location. A small arrow point protruded from the circle, showing the direction I was facing. I turned, just to watch it turn with me.

"You are so cool," I said.

"My internal thermometer indicates that I am operating at optimal temperature."

"—Good for you."

Less than a block from Ashley Drive is the Tampa Riverwalk. It's close enough that it takes longer to find a parking spot than it does to just walk there. So that's what I did, time-traveling racecar suit and all. And I was glad the passing cars couldn't see me in it.

I didn't want to stay anywhere near that door. The time in the heads-up display of the helmet showed 10:15 p.m., so I had the idea to head over. No way I was going to pass up the chance to watch a life-changing event happen all over again. Isn't that the whole point of time travel? Makes sense to me, anyway.

I proposed to my ex-wife, not too far from here. In the excitement of almost dying in what could have been a nuclear explosion that would've taken out the greater part of Tampa if my suit had been ripped open, this date was the only one that came to mind. Funny how memory works, right?

The Riverwalk runs along the side of the Hillsborough River, with parts of it going over the water as a paved footbridge. On a clear night, the moon does that thing where it reflects off the surface of the water in a long candlestick shape that looks like it brings it right to you.

And that was the main point of planning it there. I could only do this once, so it had to be perfect. I thought about taking her to the beach. Treasure Island at night is a magical place, with the residual heat of the sand warming your bare feet and the scent of the ocean on the wind. But doing it at the Riverwalk in Tampa let me frame it as a surprise evening stroll, just down the road from a good restaurant. And the lights from the downtown buildings in the background sold it.

I claimed a seat on a wooden bench along the path and waited for a young couple to comfortably stroll along, hand-in-hand. The young man was broad-shouldered with muscles like steel cables. He had a confident look in his eye that said he had everything under control and a career on fast forward. The smile on the young woman's face could stop your heart. It did mine, once.

They stopped and leaned against the outside railing to look at the nighttime skyline, across the river. He put his arm around her shoulder and pulled her close to him. She gently turned her face to him and met his eye.

"Hello? Sean? Are you there?" Clara's frantic voice came over the helmet's speakers without warning.

"Clara? Is that you?" I blurted out in surprise.

"Oh, thank God! We've been looking for you for days."

"Days? I've only been lost for maybe an hour."

She giggled. "Time suit, Sean. Time is irrelevant."

"Right. I forgot."

She giggled a little more.

"So, what happened to you? It sounded pretty exciting on your end." I leaned forward and rested my elbows on my knees as the happy couple in front of me enjoyed each other's company.

"That's not the word I would use. But yeah. It was very exciting. One of the reporters in the crowd pulled a gun out of somewhere. They shouted something about how time travel is something that only God should be able to do and shot up the console."

"Oh my god!" I sat bolt upright at the news. "Are you okay? Was anyone hurt?"

"Yeah, everyone's fine. Dr. Khatri and I ducked out of the way in time. They caught the shooter before he could turn the gun on any people and arrested him. That boss of yours was the first one to tackle him."

"That's why I'm never late for work," I said. She does have quite the management style.

"Then once that was over, it took the rest of the day to clean up the pieces of the console. He shot the electronic boards to hell so the computer wouldn't even start."

"That does tend to happen when you shoot stuff."

"You know that cute guy on the railing with that girl looks a lot like you," Clara said. I forgot she would be watching the feed from the helmet camera.

"He sure does."

The dashing young man took a step back from the beautiful young lady and softly took her hands. Her fingers were as graceful as the neck of a violin. The moon shined perfectly onto the river and reflected in its waters as the lights of the downtown buildings provided a heaven-on-earth backdrop for the most magical night either one of them had ever seen.

"Oh my… He's… He *is* you. You're getting down on one knee!" Clara shouted in my ears.

"Yep."

The dashing young man pulled out a small box from his pocket and opened it then held it up to the beautiful young lady.

"You're proposing to her!"

"Yep."

"Sean, I didn't know you were that romantic."

"Are you crying?"

"I'm not crying. I have allergies." Clara sniffled like she was crying.

The beautiful young lady looked down at the dashing young man, brought her hands to her mouth and tears welled in her sparkling eyes.

"That's so romantic!" Clara sniffled some more.

The dashing young man stood up and kissed the beautiful lady. It was a really big wet kiss. Probably the best she's ever had. Then the couple embraced and they both painted smiles of joy on their faces.

"Awwwww!" Clara exclaimed.

I smiled and asked, "Was it good for you?"

"That is the sweetest thing I've ever seen. That explains that thing you said about not dating. And why you picked this night to come back to. You miss her, don't you?"

"Of course, I miss her. But I didn't pick the date just to watch this all over again. I panicked, and this was the first one that came to mind."

"Wait, panicked? What happened?" she asked.

"I ran into the Morlock, again."

"Again?"

"Yep."

"What happened? What was it like?" Clara sounded more interested than worried. Academics.

"He looked like a walking black hole." I shrugged though she couldn't see it. "And he tried to kill me. He almost did."

"I'm glad he didn't. Oh, hey! That means you figured out Watson!" she said.

"Our relationship needs a little smoothing over but yeah. I figured him out."

"You know, if you miss your lady, you should give her a call. I bet she misses you, too," she said like she just watched a movie on The Hallmark Channel.

"I can't. She's…"

"Oh. I'm sorry."

"It's okay. Everything ends, Clara."

"Can I ask what happened? It's okay if you don't want to talk about it."

The young couple on the path started slow dancing to the music coming from one of the local bars. At least, I remember there was music. When I sat on the bench watching the whole thing, I didn't hear any. Isn't that funny?

"It's okay. It's been a long time. Maybe ten years after this happened," I said and motioned to the image of the happy couple, shimmering in the current of time. "She finally had enough of my drinking problem."

"You're an alcoholic? I'm sorry," Clara said.

I nodded though she couldn't see it. "For years, I was the stereotypical drunken detective. I kept telling her I was going to quit but then ended up spending the rent money on whiskey, vodka, and whatever happened to come up in the course of a night out. We almost got evicted a couple of times."

"And she finally got you to quit?"

I chuckled a little at that. "If only. I mean, I must've quit about a half dozen times. It just didn't seem to stick. I'd throw out everything in the house. Or so she thought. I'd always managed to forget about a stash of Wild Turkey hidden in the back of a toolbox drawer. Or a bottle of Jose Cuervo behind the washing machine. If I didn't have those, I just went to the nearest bar and none of it meant anything. I did try to stop. I wanted to do it for her. You know? Be the man she thought I was. But it was like someone else was driving. I'd just find myself with a drink in my hand and have no idea how it got there. And then there were the times my insides tied themselves in braids until I spent half the day dry heaving in the toilet."

"That's terrible," Clara said. "So, you finally quit for good when she left you?"

"Not really. It gets worse."

"How can it get worse than that?"

I put my thoughts in order for a moment and continued. "I came home one day, and she'd already loaded up her car with her things. She told me she was leaving me and why. I begged her to stay, and she wouldn't even consider it. Her face was full of tears when she got in her car and drove off. But she was so distraught that she ran through a red light."

"Oh my—So… She…"

"What? No. She's alive and well and living in Des Moines."

"Oh, thank God."

"After she left," I said, still watching the happy couple in front of me. "I went out and got so drunk that I ended up in the hospital. The last thing I remembered was telling the waitress to bring me doubles until I told her to stop. Ron from Forensics happened to be with me at the time. When I wasn't breathing, he called 9-1-1. He stayed with me in the hospital all night to make sure I was okay. If he wasn't my best friend before, he was then. I haven't had a single drop of booze since. Not long after, I got promoted to Homicide, buried myself in my work and the thought of dating again just never crossed my mind."

The me of the past looked so happy with Nicole of the past. They both leaned against the railing by the river and stared at each other.

"I don't know what to say after all that. That's horrible," Clara said.

"It's life. And it was an entire lifetime ago, so I've had a while to come to terms with it."

"You could still call her. And ya know… talk," she suggested.

I laughed. "That wouldn't be a good idea. She married some guy who works with computers. Smart guy. You'd like him. They had two kids. I think one of them is in high school, now."

"Wow. I guess that happens."

"It's okay," I said, watching the couple. "I still get to keep the good times in my brain locker. That'll never go away." I would have tapped my temple if it wasn't sealed inside my airtight helmet.

"I guess that's true."

"And you and Dr. Khatri let me see them again. That's more than a little awesome."

"And that's very true," Clara said. "So, you just haven't dated since then? Don't you get lonely?"

"No to both questions," I said and leaned back on the bench. "Ever since I got promoted to Homicide, I just haven't had time to think about it."

"Huh."

"Now how about sending me a portal? This suit is starting to smell funny from all that running around."

The swooning couple in the past was losing their charm. All I could see was what I no longer had standing right in front of me.

J.S. Johnston

"Why didn't you just tell Watson to open a portal to the present?" Clara asked.

"Because I forgot the date," I said like a question.

She giggled.

"What? I've been busy. I can't be expected to remember everything."

"You don't have to. Just tell him to open a portal to the present and he will," she said like it was common sense.

"Without knowing the date?"

"No, the present is a thing. Remember the past has already happened. The present is happening now."

"So, no date."

"No date," she said. "Just say 'Watson, open a portal to the present' and he will."

The young couple strolled away along the path over the water, holding hands. His knees shook so much that I wanted to make sure he didn't pass out, as if I could help if he did. They slowly dissolved into the shimmering waves of the current of time and disappeared. I mentally said goodbye and let them go.

"Watson, open a portal to the present," I called out, trying to keep my voice steady.

"Acknowledged. Initiating temporal gateway," he said.

When nothing happened, I stood up and looked around for it. After a moment, I turned and found it glowing in the back doorway of the building across the lot. The building was just an empty brick wall, as far as I could tell, without any sign over the door. So, the glowing purple swirling soapy membrane looked like something out of a movie.

"Why does it like doorways, so much?" I asked Clara, watching it for a bit.

"The sub-atomic particles that line the circumference of the field form an energetic bond with the enclosing structure and adhere to it like soap in a bubble blower," she explained.

"I'm not sure, but I think I just understood that. Am I getting smarter, hanging around you guys?"

"Of course, the Copenhagen interpretation of quantum physics illustrates the duality of a superposition of—"

"And it's gone," I said, defeated. "I'm just going to come home, now."

"I'll send an Uber to pick you up."

Chapter 16

She slurped her noodles. She tucked her thick shoulder-length blonde hair behind her ear. She straightened her forest green dress with the neckline that plunged all the way down to Puerto Rico. She swiped a finger under her bottom lip that was painted with lipstick the color of a 1968 Ferrari. And she slurped her noodles.

This was Clara's idea. Well, it started as Clara's idea. I told her she was being ridiculous and that I did not need to get back on the horse or camel or donkey or any other domesticated beast of burden. She told me I was the one being ridiculous. So of course, I told Ron. He agreed with her. I thought guys were supposed to stick together. Shows how much I know.

My date smiled at me from across the table and showed me teeth every bit as straight and white as money can buy.

"So, I had to wait a whole hour to be seen by the doctor and when I got in, he said that I was dehydrated and that I should drink more water and I said that I don't think it's dehydration and he said that he did some test and that it said I was dehydrated and that I'd feel better if I drank more water and then…"

I stuffed a piece of overcooked salmon in my mouth and pretended to be interested. I tried imagining she was Selma Hayek, but that didn't work.

"So, the sale sign on the rack said in huge letters that the sale ended Tuesday, not Monday and I tried explaining that to the stupid salesgirl and she said that she didn't control when the sale ended, and I asked to speak with her manager and that they shouldn't be letting little girls play with money and…"

It was Ron that convinced me to do this. He made so much sense that when I went home that night, I got online and made myself a dating profile. I think I'll punch him in the throat the next time I see him.

The waiter trotted up and almost didn't stop when he left the bill in the middle of the table and told us, "Whenever you're ready. No rush." Then he rushed off.

I pulled out my wallet and dropped my credit card on the bill.

"So, like I was saying before we were so rudely interrupted, I really think the state of the world today is nothing like the world that it used to be because back before cell phones, people would look at other people and not their cell phones and when kids get cell phones their all like insta-this and faceyspace-that and I think what's good for them is…"

I couldn't help thinking that I missed something back at William Horner's murder scene. The first one. Something I didn't know to look for. But then, the victim was already cleaned up, and most of the evidence was collected by the time I got there. Well, the stuff that Ron's team thought was evidence, anyway. I wonder if they've released the scene, yet.

"So, you're a detective," she asked, twirling her fettuccine Alfredo with her fork while not looking at it. Not a very efficient way to eat. "Is it anything like on TV?"

"Nowhere near that exciting. It's mostly paperwork." I took a bite of my overly salted asparagus with hollandaise sauce.

"Interesting," she said, raising her perfectly landscaped eyebrows that were mystifyingly thin.

The waiter came by and grabbed the bill and my credit card without stopping.

"You know, I was just thinking to myself how hot it's been and how it's never been this hot before and that well it's been hot but never this hot for this long, and I was thinking to myself is that what everyone else says and like a thousand years ago, did they say the same thing only in a different language because people from a thousand years ago didn't speak English because it wasn't invented yet and…"

All three of the victims were unrelated, as far as I can tell. Horner was a Black male traffic controller in his thirties. Sween was a White male insurance agent in his late forties. And Miller was a Black female in charge of a hospital. I researched as best I could and didn't come up when anything in their background, either. They all came from different cities. They never worked at the same company. None of them even knew each other. Maybe they were all crimes of opportunity. Maybe someone just wanted to kill and not get caught.

"So that's when I told him that I'm not paying for this latte and he looked at me and said that I had to pay for it and I asked why and he said it's because I drank it and I said that if I hadn't drunk it, then I wouldn't have known that it was nasty and he said that I drank the whole thing and I said that I had to be sure I didn't like it and…"

The Miller and Sween murders were both outdoors. The murderer just came up, killed them, and kept going. Much like the waiter with the check. But the Horner murder was different. That was inside and with his own gun. So, he had to have known the killer and trusted them at least well enough to walk away and turn his back. Or maybe he didn't. Maybe he accepted the inevitable and made them coffee.

"So, my hairdresser said that I can't make an appointment on Monday because they're not open on Monday and I mean, who isn't open on a Monday, do you know what I mean and well I told them that it was crazy, and they should get with the times, and they told me that they've always done it like that and…"

The waiter passed by and dropped off my credit card, a pen, and the receipt. I quickly signed it and added the tip. As I scooted out of the booth, I said, "I'll walk you to your car."

"Already? I like it when a man takes charge. My place or yours?"

"Let's discuss it on the way out."

She insisted on holding my hand as we walked past the tables full of people to the exit. At the car, she laced her fingers between mine on both hands and leaned her back against the driver-side door. She turned her face away from me and looked at me from the corner of her eye.

"It sure is a nice night," she said in a tone that said she was saying something else.

"Yep. The weather is nice this time of year. It's pretty late."

She had one of my hands in each of hers and pulled me closer. "I'm a night owl."

"Too bad I have to go to work. You know us cops. The work never ends." I tried to pull away, but she had a firm grip on my hands and wasn't letting go.

"I could put you to work." She pulled me a little closer, and I had to put a foot in front of me to keep from falling onto her. Then as I was leaning over her, while she was leaning up against the car, she ran her hand up my pant leg into some sensitive bits.

I grabbed her hand at the wrist and took it off my leg. "It's late. I have to go," I told her.

"No, you don't," she said in an almost whisper as her lips made for my neck.

I tried to pull away, but she kept coming for me like a vampire. I swear it was actual wine in her glass at dinner. At least, I think it was.

I tried to put a hand on her shoulder to push her away. But she had a decent grip on one hand with her fingers intertwined with mine. And my other hand was trying to keep her other hand from making a beeline for my Jujubes.

"I'm sorry," I tried to plead. "I forgot to tell you that I'm married. A lot. I'm very, very married."

"You're a bad liar," she said with a voice that could play Jessica Rabbit. "If you're worried about people watching, we can go to my place."

"Please!" I shouted, still trying to wriggle away.

I am so going to punch Ron in the throat for talking me into this.

Somewhere during the—encounter—a man casually walked just behind us. He grabbed her purse from off her shoulder and took off like a shot, breaking her cast iron grip on my hand as he left.

I took off right after him, putting all that cardio at the gym to good use.

As I ran away, I think my date shouted something like, "Get back here! There's nothing in there but lipstick and tissues and girly things!" That was probably not an exact quote.

I chased him around the building. When I turned the corner, I shouted, "Police! Stop or I'll shoot!" I didn't actually have my gun drawn on him. I just always wanted to say that.

He didn't even slow down and charged into a back alley. I followed him, wishing I'd had the chance to warm up, first. People stared and murmured to each other as we passed, probably wondering what was going on and if it was something they could

J.S. Johnston

post to YouTube.

The thief ran out of the alley and across a main street, weaving in and out of traffic that blared their horns and tried to keep from plowing right into him. He made it to the other side, so of course, I followed like an idiot.

Then cars blared their horns and swerved so they could keep from plowing into me. (Nice of them.) A blue station wagon slammed on its brakes. The driver advised me to consult an optometrist. I was touched by the concern for my health.

Meanwhile, the purse snatcher didn't stop. But they did slow down. Finally. I told myself all that cardio would pay off one day and ran him down.

He took a corner around the side of a mechanic's garage and hopped a chain-link fence that was taller than me into a brick-paved alley. And I hopped it right after him. He stopped where he was, breathing hard and holding her purse with an outstretched arm.

A glint shone in his eye and a toothy smile covered his face like the Cheshire cat. His strong cheekbones accented his narrow face and large eyes. "Looking for this?" he asked, catching his breath.

As soon as my feet landed on the other side of the fence, I pulled out my weapon and trained it on him. "Lay on the ground and put your hands behind your head," I said as I tried to catch my breath. Of course, my breath had at least twenty years on his. I bent at the waist and braced a hand on my knee, keeping the gun on him. "Christ, I'm getting old." More panting. I reminded myself how much worse it would be without all that cardio. It didn't make me feel any better.

He laughed to himself and put the purse on the ground then slowly, lazily, or one might say even lackadaisically laid down prostrate on the brick pavement, in line with the alleyway. You would think that this relaxed attitude to the idea of being imprisoned for petty theft would have tipped me off that something wasn't right. Instead, I reasoned it was a young male just being cocky as young males are known to do. I am terrible at this job.

"You got me," he said as he gingerly put his hands over his head with the speed one might use to pick up a baby bird. He did not sound scared or worried. Or even surprised that I caught him. (I know I was.) At least he noticed my gun and looked like I might shoot him with it.

"What is wrong with you, kid?" I asked. I stumbled my way over to him, covered in so much sweat that you'd think it was raining. "If you need money, there are ways to get it without stealing purses." I took one of his hands from his head and brought it behind his back. And I remembered what it was like to be as in shape as this kid. That was a lie. I was never as in shape as this kid.

"Sure was a silly idea. I can't outrun John Law," he said like a young Ben Stiller doing Zoolander. He didn't sound like he meant what he said.

I took out the cuffs and put one end over his wrist. "Damn right, you can't." I took his other hand and brought it behind his back then cuffed it, as well. "What's your name, son?"

I swear to God, he said, "Reggie Jackson."

"Reggie Jackson."

"That's my name."

"I don't think that's really your name," I said, out of breath.

"You callin' me a liar?"

"I'm saying your name is less than believable."

"Then check. Get my wallet out of my pants. My IDs in there."

Of course, I dug it out of his back pocket. I took a seat on the brick pavement against the wall of the building on the side to go through it.

"Don't mind the prophylactic." He said it like he was proud of it. But it looked like it's been in there for a while, so I'm not sure why.

"You shouldn't keep it in your wallet. The heat will degrade the rubber and you might end up with a little Reggie and—huh."

"Told ya."

"Was your mother into baseball?"

"Nah. I'm named after my uncle. He died before I was born."

Still sitting on the brick pavement, I leaned my back against the cinder block wall behind me, still catching my breath. "Sorry to hear that, Reggie. He must've been a good man to be named after him."

"Yeah, I guess. He worked for NASA. One of the guys that did the moon landings. My mom never shuts up about him."

"Huh. If your uncle worked for NASA, why are you stealing

purses?"

He laughed. "We don't all work for them, dummy. Just him. They don't pay everyone."

"I suppose not. But I'd assume they'd have enough money to put you through college or trade school. Something to keep you from having to steal purses from the dates of Tampa policemen."

He snickered and rolled his eyes a little. "My family told me they wouldn't pay for anything if I couldn't keep my grades up. They're just being cheap."

"And you could not keep your grades up, I take it."

"I never had a head for school," he said. "They kept throwing my NASA uncle in my face, telling me if he could do it then I could. 'If you bust your ass and work hard, you could be just like him.' I don't know where they're getting that. They don't work for NASA, either. School isn't for everybody."

I'd started to get my breath back and leaned forward, resting my elbows on my knees. "So just because school's hard, you said the hell with all of it. It's not worth the trouble to try to get anywhere. That how it happened?"

He turned his head from me and looked straight down the alley in front of him. I followed his gaze and found some guy with a foot out of his open door, looking at us. He stood frozen in the doorway with one hand still on the doorknob and a bag of trash in the other. He had one of those am-I-witnessing-a-crime expressions. I held up my badge as high as I could reach without standing up, and let it reflect the overhead light on the side of the building. I pointed at it with the tip of the gun in my other hand. He nodded a reply then tossed his bag of trash in the dumpster on the other side of his door and went back in.

"Just trying harder wasn't good enough," Reggie said. "Your family might've been fine with it. You don't have an uncle in NASA. 'Don't tell me you can't do it, Reggie. Look at your uncle, Reggie. If he can do it, so can you.' I hate all of them. Now, I just do what I can to get by." He turned his head to the other side of the alley, facing away from me. He was still lying on the brick pavement with his hands cuffed behind his back, so there wasn't much else he could do.

"You could've just gotten a tutor."

He turned his head back in my direction and smiled. But not the kind of smile that said I just made him happy. "You got the money for one?"

"I guess not," I said. "But it still doesn't give you the right to steal women's purses. She might've needed what's in there to make her electric bill."

"You could help her out, old man. I'm sure you're making bank at your age," he said with a half-smirk looking at me from the corner of his eye.

"It's not like that." And it's Detective Old Man to you, you little punk.

"Looked that way to me."

"Yeah well—It's not."

He laughed.

I slowly shook my head and looked down at the brick pavement. "My friends pushed me into it. You know how it goes."

"Hey, I saw her. Your friends wouldn't have to push me into anything." He had a different smile, now.

"I don't want to go into it."

"I gave. Now you have to give," Reggie said. His tone had changed to something conversational.

"Don't give me that. I didn't hold a gun to your head."

He smirked at me.

"You know what I mean. It's just complicated, is all."

"You can't be so old that you can't see her. C'mon," Reggie said and raised his eyebrows.

"I said, it's complicated."

"I don't think it is." He laughed a little.

"Well… it is. Okay?"

He snickered.

I climbed to my feet. Not an easy task after sprinting across Tampa. At least not when you've been sprinting and you're as old as me.

"Those eyes," He closed his and spoke slowly in an almost sing-song tone. "That hair and the size of her—"

"Okay, let's get you up." I cut him off. "You have the right to remain silent. Blah, blah, blah."

J.S. Johnston

"Not yet." He looked down the alley and smiled. I didn't like that one.

I took his arm, near the armpit. "Up you go."

"I said, not yet." He did not get up.

"You saw my gun, right? It's loaded and everything." I tried pulling his arm harder. But a hundred and fifty pounds of dead weight is tough.

"Did you lose your hearing, old man? I said, not yet." He raised his head and looked around.

"What're you looking for? Just get up."

Cars are so quiet, these days. Really, really quiet. Amazingly quiet. Especially for the horsepower needed to get a machine the size of a car up to highway speeds. When I was a kid, I always knew when my mother came home, even when she was still down the street, they were so loud. It was really helpful, so I could stop doing whatever I was doing before she got to the driveway. (I was not an obedient child.) But now they're astoundingly quiet.

This one—the engine barely made a peep. Standing in the middle of an alley with cinder block walls on either side of me to amplify the sound, I barely registered it over the background noise of the city. The sound of the tires crushing the detritus along the brick pavement was louder than the engine. But it was only there for maybe a few seconds, anyway. I turned around just in time for the grill of a 2001 BMW R1200C to collide with my shoulder. That's what Reggie was waiting on. I might've said something witty before it hit me, but I can't remember. So, I'm just going to say that I did. Because it's my story and I can remember it however I want.

Chapter 17

"Jesus! What're you doing here?" asked Ron with wide eyes and a slacked jaw. I met him in the dark side of the two-way mirror for the interrogation room. He almost dropped the cup of coffee in his hand when he saw me.

"Most people call me Sean. And what do you mean, what am I doing here? I work here." I shut the door behind me. "Unless you know something I don't."

He eyed me and looked like he was trying to figure out what to say.

"If you do know something I don't, you should've called and told me before I left the house."

"No, it's just—" He motioned to his face, referencing what mine looked like. I got it pretty banged up when that BMW ran me over. My right eye would be swollen for a while. I could see out of it well enough, but it still stung a bit. "Shouldn't you still be in the hospital?"

I motioned to Reggie Jackson, currently sitting cuffed to the table on the other side of the giant two-way mirror in the interrogation room. I mean questioning room. Whatever we're supposed to call them now. I give up. "You gonna come bring him by my hospital room, then?"

"Well, no. But…" Ron trailed off.

"What are you doing in here, anyway?" I asked him, finally realizing it. "You know you're not a real cop, right?" Seriously. Ron's an evidence tech. They don't even let him carry a gun.

He shrugged. "You got hit by a car and almost died. I was curious about this guy." Then, he motioned to the sling I was wearing. "Is your arm okay?"

"I didn't almost die," I said. "Well, I mean I could have. But the doctor said something about the way I was crouched over absorbed most of the impact, so it mostly just knocked me out of the way."

He gestured to his arm.

"It's fine. It was just dislocated."

"But doesn't it hurt?"

I took a nice big prescription bottle out of my pocket and shook it to let the nice big white pills rattle inside. "Nope."

He shook his head in resignation. "No one's going to think you're less of a man if you take the day off, Sean."

"What? Don't give me that. I need to talk to him." I picked up the manilla folder labeled REGGIE JACKSON lying on the desk and flipped through it.

"You can't go in there," he said, taking the manila folder from me. "It's Jean's case." He held up the folder as if to show me the name on it that I'd already read.

"I know that," I said, taking the folder back. "I'm not taking the case. Just need to talk to him." I flipped through the folder.

"You're not gonna…" He gestured with a balled fist.

"What? No! It's like you don't know me."

He cocked his head and raised his right eyebrow. "You're seeing the shrink because you…" He gestured again.

"Oh, right. Well, I got run over by a car because of him. By law, I get to ask him why."

"That's not a law, Sean."

"Sure, it is. Paragraph one-oh-two, subsection D of the Florida Statute involving handsome middle-aged detectives who get run over in the line of duty." More flipping.

Ron took a sip of his coffee and turned to watch the handcuffed and distraught Reggie Jackson on the other side of the glass. "So, how'd your date go?"

"It was fine."

"Fine?" he asked like he didn't believe me. He turned away from the window to compound that with a disbelieving look.

"Yeah, it was fine. What?"

He chuckled. "What happened?"

"Nothing happened. It was fine."

"Dates are never fine. They can be great, horrible, wonderful, dreamy, terrible, ordained, fated, and I think sometimes they can even be nice. They're never—ever—fine."

"It was fine. Really." I hid my eyes in more of the stuff in the folder.

Ron took it from me, again. "What happened?"

"She was just a little boring, is all." I tried to take the folder back from him, but he pulled it out of my reach. His arms are very long.

"And?"

"And I don't want to talk about it. It was fine."

He put the folder back on the desk.

"It was a long time ago, Sean. She's moved on."

"It has nothing to do with that."

"Then what?"

I leered at him and sighed.

"Oh. Oh!" His eyes popped open then he settled into a good chuckle. "What'd you do?"

I motioned to Reggie on the other side of the window. "I ran away."

"So, are you going to call her?"

I shrugged. "She's texted me a few times since then. I should probably tell her I got her purse back."

"I'm sure she'd appreciate that." He smiled and looked back at Reggie.

Just then, Jean came through the door, dressed in a blindingly white button-up shirt, black slacks, and black flats. And her long blonde hair pulled back in a very professional-looking ponytail. She held a cup of coffee in her hand, as well. "Oh my god, Sean. What did she do to you?"

"Do to me?"

She closed the door behind her. "Your date. From last night?"

I adjusted the strap of my arm sling and made an evil eye at Ron.

"Hey, you never told me to keep it a secret," he said, shrugging.

I grabbed the folder from the desk and turned to Jean. "I'm going to go talk to your suspect, now."

She laughed and said, "Okay." She took a sip of coffee, leaving a lipstick print on the side.

We like to keep suspects waiting for a while before we come into the interrogation room. If you're ever taken in, you could be in there for an hour or more before we ever get there. We'll tell you we're busy and apologize. But the real reason is it makes people want to talk. They get comfortable with their surroundings and tell us whatever we want to know just to get out of there.

As I opened the door, I said, "Your uncle didn't work for NASA."

He lost three shades of melanin when he saw me with a swollen eye and my arm in a sling.

"You don't have an uncle." I closed the door. "You did have your name legally changed three years ago." I put the folder down on the table in front of him. He glued his widened eyes to me and not it. "You were born Martin Edward Jackson." I sat down in the chair across from him and opened the folder.

"I'm a D.J. as a side hustle. I thought it would help me get more gigs." He looked like I'd caught him at something. "Shouldn't you be—"

"I didn't ask you about your name."

He sat at attention. His wrists squirmed just a little in his cuffs.

I pulled out the papers for the driver of the car that hit me and dropped them in front of Martin. He looked at them then up at me and shook his head.

"I don't—"

"I didn't ask you about him. Now, did I?" I cut him off.

He shook his head, quietly.

"His name is Gerald Howell," I said and slid out his mugshot. "He'd already been busted for drunk driving before and had his license taken away. Now he's locked up in a jail cell with a guy twice his size who thinks he's pretty. The night he hit me, he just happened to be at a new bar that wouldn't turn him away. He went there, got drunk out of his mind, and took that back alley to keep out of sight of cops. If he saw either one of us at all, he sure as hell didn't have the reaction time to do anything about it."

"Hey, I didn't have—"

"You didn't have a damn thing to do with him!" I stood up and planted the balled fist of my good arm on the desk, leaning toward him.

His mouth fell open a little.

"You didn't know him. You never met him. You had absolutely no reason to think he'd be there to run me over. But you still told me that bullshit story about your nonexistent uncle in NASA and how hard it was to be a kid in a family with him in it all to keep me there until he did." I took a breath and continued. "You even laid in line with the alley to make sure you didn't have to worry about him running you over, too." I paused for a moment to see if he'd offer anything. "Well? What the hell was that?"

He looked down and shook his head like he realized something. I craned my neck to get a look at the expression on his face. The corner of one side of his mouth came up in a half-smile.

"I'm waiting."

"I think I should have a lawyer," he said in a voice so quiet that it was barely more than a whisper.

"So, do I. Now tell me what in god's name is going on. Who are you and why did you try to kill me like—like... *that?*"

"I'm exercising my right to remain—"

"Oh, stop it, Martin." And I made sure to say his name like I'd just punched him with it. "As if I came here to find out if you're guilty. I already know what your guilt is. I was there! When somebody tries to kill me, I get to ask why."

He shook his head. "I can't tell you."

"Sure, you can. Just open your mouth and start talking." I mocked him, a little. "Hello. My name is Martin and I'm a dumbass. I tried to kill a cop, because—"

"No. I mean I said I wouldn't tell anyone." He looked up at me with sincere eyes.

"Huh."

He looked back down at the floor.

"Someone put you up to it."

He kept looking at the floor.

"Did they pay you?"

Nothing.

"Did they say something to you?"

He looked up at me and then averted his eyes.

"Look. Man-to-man. You tried to kill me, and I survived. Your part now as a man is to own up to what you did, look me in the eye, and tell me why. I deserve that much. I won't tell anyone. You have my word."

He looked at the two-way mirror on the other side of the room. I followed his gaze.

"Good point." I uncuffed Martin Edward Jackson to his complete surprise, took him by the arm, and led him out the door.

Both Ron and Jean burst out the door of the adjoining room with ghost-white faces.

"Sean! Where are you taking him?" shouted Ron as I led Martin down the hall.

"We're going for a walk. It's good exercise," I told him.

"You can't do that!" shouted Jean as I got farther away. They started to follow me. I still had a good grip on Martin's arm, and he became less willing to accompany me down the hall.

"Should I be scared?" Martin asked me, sounding scared.

"Only if you're claustrophobic," I replied.

"What?" he exclaimed.

I didn't answer him.

"Sean! Please!" shouted Ron as the two of them followed us down the hall. The other people stopped what they were doing and took notice.

I brought Martin to a closet and opened the door. As I pushed him in, he asked me, "Isn't there a law against this?"

"I dunno. Probably," I answered.

As Ron and Jean shouted their protests, I followed Martin into the closet and shut the door behind us. I pushed him toward the bright stainless-steel shelves and let him go. He looked at me like I'd just grown a third head.

"There," I said. "We're alone. No one can hear us. Whatever you tell me stays here. I promise." I leaned back against the door and folded my arms.

Martin rubbed his wrists. "Thanks," he said like he knew what I'd just done for him.

"No problem. So, who was it? And what'd they tell you?"

"I don't know who they were," he began. "They called me on my cell."

"Did you get a number?"

He shook his head. "It was unlisted."

"But you answered it."

"Not at first. They kept calling, never leaving a voicemail. Eventually, I got sick of it and answered, just to tell them to leave me the hell alone. Ya know?"

"And they weren't just trying to tell you that your car's warranty was about to expire."

He chuckled. "No. They weren't."

"What did their voice sound like? Man? Woman? Young?"

"Distorted," he said with a creased brow. "They were using one of those voice changers."

"Figures. What'd they say?"

"They called me by my name, for starters."

"They knew your name was Reggie—"

"No," he cut me off. "I mean my birth name. Martin Edward. Scared the hell out of me."

"Huh. So, what'd you say?"

"Nothing. I was so much in shock, I just listened. They told me that if I didn't do this for them, they'd take my dog out and drown him in the bay."

My eyes widened at that, and I asked, "They didn't even bother with money. Just went right for your dog?"

He nodded. "Yeah, man. Who would do that?"

"I don't know. But you believed them?"

"Yeah. They told me exactly where you'd be with that lady, where to stand to take her purse, where to run to… I figured if they knew all that, they'd know how to get to Jerry. And he's not the best guard dog. If anyone ever broke in, he'd just want to be their friend."

"You could've called the cops," I said. "Reported them."

"What would they do? You can't call the cops if someone threatens your dog."

"I guess not. What else did they say?"

"Just that if I ever told anyone, they'd still come after Jerry. He's not Cujo. My ass weighs more than he does," Reggie said and looked a little desperate.

"Okay," I said with a sigh and a nod. "I haven't heard a word you've said. I mean that."

"Thank you." Fear came through in his voice.

I opened the door to find Ron and Jean standing just outside, looking worried. A crowd of other people surrounded them like rubberneckers near a traffic accident.

"What the hell was that, Sean? What's wrong with you?" shouted Ron, waving his arms in the air.

The expression on Jean's face was a mix of bewilderment and anxiety. The sculpted brow over her dark blue eyes creased like an old newspaper. "There's been a mistake," I told her. "This boy is completely innocent. Let him go."

As the two of them looked confused and professed their disagreement, I walked down the hallway filled with people staring at me and left.

Chapter 18

She stood with her back toward me. Her hair was in an afro. Delicate spindles of dark, teased-out follicles crowned her head. Her bare, muscular arms showed off skin the color of coffee with cream. Her long, slender figure looked exaggerated by the curves sewn into her thin white dress that came down to mid-thigh. Fishnet stockings wrapped around legs that you only ever see on the cover of women's fitness magazines in the checkout line. The kind you tell yourself must be Photoshopped and don't pay any attention to because humans aren't shaped like that in real life.

This was how I met Peppermint, or rather the first time I saw her; standing behind her in the checkout line of a gas station, in the middle of the night. I didn't introduce myself until a few minutes later.

Her white purse was the same shade as her dress and just big enough to carry a handful of tissues. She adjusted its thin gold chain that ran across her body from her right shoulder to her left hip. Then after a moment, shifted her weight on painful-looking high heels as she waited in the checkout line of the 7-Eleven, holding a bottle of blue Gatorade and a couple of packages of peanut butter crackers.

An overweight man stood in front of her at the checkout counter. His hair had receded into a thick ring around his head. The remainder of which looked like it had been graying for years and was now almost white. The back of his charcoal gray t-shirt cleverly displayed Mickey Mouse's backside, as if he was turning his back to me as well. Something red was smeared across it and I told myself it was just ketchup.

The kid behind the counter looked like he may as well have been on Mars, as he scanned the man's bag of Ruffles.

At the time, I was working a break-in case—a broken window

downtown, a two-time convicted felon. Yadda, yadda, yadda. I'd knocked off late that night and stopped to get some gas, a case of beer, and a pizza on my way home, like a lot of other nights.

My phone chirped the notification for a text, but I left it in my pocket; it wasn't worth digging out. It was Nicole, my wife. I hadn't bothered to call her to let her know I'd be working late like I said I would. At the time I didn't understand it, but I hadn't been any kind of husband to her for the last year. I did, however, plan to be very drunk as soon as I got home. And I was fine with it.

When I checked out and carried my armload of goods to the car, the woman in white was at the driver-side door of her yellow Toyota Scion on the other side of the gas pumps, fishing her car keys out of her tiny purse. The guy in the gray Mickey Mouse t-shirt came up to her with that look in his eye. She saw him walking up and pretended she didn't.

"Hey!" he shouted as he trotted up to her before she could get in her car and drive away. "Hey, you!"

Her hand emerged from her purse holding the key fob to the Toyota, then dropped it on the asphalt ground. "Shit," she said under her breath as she quickly knelt to retrieve the key ring.

The man caught up to her, a little out of breath, and put his hand on her door. "Hey, I was trying to get your attention."

"Yeah?" she asked like the answer was already no.

"How much?"

"For what?"

"A little… You know."

Another local prostitute. I opened my passenger side door and put the pizza and case of beer on the seat. I really didn't care. Everyone's just trying to pay the bills the best they can. As long as no one got hurt, as far as I was concerned, I was off work and late for the first beer.

"No." She stepped back from him and crossed her arms.

He positioned his whole body in front of her driver-side door and leaned back on it. "No, what?" he asked, annoyed.

"No, I'm not in the mood. Now get away from my car."

"What do you mean? You're getting paid to be in the mood." He gently grabbed her elbow, which she jerked away from him, dropping her Gatorade. The smack on the pavement got my attention.

"Just leave me alone, okay?"

"Come on. I got money." He took a step toward her.

"I said no." She was getting angry.

"C'mon!"

"Hey!" I shouted across the parking lot. "She said no. Now leave her alone."

"Shut the hell up," he shouted back. "This is none of your business."

When she looked back at me, he snuck a feel and grabbed her left breast. He squeezed and dropped his jaw, enjoying the moment.

She slapped his hand away and backed off.

I ran past the pumps, across the parking lot, and connected my fist with his eye. While he was in a daze, I followed it up with a left hook to his jaw that he managed to block. He threw a solid right to my nose and broke it. I fell back to the hard, unforgiving asphalt, smacking my ass and then the back of my skull, sending waves of pain all through me. Before I had time to shout, the guy in the Mickey Mouse t-shirt was on top of me, taking swings at my face. I raised my arms to shield myself from his blows, but they still hurt like hell.

On one of his swings, I managed to wrap my arm around his in an armlock. He stopped for a second like he'd given up. But he reached around to his back and produced a knife. I was in such a hurry to pound his face in, that I never bothered to consider that he might have a weapon. There it was, reflecting the fluorescent lights of the gas station awning. He raised his arm, aiming the point of the knife down at me. The muscles in his hand flexed, tightening his grip.

Then all those muscles tensed over his whole body in this forced, mechanical convulsion. As if he'd suddenly turned to wood. His face scrunched in a pained expression. His mouth clenched shut hard enough to break his teeth. He made a gurgling sound; spittle trailed down the corner of his mouth. The rapid tac-tac-tac of electricity froze him in place on top of me.

Then as if someone switched him off, he fell face-first onto my chest. He was somewhere around three hundred pounds, so I had to shove hard to roll out from under him. The woman in white stood just a few paces off, legs spread and holding a taser in both hands like a gun. The thin leads streamed from the front of it to the back of the man who was now unconscious on the ground, beside me.

"Where'd you get that thing?" I asked, still pulling myself out from under the man's girth.

"Off your belt. Is he out?" she replied, leaning in, and looking at him like a specimen in a zoo.

I checked my belt holster and found it empty. I didn't even notice her take it. Nice. "Yeah, he'll be out for a while. You okay?"

She snapped her eyes to me and tilted her head. "Am *I* okay?"

"Yeah. You okay?" I stood up to my full height, touched my nose, and winced. It stung pretty bad. I tried to wipe off the trailing blood with the cuff of my sleeve. "Damn. I liked this shirt."

She fished in her tiny purse, came out with a few tissues, and handed them to me.

"I didn't need you to do that," she said as I took them.

"Do what?"

"Come to my rescue. Guys do that all the time, you know. I can take care of myself."

"I see that," I said and passed a hand over the empty Taser holster on my belt. "Now you won't have to. Not with him, anyway."

She looked down at the unconscious idiot, drooling on the blacktop. "I'm Peppermint," she said after a minute, a sigh, and a head shake. She extended her hand to me, and I took it.

"That's what you go by? Peppermint?"

"Yeah. We can't tell guys our real names. So, a bunch of us use types of candy as... you know—our hooker names. It's supposed to be sexy. I'm Peppermint. There's Caramel, Licorice, Butterscotch, Marshmallow—"

I snickered.

She smiled just slightly, from the corner of her mouth. "What?"

"Please tell me Marshmallow is a little pudgy."

She giggled and slowly grew her smile to full, connecting both ears. It was contagious, and I smiled back at her. "A little. But don't tell her I said that." She pointed at me to drive it home. "She's sensitive." The woman in white squatted down to pick up the bottle of blue Gatorade that she'd dropped then leaned back against the side of her car.

"I'm Sean. Do you have a real name?" I stepped closer to her, taking the invite.

She shook her head and took a drink. "My name is Peppermint. And you're a cop."

"I'm not that kind of cop. At least not right now."

She shook her head again. "Peppermint." She handed the Taser back to me, butt end first like a real gun.

"Keep it. So, this is what guys do all the time?"

She shrugged.

"Don't you ever get tired of it?"

"This is just until my book deal goes through."

I laughed at that. Then stopped when the kid inside the 7-Eleven pulled out his cell phone and made a call. He leaned over the counter to get a better look out the window at us. From the look on his face, he was calling 9-1-1.

"Alright, Sean. Time to go," she said, taking another drink.

"Right. I'll stay and explain Captain Inappropriate." I gestured to the unconscious man drooling on the pavement of the gas station.

"Yeah, I know better than to hang around." As she stood back up, she handed me the Taser again. When I looked at her, she qualified it with, "I'd just end up tasering myself one day. That would not be very sexy."

I smiled and took it back from her.

Before she got in her car and drove off, she stood with her hand on her open driver-side door and said, "And Sean, thanks for coming to my rescue."

I made a gentle half-nod then went into the 7-Eleven to talk to the kid and wait for the uniforms to show up.

* * *

"Whiskey on the rocks," Mark said dispassionately as he slid the drink to me across the bar and left. After today, the first place I ran was The Hollow Giraffe to get eviscerated in a tsunami of alcohol. I was ready to forget all those dry years like they never happened. After all, I'd earned it.

J.S. Johnston

Mark didn't try to talk me out of it. Didn't tell me how disappointed he was in me, how he'd been rooting for me, that I needed the money to make rent knowing how much I got paid working as a public servant for the City of Tampa. And he absolutely didn't shake his head and look at the floor as he walked away. He just said, "Whiskey on the rocks," as casually as he might say, "Steak and onions." Then he went to help other people trying to reach a level of intoxication so legendary that songs would be written about it and sung for generations afterward. No, wait. That was *my* plan.

Blind Lemon Jefferson played "Hard Time Killin' Floor", sweet and slow over the speakers of The Hollow Giraffe. The constant white noise of the crowd always quieted down when he came on. The owners typically gave whoever was tending the bar free rein of the playlist, though restricted it to about a thousand or so blues songs, to keep up with the theme of the place. Mark was partial to Blind Lemon. He's never explained whether it was because the crowd didn't shout so much, or he just liked him. But he played him a lot on the nights he was on duty.

Melting ragged chunks of broken ice glistened under tiny overhead spotlights, as they carelessly floated in the amber-brown liquid. The refracted bar lights made it all glow, almost as if it had willed itself to do so. As if it were making itself noticeable to me. Me, specifically. Only me. It wanted to become part of who I was. It wanted to flow through my body and envelope my brain in a tender caress of amnesia. The gentle touch of a loving mother that smells of oak and turpentine.

I came here to relieve myself of my mortal terror. Or forget about it for a little while, anyway. Maybe just turn down the earthquake in my hands. My heart pounded like I was running the hundred-meter dash while I was still sitting on my barstool. I swear it almost escaped out of my throat. Maybe with some whiskey, it might decide to stay.

"What're you doing?" asked Peppermint, who had sat down on the stool beside me. I swear she wasn't there a minute ago. Funny how whiskey can do that.

"I like this place. It has good music. The stools are comfortable. Plenty of parking." I ran my fingers across the flawlessly smooth surface of the glass, through the newly formed droplets of moisture.

"You know, that's not what I mean," she said with a smirk. "You don't drink, anymore."

"I do, today." I brought the glass to my lips. An aroma of claws and teeth gently kissed me and sauntered into my nasal passages. I took a breath and let it fill my lungs. It was—comfortable. Like I was home.

Peppermint stole the glass from my hand like she owned it and set it back down on the bar before I could take a sip. It came down with a knock of glass on wood and I had a mini heart attack when some of it almost spilled out. "You don't today, either," she said. Damn her.

Mark stopped cleaning glass tumblers and looked up to notice us. His eyes were wide like he just walked in on Mom and Dad doing something they later had to tell him was wrestling. He quickly turned around, pretending to be summoned by another customer.

"I didn't realize your services included fortune-telling." I picked the glass back up.

"Baby, I have all kinds of services." She took the glass from me and set it down on the bar, again. It looked so far away.

Mark pretended like he wasn't paying attention. "He didn't give me this." I gestured in his direction. "Why do I need to get it from you?"

She leered at him with a force that he had to have felt boring a hole in the back of his head. "I'll talk to him, later," she said continuing her death stare. "I care about what happens to you, Sean. And what happened to your arm? And your eye?"

"I had a rough day. I needed a drink." Seemed like a reasonable enough explanation to me.

"What kind of a rough day gives you a black eye and puts you in an arm sling?"

"A really bad one."

"And you know you can't just have one drink to relax. You keep drinking until… Last time, you wound up in the hospital and almost died."

"Right now, I'm fine with that." I picked the glass back up.

She sighed, grabbed my drink, and set it back on the bar. "What happened?"

"You know, that costs the same, whether I drink it or not." I pointed to it.

"You don't talk to your shrink, either. Do you?"

"I'd be a lot more talkative with that whiskey in me."

She glared at me with a waiting expression.

I checked to see if someone had maybe been trying not to overhear us. Even Mark was engaged with a college-aged group of kids, ordering big curvy glasses full of neon-blue diabetes. Tourists. I don't think the curvy glass makes it taste any better.

"Someone tried to kill me," I told her in a hushed voice. I shoved it out of my mouth as quickly as a note smuggled between desks in math class.

"Huh?" she asked. I guess it was too hushed.

"Kill me. Someone tried to kill me, today." I used my good arm to motion to my arm sling and my black eye.

"Baby, I'm sorry. But I know that's not the first time—"

"I don't mean like that. Someone tried to *have* me killed. I have no idea who and they're still out there."

Mark turned his head to look at us, still at the other side of the bar, bending over to scoop ice from the bin. His half-smile told me he didn't understand what I just said.

"Oh, my God. How? What happened?" she asked.

"It's a little complicated. But they got me to chase someone to a back alley where someone else hit me with their car." I adjusted the shoulder strap of my arm sling. "Woke up in an emergency room."

"How do you know it was planned that way? It could've been an accident."

"The kid told me so, himself. He said someone threatened to murder his dog if he didn't do it."

Peppermint shook her head and put her hand on my good arm. "Who would do that?"

The lights danced in the glass of whiskey and for a moment, I forgot she expected me to answer her question. "I'm working on a case that keeps getting bigger. And I can only assume that it's someone who doesn't want me to solve it." I left out the part where I'd reasoned that whoever put the kid up to it knew me well enough to know exactly where I'd be, exactly when I'd be there, what they'd needed to do to get me to chase them, and where to get me to chase them.

Peppermint raised her hand to get Mark's attention. "Coffee. Extra sugar, no cream," she called across the bar, pointing to me with her painted forefinger. She took the glass of whiskey from me and put it on the far side of the bar, a long way out of reach.

"I wanted to drink that."

"No, you didn't."

"Are you a mind reader, now?"

"I told you. I have all kinds of services. What are you going to do about…?" She rolled her hands.

"The purse snatcher? As far as I'm concerned, he's innocent. I mean, of attempted murder, anyway. I told Jean to let him go."

"You her boss, now?"

"Good point," I said. "I probably should've said please."

Mark came over and put the Styrofoam cup of coffee in front of me, along with half a handful of sugar packets. "Your coffee." Peppermint picked it up and set it a little closer to me, for good measure.

"Did Robbie McSnatcher tell you who put him up to it?" she asked.

"If he did, I wouldn't be in here. I'd be arresting them.

"How did they talk to them?"

"Phone," I said, holding my coffee and eyeing the whiskey.

"Their own?"

"I don't know. I haven't checked the kid's phone records, yet. But smart people don't make calls like that from a phone worth tracing, anyway."

"Having you killed sounds like something a desperate person would do," peppermint suggested. "People make mistakes when they're scared or desperate."

"That's also a good point." I took a sip of my coffee, and I don't know why. It was terrible. "This is wretched," I said, fighting to swallow it.

Peppermint grabbed the cup and took a sip without bothering to ask if it was okay. "Oh, God. It's horrible." The look on her face confirmed the truth of her statement.

I half-stood up from my stool and stretched my good arm across the bar for the glass of whiskey.

Peppermint took it from me and put it back where it came from. "You don't want that."

"I bought the drink. Why would you think I didn't want it?"

"Because if you really wanted it, you would've gone to another bar," she said.

I reached for a witty and insightful retort to snap back with but didn't find any. Instead, I did my best to leer at her for a good long moment.

Peppermint raised her thin, feminine eyebrows back at me. She tilted her head down, just so she could look up at me with gotcha-eyes.

"I have to pee," I said as I stood up from my barstool. As soon as it was in reach, I stretched out my good arm for the whiskey.

Peppermint snatched it, plucked the ice cube from the glass, and tilted her head back to down the whole thing in one gulp. I wonder if guys ever pay to see that. She dropped the ice cube back into the glass with a clink and smiled at me, the caliber of which was medically impossible to be angry at.

I snatched the ice cube, popped it in my mouth then held it between my front teeth and grinned at her as spitefully as I could manage as I stepped backward.

She rolled her eyes and looked over to Mark, who forgot he wasn't supposed to be paying attention and tilted her head at me to him. He held up his hands in a not-my-fault gesture then turned to attend to one of the college kids.

When I turned to head to the little detective's room, I bumped right into a guy, almost running him over. "I'm so sorry," I said before I recognized him. "Hey, Allister. What're you doing here?"

He was still dressed in his work clothes, a solid pale-yellow button-up shirt, black pants, and brown wingtip oxfords. And he smelled like cheap beer. "Hey, Sean. Someone recommended this place, and I thought I'd come and check it out." His eyes were wide, and his voice was shaking. His line came out—rehearsed. Like something in a speech or play. I probably should've picked up on that.

"Well, I'm glad you came out." I patted him on the shoulder and added, "I'm on my way to see a man about a horse. But I'm sitting just over there at the bar if you want to have a drink."

Behind him, a table of what looked like a middle-aged boy's night out, who were at least two pitchers into hearing loss, shouted to each other about batting averages. The baldest one was very passionate about the Tampa Bay Rays and how an enclosed field like Tropicana changes the game. He shouted louder than the others but as far as I could tell, the others did not accept that to be an indicator of his point being any more valid than theirs.

Allister quickly nodded. "Yeah. Sounds good," he shouted over the enthusiastic table. He flashed me a forced, artificial smile then crowded into a barstool on his right to let a lady in a green sundress squeeze past.

"Alrighty, then. I'll be back in a minute," I replied then turned around and left. As I weaved my way between the fully manned tables, a passerby came stumbling the opposite way to me. Before I could get out, I had to squeeze past someone standing in the middle of the aisle while he shouted to a table of women. And he thought wearing an expensive Hawaiian shirt tucked into his khaki shorts would make his protruding belly unnoticeable. He was mistaken about that.

I always wondered if Allister had a social life. I'm not sure if he's ever been more than ten feet away from Ron, up until that night. And when he actually talked, it was usually about bugs or some new chemical test for human blood or something. So, I expected an interesting conversation when I got back to the bar.

The bathrooms were tucked out of the way, behind a wall divider; it was almost like they were hiding their business from the rest of the bar. The men's room was indicated by a sophisticated-looking 1920s-style cartoonish, anthropomorphized giraffe in a tuxedo with a monocle, holding up a long cigarette holder in its cloven hoof. The lady's room had a giraffe in a dress.

A guy in a black cowboy hat and shirt that looked like he got it from the Dollywood giftshop walked out of the door with the giraffe in a tux. His face was flushed red and covered with about three days of neglected beard growth. His eye movements looked delayed. Like he was about two and a half seconds behind the rest of the world. He smiled and threw me an exaggerated nod as he passed me. I smiled back and wished I was in the same place he was in.

Once inside, I had the place to myself. The constant roar of the bar crowd dampened as the door closed and somehow I could breathe a little easier. Like a strange kind of temple where I could take a pee. The urinals were along the far wall, all topped with framed posters of overly Photoshopped, and under-fed girls in bikinis. I picked the one with the swimsuit made out of an American flag and took my place.

The posters were all covered in a sheet of clear, reflective plastic. It was reflective enough that I could watch Allister come through the door to the men's room and purposefully close it behind him. He made jerky motions as he looked around. He turned the key for the deadbolt on the door and the SHUNK sound of it locking echoed off of the tile walls of the bathroom.

I almost got out the words, "What's wrong?" before he pulled up his pant leg and produced the rectangular form of a Glock 22 from his ankle holster. They're standard issue and semi-automatic, not that it matters. It only takes one bullet to ruin your day. I'm not sure where he got it from. Like Ron, he's not an actual cop, either. Allister is another evidence tech. He must've lifted the gun from one of the cops at the station. I never see him at the range, but that also didn't matter. From where he stood at the door, only a few feet away, a drunken blind man could sneeze and put an end to a dashing middle-aged detective.

I could easily make out his form in the wavy reflection of the framed poster take it in both hands, the way they teach you at the academy, and aim it at my back. So much for sacred ground.

Chapter 19

"It does make sense now that I think about it. You knew about the butterflies like it was all common knowledge. Hell, you fell in love with the thing as soon as you took it out of the bag. And a degree in forensics is basically the same as one in how to murder someone without leaving behind any evidence." I tried to keep my voice conversational and soothing. "You did good work. Those sites were the cleanest I've ever seen. But do you think pulling a gun on me will help?"

The Glock 22 shook in his hand like a Christmas present. "Shut up," he said with his equally shaky voice.

"I know what you mean. I'm not a talker, either. It drives Dr. Striker crazy. Which is funny because he's a psychologist. Or is it psychiatrist? I never did ask. Have you ever been to see him? No, I guess, you haven't. Well, he—"

"Shut up," Allister ordered.

"Yeah, I know what you mean." I half-chuckled. "I don't like to talk about my sessions, either. No shame in going to see him, though. I think everyone in the precinct has seen him at one time or—"

"I said, Shut up!" He added his other hand to the Glock.

"Okay, okay. You're the guy with the gun. You're in charge of the men's room."

"For the love of God, shut up!" He punctuated the sentence with his Glock. "I absolutely cannot stand you. Do you know that? Cannot stand you! You and your good looks, walking around the station like you're the whole reason it's here. It's like you think you're in Miami Vice or something. Even Ron doesn't shut up about you."

"So that's what you've had against me, this whole time? You think I'm handsome?"

J.S. Johnston

"I said shut up!"

"Alright. You're the boss." Poster Bikini Lady was no help at all.

"Put your hands where I can see them."

"One of my hands is in a sling." I wiggled it a little like he wouldn't have noticed, otherwise. "Is it okay if—"

"Fine. Just put your good hand where I can see it."

I held it in the air. "Can I ask why it matters where I put my hands if you're going to shoot me, anyway?"

"Jesus. Do you always talk this much?"

"My mom used to ask me the same thing."

His reflection on the poster fought a smile. The gun in his hand wasn't so amused. It rattled like an angry dog tied to a stake.

"You know, you're not making things any easier for yourself," I said. "This place is full of people. If you fire that, a dozen guys will bust down that door before your ears stop ringing."

He stood up straight and creased his brows at me. "You can be so dumb, sometimes. With everything in the news, do you really think they'll all rush in and play the hero as soon as they hear a gunshot? Once I shoot you, they'll all flood to the front door, climbing over each other to get out. I'll run out with them, and no one will have a clue what happened." He adjusted his grip on the gun's handle as if he wanted to remind me it was there.

"That's not a bad plan. I mean, you'll never get away with it."

He breathed so hard, either from a few pitchers of liquid courage or from the sheer terror of what he was about to do, that the sound of his breath filled the men's room. His nostrils flared and his chest heaved in his reflection. His face, normally sour cream white from days spent under the fluorescent light of the police station, was now flushed red. "I swear to God if you don't shut up—"

"Okay. Fair enough. Then can you talk? You still haven't explained the connection between those people, why you killed them, and how you did it. You didn't leave me a ghost of a clue to go on. So, I've been racking my brain over it for days. Can't I have that much, before you shoot me?"

He shook his head. "I never killed anyone."

"Wait. What? Then what's the gun for?"

"Because you *think* I did, which is just as good," Allister said. "I

166

know how the system works. You were going to arrest me for it. You said it yourself. I know about butterflies, and I know how to keep from leaving evidence because I work in Forensics. Good enough for you. Right? I can't afford a real lawyer, so there's not much hope for me. Do you know how they treat people in jail? Not just the guards, but the other prisoners. The bigger guys. They do horrible things to you—things people don't talk about—things you never stop having nightmares about. And they'll keep doing it for as long as they can get away with it. And do you know what it's like to try to get a job after you've been to jail?" He spoke in a strangled voice like he was trying to reign in whatever was trying to get out. "Even if I somehow don't go to jail, I'd still be all over the news. People don't see someone accused of murder on TV and think they didn't do it. My life would be over."

"You were never a suspect, Allister. Why would you think that I was going to arrest you?"

"Liar! Your boss called me and told me. She said she was warning me out of professional courtesy."

"Sargent Martinez called you?"

"Who?"

BANGBANGBANGBANG! "Open this damn door!" shouted a drunken angry voice. The sound ripped through the men's room, echoing off the tile floor, and shattering the tension. Allister instinctively turned his head to look.

As soon as he got distracted, I spun around, deflected the gun in his hands with my arm in the sling then brought a fist across his chin with my good arm, knocking him out. The Glock 22 slid across the floor and came to rest under the row of sinks. And I spent the next ten minutes screaming like a six-year-old kid from waves of pain, provided at no charge from a dislocated collar bone.

Pain flooded into the raw, exposed nerves of my entire left side. Like someone dipped them in lemon juice, used them to flog someone for shoplifting, then when that wasn't enough, assaulted them with a can opener and dragged them over T.J.'s litter box for good measure. I was completely unaware that amount of pain all at once was even possible. It was invasive, springing from inside me and somehow pushing its way down to my toes with absolute entitlement.

J.S. Johnston

The guy outside the bathroom asked me if I was okay, with a lot more of a concerned voice than I was comfortable with. When I told him I was okay in my distinctly middle-aged man-sounding voice, he told me to take all the time I needed and walked away. I'm still not sure what he thought was going on in there.

As he lay on the men's room floor drooling on himself, I took Allister's ankle holster off his leg, put it on mine, and tucked his gun away, safely inside. I'd find out who it belonged to and return it to them, later. Then I threw Allister's arm over my shoulder and walked him out. The going was rough with me with only one good arm and him dragging his feet along the floor. But, once I explained things to Peppermint, she helped me get him to the car with only a small lecture on how I needed to be more careful and how one day I wouldn't be so lucky. I remember saying the same thing to her, not long ago.

On the way out, we passed a couple on their way in. They were genuinely concerned when they asked about him. Coming from a bar, an explanation of too much to drink was all they needed to not pay us any mind. His distinctive odor helped with that.

I got Allister's address from the driver's license in his wallet and took him home in my car while Peppermint followed us in his. Of course, his apartment was up on the third story. I bet the view was awesome but bringing in groceries must've sucked.

His living room was a lot more normal than I'd expected—something in the realm of a grownup teenager. Framed posters of early 1980s video game cover art hung on his wall, like Space Invaders and Galaga. A very large 4K TV stood in front of a very pillowy deep red couch. He had surround sound speakers equally spaced around the room and black soundproofing foam hanging on the wall, here and there. I guess someone complained.

I dropped him on the couch so he could sleep off an eventful night, resting his head on a pillow with a portrait of Captain Kirk from his glory days.

He had one of those coffee tables that doubled as a mini-fridge, but a leg was missing from the left-hand corner. A stack of worn paperback novels replaced it. I pulled the drawer out, shielded my eyes from the interior light that flicked on, and pulled out a can of

Dr. Pepper. My fee for taking him home. "Want one?" I asked Peppermint without looking at her.

"No thanks."

"Suit yourself." I put it on the coffee table so I could pop the top with my good arm.

"Hey, look at this," she said, picking up a DVD from a stack of them on the top of the table, beside a pair of video game controllers. It was the first season of *Detective Ian: Space Detective*. It looked like one of those serials that used to come on before feature films in movie theaters, from back before anyone owned a TV, like Buck Rogers and Commando Cody. He stood heroically, holding up a ray gun in one hand and his arm around a gorgeous starlet who huddled close and looked very worried. Costumed villains loomed behind them. Their rocket-powered spaceship took up most of the background. Peppermint opened the case and remarked, "It must be in the player."

I traded her the Dr. Pepper for the DVD case to look at it a little better. "So that's why he hates me." It does make more sense. I'm not that handsome.

"He hates you so much that he tries to shoot you and you feel the need to take him home and put him to bed?" She took a drink of my soda.

"It's… complicated."

She chortled a little. "I bet." She took another sip. "So, are you going to see that girl again?"

"What girl?"

"The one from your date, last night."

"Oh, not you, too." Suddenly, my shoulder started to ache. I returned Detective Ian to the top of the stack on the coffee table and took my soda back from Peppermint.

"It's good for you, Sean. You need to socialize more."

"I don't need to do anything." I took a drink of Dr. Pepper. "And I'm tired of everyone thinking they know what's best for me. Sex isn't vitamin C. I won't get scurvy if I don't date."

"I don't mean that. What happened with Nicole was a long time ago. You wouldn't be disrespecting the memory of your relationship if you got out once in a while." She switched on the floor lamp beside the couch that looked like those old spotlights from movie sets. It made a dim glow that didn't go much farther than the coffee table. Good to know Allister is a troglodyte.

A shallow bookshelf lined part of the back wall, full to over capacity with more paperbacks. Even more books were stuffed in the space between other books and the bottom of the upper shelves. More books lay in stacks on top of the bookshelf. Some of them were epic fantasy, some were sci-fi.

Most of them were detective mysteries. So—so many detective mysteries. Men detectives, women detectives, adolescent detectives, vampire detectives, dog detectives… He had one about a detective who solved cases in a zombie apocalypse. (Not sure what the point of that would be.) He had a full shelf of thick comic books of young girl anime detectives with giant eyes. I think they call them manga. I wonder what the medical implications would be, having eyes that huge. They look like they can see your soul. I'd read the hell out of that book.

"I really need to introduce you to Clara," I said under my breath.

"Who's Clara?" asked Peppermint.

"Someone I work with. And I get out plenty."

Peppermint grabbed the soda from my hand, took a sip, and handed it back. "Talking to people at your job isn't the same."

"You know if you want your own, he has more in the coffee table."

"I'm fine, thanks. You want to end up like this guy?" She motioned to Allister, still resting comfortably, laying on his ridiculously overstuffed deep red couch. His mouth hung open and a stream of drool began to pool on the Captain Kirk pillow. I checked his breathing, just in case. You never know.

"What's wrong with him?" I asked.

"He did just pull a gun on you."

I paused for a moment and said, "Stop making sense."

She smiled at me. I hated that smile. It's wide and toothy and warm and soothing and you can't help but smile back. I did my best to stifle one, but I don't think I did a very good job.

When Allister had the gun on me at the urinal, he said that someone called him and told him that I was about to arrest him.

Reggie Jackson also said that someone called him to put him up to leading me to what was supposed to be my death. In both cases, it was someone they didn't know. And in both cases, they were told something they'd be willing to kill for.

It not only meant that the murderer knew people well enough to know where their line is, that line where you think the only sensible thing to do is to murder someone, it meant that they knew the people around me—who my friends are, my acquaintances, the people that hate me, the girl that I took out on a date, and even where I took her to. I think the idea that it could be so personal is what scared me more than anything else. But the creeping dread of vulnerability from my innermost circle aside, it narrowed down the suspects a good bit. That's turning lemons into lemonade. It was time to start going through my friends list.

Chapter 20

"You didn't arrest him," noted Dr. Striker, sitting back in his comfortable, washed-out red fabric upholstered chair with tiny green flowers machine knit into it. He rested his elbows on its high armrests and made his arms into a triangle, lacing his fingers together at the top. He crossed his legs in a tight pretzel twist, one over the other. He tapped his top foot, the one hanging in the air as if reminding himself that the shoe it wore cost more than my mortgage payment. He forgot about his laptop on the rolling stand to his right, where he normally typed in his innermost thoughts about me. As far as I was concerned, it could stay there.

I shook my head and said plainly, "No. We took him home to let him sleep it off. I should stop by Forensics and see if he shits himself." I sat back in my identical chair, matching his arm triangle. Those chairs *were* comfortable. Really *really* comfortable. I did my best to keep from making it obvious that I was enjoying sitting there.

"But he pulled a gun on you."

"I stole a soda from his coffee table, so it's all good."

"I mean, doesn't that confirm he's the murderer?"

"It confirms that he was scared that I'd *think* he was," I explained. "Scared enough to pull a gun on me. But he wasn't the killer. And he wasn't about to shoot me."

"But how can you be so sure?" he asked. "He got drunk to build up the courage, waited for you to be alone in the men's room, locked the door, had an escape plan—"

"Because it's all wrong," I said, cutting him off.

"How is that wrong? It sounds like he had it all planned."

"Well, yeah. He planned that part. But you see," I held out my hands like I was shaping a clay pot as I explained this next part. "Murder is really messy. I mean, three-year-old-kid-having-a-temper-tantrum-in-a-mud-puddle messy. Most of them—and I stress *most*—are crimes of passion. The murderer knows the victim well. Usually very well. There's a bad argument. Maybe someone does someone dirty, or they think they do. And they truly believe with all their soul that they just have to kill that other person. They think they have no other choice but to remove them from the face of the Earth and do whatever they need to do to make that happen. Then there are the robberies and drug deals gone wrong, gang rivalries, or someone taking the wrong drug at the wrong time, and someone is just there… It's almost never thought out ahead of time. It just happens and evidence explodes all over the scene. Blood on the carpet, the walls, the murder weapon. They try to wash it off their hands and we find the chemical signature in their sink and drain. I mean all over and everywhere. And that's just the blood. Then there are fingerprints, footprints, mud, DNA, textiles, grass pollen, cell phone GPS records—"

"Okay, okay," Dr. Striker said. "I get it. I watch all the CSI shows."

"But the case I'm working, there's none of that. It's neat. It's clean. More thought out than your average game of chess. They didn't leave one single thing behind that could possibly allude to the fact that they were ever even there in the first place. Other than the fact that there's a victim, anyway. The time suit is probably the only thing that'll lead me to the murderer."

"I think I see your point," he said and scratched his chin.

"But last night, Allister was ready to explode all over that men's room, himself. He smelled like he'd been drinking all night to build up the courage just to walk up to me. Even then, the gun rattled in his hands and the tears poured out in his voice. Does that sound to you like the same guy?"

"I suppose not."

"Allister is a waste of time," I said, adjusting my arm sling. "I didn't arrest him because the more time I spend on him, the more time the real killer has to do more killing. They're still out there."

"But he could've been just intimidated by you. None of the other victims were cops. What if they were all just practice, and he was actually working up to you?"

"I thought of that. I think I talked so much that if there was any killer instinct in him, he would've shot me just to shut me up."

Dr. Striker raised his eyebrows and sat up a little straighter.

"I get talky when I'm nervous," I said.

He didn't say anything.

"What?" I asked. The way he looked at me was a little weird.

"Nothing," he replied, eyebrows still raised. "I just think it's interesting."

"I really hate it when you do that."

After a pause, he said, "So, you just took him home and put him to bed. No blood, no foul?"

"Yep."

"But he pulled a gun on you. Isn't that illegal?"

"If you wanna get technical."

"Technical? Allister pulled a gun on you. He could've shot you. He could've coughed, accidentally pulled the trigger, and killed you."

"Allister wasn't going to shoot me," I said, shaking my head.

"He had it out and trained on you when you had your back to him. How could you be so sure he wouldn't shoot?"

"Because I could tell," I said.

"But how?"

"When was the last time you tried to convince someone else you were going to do something before you did it?"

"You make a good point," he said with a nod. "But what if he accidentally shot you? What if the gun just went off when that guy banged on the bathroom door?"

"Then I would've been very upset. I might've even arrested him."

He smirked at me.

"Allister is a diversion," I said. "The real killer is still out there. And I need to find them before they kill someone else. Or me. I don't need to be wasting time worrying about what a kid does when he's scared."

"Fair enough." Dr. Striker shrugged his shoulders.

"But just between you and me, I think you might see him in here, soon."

"That tickles you, doesn't it?"

"What does?"

"The fact that you're making him want to go see the station

psychiatrist," he said.

I chuckled. "Yeah, I think it does."

Dr. Striker pointed to the clock on the wall. "You made it."

"Made what?"

"To the end of the session. I think this is your first time."

I dug my phone out of my pants and looked at the time on the display. "Sorry. Didn't mean for that to happen." I got up from my comfortable, washed-out red fabric upholstered chair with tiny green flowers machine knit into it. It really was a comfortable chair.

"Very funny."

"I mean, I actually do have another appointment. Detective stuff."

"Before you go," Dr. Striker said with a pointed finger. "How long has it been since you had a nightmare?"

"Nightmare?"

"Yeah."

"I don't know. Why?" I asked, standing to my full height, and adjusting my arm sling.

"Just take a guess. Has it been a day? Two?" He was still sitting in his chair with his legs crossed, looking up at me.

"Maybe a week… ish."

"Was the last one before or after you started going back in time and seeing your Morlock? Do you remember?" Dr. Striker asked, cocking his head.

"Well, it was—" I stopped mid-sentence and looked at him.

He looked back at me.

"That is messed up," I said.

"It was before. Wasn't it?" Dr. Striker grinned at me like he just found Waldo. "You haven't had a nightmare since that thing started chasing you around the in-between time. Have you?"

I stammered for a moment. "What does that mean? Do I need to be committed?"

"We can talk about that on your next visit. Your time is up." He was still grinning.

"This isn't fun anymore. I'm going to go, now."

"I look forward to our next visit." He raised his hand in a goodbye as I walked out the door without closing it behind me. I really hate that guy.

***

Now that the hard part was over, I could fight the midday traffic and get to the University of South Florida for something a little more fun. Dr. Khatri said she needed me for something important, regarding the development of the time suit. That was how she put it when I talked to her over the phone. Something important regarding the development of the time suit. She didn't tell me what she needed. I didn't too much care, either. Not in a bad way. I just didn't think I'd understand whatever technical explanation she was sure to throw at me, so I didn't ask. She and Clara were wholly on a different level than me and I was okay with that. Besides, I was so happy to take any excuse to go play that it didn't matter. So, I told Dr. Khatri that I wasn't Clara, but I'd move whatever couch she needed. She laughed at my joke. I'm getting good at making them.

When I got to USF, I found her sitting in a rolling office chair, leaning over at the console in the Physics lab. She was intently staring at a computer screen, filled with gobbledygook in neat columns that clearly meant something important. The time suit's helmet sat perched on top of the upper part of the console with three or four thick, black cables plugged into its back like hair. Almost like the head of the guy from the Predator movies, only a lot less scary.

"Why do people wear those white lab coats?" I asked, walking up to her at the console. I wasn't complaining. She looked really good in it. Something about the not quite whiteness of the fabric against her light-brown skin brought out an approachable beauty in her. Or maybe it just reminded me of my sixth-grade science teacher. I used to have a crush on her. I might've said that, already. Well, it's still true. "Is it just in case you have to get medieval on one of your students for handing in their homework late?"

"Detective Papadopoulos," she said in a friendly, excited tone. She turned around in her chair to meet my eyes and wave me over. "Come, come. Glad you could make it. I need you for this."

"Is Watson sick?" I gestured to the time suit helmet with the cables running out the back. "I promise I didn't break him."

"No, no. I assure you, Watson is perfectly healthy. Please come and have a seat."

I walked around to get a better look at where the cables plugged into the helmet. "Are you trying to wire him up with surround sound? Because that's what the back of my TV looks like."

She snickered. "No. I'm debugging his operating system. Give me just a moment to log out of the application and close up." Her slender lady fingers continued to tap keys. Gobbledygook continued to scroll up the screen.

"Hey, I understood most of those words," I said, still looking at the cables. "Didn't even need Clara."

She chortled a little as she typed away.

The rest of the time suit hung on a mannequin that stood beside the weird empty doorway in the middle of the room as if it were on display at Macy's. Its faceless head looked off into the distance like how T.J. watches ghosts in the closet. The suit still had some of the streaks of dirt and grass around the elbows and hindquarters from when I crawled on the ground to hide from the Morlock. More streaks of dark and light ran across the chest like it was at one point completely covered in dirt and someone blew cleaner across it. Scratches covered the knees, like a kid who fell off his bike.

"I still haven't had your suit cleaned," said Dr. Khatri, still typing away. "You can't just throw it in the washing machine, you know."

"Do you have to clean it?"

"I'm sorry?"

"Do you have to clean it?" I asked, turning to her. "I mean, all the scratches and grass stains tell a story."

She looked up from her monitor and gently smiled at me. "It smells very bad."

I took a sniff. "Yeah. Yeah, it does."

She shook her head and turned back to her monitor, still smiling. "Boys." The rhythmic light tapping she made on her keyboard was soon followed up with, "And done."

"Do Clara's parents ever come around?" I asked, centering my head to look into where the mannequin's eyes should be.

"Her parents?" Dr. Khatri sat back in her office chair and ran her thin fingers through her short salt and pepper hair.

"You know. To see what she does in the lab for hours every day.

Tell you how proud they are of her and to see what her genius hath wrought."

Her gentle smile faded, a little, and she folded her arms across her chest. "Unfortunately, Clara's parents died when she was a little girl." Somehow Dr. Khatri's light Indian accent softened the blow of something so tragic.

"Sorry to hear that. I'm sure they would've been proud." I stepped over and leaned forward against the back of the console, facing Dr. Khatri. Her dark, clear eyes met mine. They were—comfortable. "Does she ever talk about them?"

"Yes. All the time." She stressed that part about all the time. "What they did for a living, how they used to give Clara those little peanut-shaped peanut butter cookies when she brought home good grades. I feel like I know them."

"And they died when she was a little girl?" It might've just been my imagination because she pointed it out, but I could swear the funk of the time suit still hung over me where I stood, by the console. The scent of man musk was as heavy in the air as the cigar smoke in a cartoon poker game.

"Oh, yes. But you wouldn't think it, the way she speaks of them. They're still alive to her."

"So how do you know they died when she was little?"

"I asked her about them, one day." Dr. Khatri said with a nod.

"Oh, really? How did that go?"

Her face scrunched up, slightly. "Awkward."

"What happened?"

"We were just chatting casually while working on the schematic for the processing unit. The current scale of transistors is reducing so fast that they're approaching the plank length limit where quantum tunneling becomes a factor and—"

I cleared my throat.

She tilted her head and made eyes at me that said I was adorable. It's true. I am adorable. "Sorry. I mean we were talking while working on the suit."

"Thank you."

"We came to the subject of the rising cost of tuition," she said. "USF had just gone through a series of revisions due to inflation, the economy, the loss of public support for government funding… I asked if she was able to get a grant or if her parents were helping her."

"With as smart as she is, I expected her to be on a full scholarship."

"She's a genius," Dr. Khatri said and nodded. "But college is still expensive."

"How smart is she, exactly?"

"Very smart." She shrugged. "She's in Mensa."

"Wow."

"She's been at the school only three years and already taught me a few things I never knew," Dr. Khatri said.

"So, what did she say when you mentioned her parents?"

"She broke down in tears."

"Really?" I asked. "What did you do?"

"Well, of course, I asked her what was wrong, but I couldn't understand her. She'd buried her head in her arms, here on the console, sobbing. I thought she and her parents had a huge fight, and they threw her out. I came over and sat in the other chair and rubbed her back to calm her down for a few minutes. Once she was through sobbing enough to talk, she told me that they died years ago."

"Really? And there's still enough sting to do that to her when someone asks about them?"

Dr. Khatri nodded and said, "As she cried, she told me she didn't have them to help her through these years, like the other kids."

"I see. So, because they're not around to help financially or emotionally—"

"She's on her own. It's very scary for a young person to be out in the world without a safety net. You remember how huge the world seemed when you were twenty-three."

I snorted. "I was born at forty."

She returned my snort.

"But I can see her perspective," I said. "It would be frightening. What did they die of? I mean if you don't mind me asking. Did she say?"

"Traffic accident. She went on for a while. She's really angry about it." Dr. Khatri reached to her right and picked up an old paperback novel with a crumpled cover and yellowed pages, looked at it for a moment as if it were Clara herself, and sat it back down.

"Did she say what happened?" I asked.

"She said a semi-truck slammed right into them."

"Oh my god."

Dr. Khatri nodded. "She was with them at the time. She survived, and they didn't."

"Wow. That would stick with me too. What happened to the driver of the semi?"

"She didn't say. She was more focused on how her parents wouldn't be here to help her through her college years."

I came over and sat down on the empty office chair, beside Dr. Khatri. "I might cry a little, too," I told her.

She sighed and ran her fingers through her hair, again.

"Well, one of these days, we'll all have self-driving cars and that won't be a thing, anymore," I said, trying to keep her from dwelling on what had happened. It was clear that she cared for her. But she can't change what happened to her any more than I could.

"I will be the first to buy one," she said. She looked into the computer monitor embedded in the console like she was watching a thought play out in her head.

"So, where's your couch?" I asked, trying to make my voice lighthearted.

"My couch?"

"The one that must need moving. You said you needed my help, and I don't have anywhere near the education or the I.Q. to help you with anything else."

"Oh, that!" She patted my outstretched knee. "The first one might be true, but certainly not the other." She stood up, rolled her chair away, and motioned me to move mine into her spot in front of the keyboard and monitor. "Please."

"You really want me to sit there? With all those buttons? Maybe you're not as smart as I thought."

She smiled. "We're making a new suit, remember? We need your feedback about using the one hanging up." She motioned to it with her head.

"I completely forgot I was supposed to be taking notes!" I

exclaimed.

Dr. Khatri laughed at me.

"Seriously, what do you need my feedback for? Haven't you guys worn it?" I asked.

"Yes, but we're not detectives. And that's who the State of Florida, huge corporations, and private donors have paid us to make it for."

"A scientist doesn't see the same things that a detective does."

"There you go," she said. "I need you to answer the questions on the computer about your experience. What you liked, what you didn't. Suggestions about what you hope to see in the next model. Things like that."

"You know, I could've done that from home. There's this thing called the internet where I can send you stuff."

"But then I wouldn't be able to see your smiling face." She put a hand on my shoulder and gestured to the empty spot. Her hand was so tiny, laying there.

"That's true. My smiling face is the subject of many scientific papers."

Dr. Khatri looked at me with amused eyes.

"That didn't sound the way I wanted it to sound, did it?"

"No. But that's alright. I know what you meant."

I rolled over to her recently vacated spot and read the questions on the screen.

"All the questions are free-form," she said. "So, answer them in your own words. Feel free to add whatever extra suggestions you can think of."

"So, is the next suit going to be able to go forward through time? Is that something I can ask for?"

"What do you mean?"

"Well, Clara said that it only goes backward, to the past." I pointed with my thumbs to an imaginary place behind me. "It can't go to the future."

She squinted at me.

"That is right. Right?" I asked.

"If Clara told you that, you must've misunderstood whatever she said."

"So, it *does* go to the future. Why haven't I been doing that? Maybe

I can see who I arrest and save myself some time."

Her face changed to a knowing look, and she giggled, a little. "I think I understand why she told you that."

I waited patiently for an answer I was sure I wouldn't understand, anyway.

"It doesn't work like that. You wouldn't be traveling to a contiguous timeline. When you open a portal to the future, the train of causality bifurcates, duplicating into parallel—"

Nope. Not a word. "Doctor, have a heart," I pleaded. "Clara isn't here to translate."

"Sorry." She drew a breath and began slowly. "You've seen movies that use the idea of a multiverse. The idea that slightly different universes exist simultaneously, alongside our own. Right?"

"Sure. It makes for good sci-fi. I'm with you so far."

"When you open a portal to the future, a new universe splits off from ours." She put her forefingers together in the air. "When it's initiated, it creates what we've been calling an apex." She separated her fingers, raising them as if tracing out an invisible fork in the road. "After that point, anything that happens in our universe won't affect the new, separate universe and vice versa, like two different copies of the same book. But it's not like what you're used to seeing in the movies. The dimensions lay on top of each other on the quantum level. There is a—"

"Ut, ut, ut, ut, ut… Abraca-science" I said, interrupting her. "Let me stop you right there. Portal to the past—same universe. Portal to the future—different universe. If you start going into quantum things, my brain will explode and make a mess all over your console."

"I've cleaned up worse things."

I started to chuckle. "Wait. What?"

She grinned playfully at me.

"So why don't you guys use the suit to get the winning lotto numbers?" I asked. "You wouldn't have to work so hard to get funding."

"Because it would be in a different timeline." She held out her hand, palm up in an isn't-it-obvious gesture. It was not.

"How silly of me?"

"When the realities split, the events that happen after that point will happen differently, unconnected to the other." She spoke slowly as if I could understand her better.

"Right."

"As a consequence, probabilities will have different values and therefore outcomes when their wave functions collapse."

I stared at her silently, with eyes as wide as I could manage.

"Remember when Jeff Goldblum explained chaos theory to Laura Dern in *Jurassic Park*?" she asked.

"Now I got you." I nodded in approval. "Please continue."

She snort-laughed. It was cute. "There are so many factors that can affect the smallest of things that—"

"The lotto numbers that come up in one timeline are only for that timeline and would be completely unrelated to ours."

"Yes!" she exclaimed like an excited sixth-grade science teacher. "Now, you've got it. Even if we were able to get the numbers, it wouldn't do us any good in this timeline."

"But the bigger events—"

"Would be mostly the same," she explained. "However, the timelines would diverge more and more the greater the reduction of scale. They would be unrecognizable on the quantum scale, almost instantly. And as a consequence of that, events would diverge more and more the farther in the future you went. You from the present and You from the alternate timeline might both get a flat tire on the same day you went through the portal. But a year from then, one of you could marry and move to Montana and the other might become president."

"Well, that's a bit disheartening," I said. "It takes the fun out of a time machine, a little."

"Would you want to see your future, Detective?"

"Call me Sean. Please."

"Would you, Sean?" Dr. Khatri asked.

"Actually, not really. At least not that much of it."

"You would prefer the mystery? A true detective." She smiled at me.

"Well, it's not that. Not, exactly."

"What, then?"

"What if I find out that this is my best life?" I explained. "This is it and it doesn't get any better."

"Would that be so bad?" She shrugged. "You seem to have a good life; a nice job, and friends."

"No, it's not that."

"What?"

I drew a breath and explained, "You know how all the little aggravations in your life—having to get up for work in the morning, dealing with frustrating coworkers when you get there, traffic jams when you go home, annoying kids making your coffee order wrong—they all go away when you tell yourself 'This won't be a problem when things get better.' You know? When you get that promotion. When you buy that new car. That new house in that good neighborhood. When you retire and spend your days getting skin cancer on a beach in the Keys. Right now, I can confidently get out of bed in the morning and none of that stuff bothers me because I can tell myself that it doesn't matter. It's only temporary. I won't have to deal with it when… Whenever. Right now, I can just imagine whatever that is, and it's as good as real. But if I saw that it never does get any better, that this is as good as it gets—"

"Then you can't do that, anymore."

"Yeah," I said. "I know I have a good life. A great one, actually. It really shouldn't make sense."

"Humans don't make much sense." She leaned forward in her office chair and put her hand on my forearm which was resting on my leg.

"I guess not. What about you?"

"I don't make sense, either."

"No." I laughed. "I mean, would you want to see your future? If you knew it was guaranteed to be your real future."

"That depends," she started. "If I was unable to change it, then no."

"For the same reason?" I asked.

"I wouldn't want to know if things got worse if I wasn't able to do anything about it."

"Oh, so you wouldn't want to know if you were going to get in a traffic accident if you couldn't use that information to take a different way home that night."

"Yes. Exactly. I would rather go on thinking everything would be fine and be very surprised when it happens," she said.

"I could see that. That would be a terrible feeling."

"I would be more interested in seeing how different my life will turn out in a different reality," she continued. "What happens if I have the tuna or the steak dinner? Or if I were to have gotten a teaching position at UCLA instead of here at USF. Or gone into a different branch of physics, altogether."

"I get it. Everyone always wonders what would've happened if they made a different choice. It would be fun to find out. But what if you met yourself and it turned out her life is way better than yours? Wouldn't you be jealous?"

"I might," she said. "But then, I would look exactly like her. And no one would notice if I replaced her and disposed of her body."

"Wait, what?"

She smiled, got up from her chair, and walked toward the door. "Come get me when you're done with your questionnaire."

"Hey, wait! What did you mean about disposing of the body?"

She stepped out the door and closed it behind her.

Just then, my pants chirped. I dug out my phone to find a text from Sargent Martinez and my stomach tied itself in a knot. Suddenly, I remembered Reggie Jackson.

I open the text. It read, "Come to my office."

I replied, "Sure. I'm doing some work with the time suit at USF. As soon as I'm done, I'll be right there."

To which she replied, "NOW!"

The knot in my stomach got a little tighter. At least she didn't add an angry emoji.

"On my way," I texted back.

Chapter 21

"What is wrong with you?!" Sargent Martinez screamed at me from her desk as soon as I walked into her office.

"Did I do something wrong?" I asked as I shut the office door. Yes, I knew what I did wrong. But you should never volunteer information to a cop. Even if you are one.

"What did you—" she cut herself off mid-sentence so she could turn her laptop around to face me. It showed a freeze frame of a video from a security camera. It was me leading Reggie Jackson down the hallway by the arm. Reggie looked pretty worried.

I pointed to the picture on the screen. "That's not what it looks like."

"That's not what—Sean! You went to cop school, right? You understand why this is not okay, right?" The expression on her face made her look like a completely different person. "And he asked for a lawyer, and you didn't stop questioning immediately and provide—"

"Hey, he said, 'I think I should have a lawyer' which is completely different than—"

"Sean!"

"It…"

"What, Sean?" she shouted. A little spit came out with that one.

"The suspect indicated that he wasn't comfortable giving testimony in the interrogation, I mean questioning room, and—"

"So, you just took him out of it?"

I raised my hands to chest level, palms up. "Well, he wasn't going to talk, and—"

Sargent Martinez slammed a fist on her desk and the laptop jumped a few inches. She pinched the bridge of her nose. "Damn it to hell, Sean." She took a breath and continued. "You're already on disciplinary action for assaulting a suspect. What were you planning on doing to the poor kid? The people who watched you drag him out of that room thought you were going to kill him."

Standing up my full height I said, "I assaulted Randal Jablonski because he was a serial killing pyromaniac who threatened you. I promise not to do it again."

She looked at me with a cold gaze. "What were you planning on doing, Sean?"

I pointed at the display on the laptop with an accusing finger. "Somehow that kid knew exactly where I'd be. And knew exactly where a drunk driver would be and led me to him. And put me in the hospital." I straightened my arm sling. "I wanted to know why. He wouldn't talk in the interrogation room. So, I brought him to the supply closet."

She stared at me and didn't say anything.

"Once I got him in there, he answered all my questions," I added.

She still didn't say anything.

"What?"

Martinez ran her palms over her face from top to bottom and took a big breath. Then she turned her head and looked to the side at nothing. "I should fire you for this."

A hole burned in the pit of my stomach. I leaned forward and put my hands on her desk.

She met my eyes.

I said slowly, "Reggie told me someone wants me dead. He was supposed to kill me."

Sargent Martinez narrowed her eyes. "What?"

"Reggie told me that someone wants me dead. Whoever it was knew exactly where I'd be and when. They knew how to get me to chase him. And they knew exactly where a drunk driver would just happen to be." I left out the part about Allister also trying to kill me. One thing at a time.

Sargent Martinez leaned back in her chair and asked, "Why?"

I stood up to my full height and shrugged. "He didn't say."

"Could it have anything to do with the case you're working on?"

"Sure. Maybe. Or a past case. I've put a lot of people in jail. Sometimes they hold grudges."

Martinez looked at me for a moment. Then, she turned the laptop back around to face her. "I should really fire you after what you did. But Reggie, Mr. Jackson, isn't pressing charges. And we've been short-staffed for a while. And it doesn't look like it's going to get any better, soon."

I breathed a little easier.

She hardened her gaze at me and said, "You are to stay away from Mr. Jackson." I stifled a grin when she pointed at me and continued. "Far away from him. Don't come anywhere near him. If you go to Starbucks for coffee and you see him there in line, go to another Starbucks. Do you understand?"

I nodded. "Yeah. I get it. I don't go anywhere near him."

"One more infraction and you're gone. I don't care how short-staffed we are. And I mean *any* infraction. If you use the bathroom and forget to wash your hands, you're done. Do you understand?"

I nodded, again. "Absolutely." I tried not to smile.

Sargent Martinez expelled a long dramatic sigh as she gently shook her head and looked off into the distance. I stood in front of her desk and waited for her to say something. After a moment, she turned her head toward me and added, "I'm taking you off of the time suit project."

The words hit me like someone just told me Santa Claus wasn't real.

"What?!" I shouted without meaning to. I bent over and slapped my hands on her desk, putting my face inches from hers.

"Don't look at me like that," she said with indignance. "Everyone saw what you did with Mr. Jackson. Letting you keep using the time suit would be telling everyone it's just fine to do whatever the hell you want, laws be damned!" Her eyes widened mockingly.

I didn't know what to say. So, I didn't say anything. I stood up, removed my hands from her desk, and looked at her in shock, my mouth hanging open.

Sargent Martinez shook her head. "Come on, Sean. You really thought nothing was going to happen?"

"But… I've already put so much work into it. And… the case I've been working on…"

"Right. Turn over all the notes you have on the suit. I'll get someone else to pick up where you left off." She looked at something on her laptop and tapped some keys.

"But the case…"

She stopped typing and looked up at me. "People have been solving crimes for thousands of years without needing time suits. I'm sure you'll be fine." She looked back down at her laptop, read something, and tapped more keys.

"But there are no clues with this case, Sarge. None!" I shouted at her. "The time suit is the only way I'm going to catch—"

The look in her eye was like a knife in my heart. "Then your replacement will have to figure it out with the time suit. Because you're off the project." She returned to typing.

I stood in front of her desk, waiting for her to say something.

She tapped more keys and clicked something with her mouse.

After a few moments, she looked up at me and asked, "Do you have any questions?" I was a little insulted by the lack of emotion on her face.

"No. No, I guess not."

"Good. Email me all the materials involving the time suit by tomorrow morning," she said.

I didn't know what to say.

"You can go now," she ordered, returning her gaze to her laptop.

I turned and left.

* * *

"Boy, Captain Cosmos. The multiverse sure is a dangerous place."

"It certainly is, Ensign Jimmy. You'd better stick close. My disintegrator ray is more than a match for any beast from Earth 4253."

Captain Cosmos and Ensign Jimmy stood bravely in their gleaming white Space Guard uniforms, chests out and shoulders back. They each wore giant Space Guard emblems on their left shoulders and short capes over their backs. Captain Cosmos held out his Space Guard-issued X-9 quantum disintegrating ray gun, ready for action. Together, Captain Cosmos and Ensign Jimmy were the multiverse's last hope against the ever-encroaching forces of darkness. Though they may have been in black and white, their vibrant color exploded out from my TV, all the same.

Sargent Martinez taking me off the time suit project ate at my gut like I'd just swallowed a highball glass of Drāno. So, I watched Allister's stupid sci-fi serials to try to calm down. It didn't exactly help.

"Do you think the Vulture Men will be back? They sure were angry when we stole their power gem," asked Ensign Jimmy, stoically hiding the mortal terror after narrowly escaping the clutches of said Vulture Men. His short blonde waved hair was flawless. His communicator wristwatch would call the chief of Galactic Operations in every emergency. (He was sure to show up at least once every episode.)

"No, I think we've heard the last of them. After I defeat their leader, King Voltar, they'll think twice about tangling with us." His voice was strong and commanding. His chin was angular and manly. The Space Guard-issued X-9 quantum disintegrating ray gun that he held aloft looked like what everything in your junk drawer would look like if you glued it all together and painted it silver. But held in the hands of a Space Guardsman, it was hope. I still don't know why Ensign Jimmy didn't get one.

What the hell is Martinez thinking, taking me off the project? I've already put so much time into it. Whatever the hell that thing is we've been calling the Morlock will just slaughter the next person who puts it on.

"Should I get on the interdimensional radio and signal Earth 1 that we were successful in our mission?" asked Jimmy to Captain Cosmos.

"Not yet, Ensign Jimmy. We may have the power gem. But Princess Esmalda still has the glove of dreams. We must obtain it from her before we can return home."

"Gee whiz, Captain Cosmos, all the firepower in the multiverse can't defeat Princess Esmalda. She'll never give up the glove of dreams."

"Oh, I think my powers of persuasion will convince her, Jimmy. Once I—"

"Captain look! In the sky over those hills! It's the Vulture Men!" exclaimed Jimmy.

Using the time suit was my only hope to find whoever's been behind the murders. They didn't leave me anything else to go on. No DNA or prints. No textiles or residue of anything traceable. No witnesses. My best hope was to go back in time, and then sit and watch it happen. Now, I can't even do that. This will be one more case for the unsolved files and the grieving families of the victims won't have the closure they need.

Ensign Jimmy needed to take his meds and calm the hell down.

A flock of very angry vulture men soared through the sky in V formation against a well-painted backdrop of clouds. Their rigid feathered wings were half as tall as they were and slowly flapped up and down on obvious hinges as they flew. Their broad, muscular chests were bare, except for leather harnesses that bore their king's emblem, a golden screaming vulture head. The head of the flock at the point of the V held a long scepter with both hands that was topped with a sculpture of a flying vulture with wings in a flying position. The man's face was bearded and angry.

"Quick, Jimmy! Let's fall back to our interdimensional spaceship, the *Relativity*!"

"Right behind you, Captain!"

Cuts of flamboyantly costumed actors valiantly stepping into frame cycled as the strong-voiced male narrator boldly asked the audience, "Will Captain Cosmos and Ensign Jimmy escape the talons of the Vulture Men? Will Princess Esmalda part with the glove of dreams? Will our heroic duo ever return home to Earth 1? And what in the multiverse is in store for them? Join us next week for Captain Cosmos and the Multiverse of Madness and find out!" The screen faded to black then faded to a list of credits over a backdrop of the words Captain Cosmos in giant, exciting font. The closing credits only listed Ensign Jimmy's name, just below Captain Cosmos. Poor Ensign Jimmy. No wonder he's so excitable. He probably thinks his boss will take him off the project.

These stupid shows aren't bad. I can understand what Allister sees in them.

T.J. lay stretched out on the back of the couch, cleaning his paws. His full coat, gray with black stripes, was always cleaner than mine. He looked back at me with his giant green eyes and licked his lips.

"What?" I asked, pausing the video playing on the TV. "Captain Cosmos is research. Dr. Khatri said something about a multiverse and as a good detective, I have to know all about it. This could crack the case wide open." I wasn't sure if she said multiverse, exactly. I think it was alternative realities or timelines branching off or something science-y. Anyway, it sounded good on paper.

I got the name of the show from one of the stacks of DVDs at Allister's place. And thanks to the twenty-first century, everything is available for streaming. I still think he's weird. But Captain Cosmos is growing on me.

T.J. took a big breath then let it out in a long, drawn-out sigh and I relaxed along with it. (Funny how that works.) He put down his paw that he'd finished cleaning. (I couldn't tell it was dirty in the first place.) His giant green eyes with giant black pupils blinked at me, slowly. (You know because they're so big that they can't blink quickly. I mean, they really are huge.) A halfhearted meow eased out of him. And by halfhearted, I mean that it was more like the creek of a door hinge than a meow. I think my cat is broken.

I pointed an accusing finger at him and said, sternly, "Captain Cosmos would not approve of such language."

He straightened himself out along the back of the couch and laid his furry gray chin down on his impeccably clean paws.

"You're right. They do need more episodes with the cat women from Venus." I reached over to the coffee table and took the last swallow of sweet tea. "I need a refill. Want anything?"

T.J. curled his tail around his body, like a furry sleeping dragon. At least I think that's what dragons do. I mean when they're sleeping on piles of gold and not snacking on knights.

"I'll just surprise you, then."

The fridge stood right next to the sink which was overflowing with dirty dishes. Piles of them stacked tall enough to come over the top and some laid on the counter next to the sink because I just couldn't stack them any higher without it all crashing down. I do like to cook. And I've been so busy with the recent murders that it'd been a while since I'd been able to clean any of it. So, there had to have been at least a few days' worth of plates smeared with peanut butter and half-eaten bowls of guacamole. (The fresh guac was really good.)

There was also a pizza pan with leftover tomato sauce and burnt cheese stuck to it, shoved in on the side. In all, it made the kitchen look like it belonged to any bachelor in your average sitcom. Also, it stank. I'd gotten good at ignoring that, too.

Seriously, do sitcom writers think all bachelors live like that? I mean, really.

About as soon as I opened the fridge door and moved aside the jar of pickles to grab the handle of the jug of sweet tea, my phone started playing Chopin's Funeral March. It was still sitting on the endtable, beside the couch in the living room. T.J. looked at it like it was swearing at him.

"You have got to be kidding me," I said, practically stomping my way back over to read the name Sargent Martinez on the display like I needed to. "No!" I spat at it. "No! You do not get to take me off of a project like that and call me afterward!" It continued playing the Funeral March. "I don't care what it is, do it your damn self!"

T.J. raised his head from his front paws and looked at me, expectantly.

"You make a very good point," I told him. "Good thing I have you around." I reached down and swiped the icon of the little red phone and the music stopped. I took a long, deep breath. "There." Another breath. "Now I feel better. Thanks, T.J."

On my way back to the kitchen, my phone started playing Cheeseburger in Paradise. I stopped and chuckled. It was Ron. I let it play for a while, so he doesn't think I sit by the phone, waiting on his call. Besides, I like that song.

"I got a lot of detective work, going on," I said, answering it.

"Oh, yeah?" he asked. "What do you have going on at this time of night?"

"You know. Detective things."

"Detective things, huh?"

"Yep. Doing the City of Tampa proud." I put him on speakerphone, so I could get back to refilling my glass of tea without having to juggle anything with my bad arm.

"I heard what happened," he said. The last time he used that tone of voice was when Nicole walked out on me. "You're sitting around at home sulking and watching movies, aren't you?"

J.S. Johnston

I set the phone down on the counter, beside the fridge and opened the door. "Of course not," I said, picking up a jar of mayonnaise from the top shelf to check the expiration date. It expired three years ago. I should probably start buying smaller jars of mayonnaise. "You know how busy I like to keep. I don't have time to sulk about being taken off the only thing that'll solve a series of murders and let a city of people sleep at night."

He snort-laughed. "So, what're you watching?"

"Captain Cosmos," I said, refilling my glass. My arm didn't hurt that much with the meds from the hospital. But I was still getting good at doing everything one-handed.

"Is that a new Marvel movie?"

It took me a minute, but I chuckled when I got the joke. Then I almost spilled my tea. "Because Captain Cosmos would outrank Captain America?"

"Well, does he?"

"I don't know. He might. It was one of the DVDs lying around at Allister's place. I got curious and decided to stream it." I set the jug on the counter and replaced the cap. "It was one of those serials from a hundred years ago that used to come on before the actual movie."

Another snort-laugh. "Sounds like something he'd watch. Is it any good?"

"Ah—well…"

"Oh, one of those."

"Yeah. One of those." I said and put the jug back in the fridge then grabbed my full glass of sweet tea.

"Oh, hey. Did you ever call that girl to let her know you caught the guy who stole her purse?" Ron asked.

"Ah, dammit!"

He laughed. "Guess not."

"No. Do you think she still wants it back?"

"I imagine she does," Ron said between chuckles.

I put the glass of tea on the endstand beside the couch and walked back to the kitchen to grab the phone.

"She texted me. A few times," I said.

There was amusement in his voice. "So, what do they say?"

"Probably nothing I want to read."

"You are really shit with people. How did you make detective?"

"My roguish good looks?"

"You're not that good-looking," he said with indignance in his voice.

"Yeah, that's true. Beats me, then."

I wandered back into the living room. T.J. raised his head to look up and creaky-meow at me.

"What?" I asked him.

He just looked at me.

"Oh! Right. Sorry."

"Who's there with you?" asked Ron over the speakerphone.

"Just T.J. Why?"

"You're talking to him, now?"

"Of course, I'm talking to him. I'm not telepathic, Ron." I went back to the kitchen and filled a bowl with some water and set it down on the table that runs behind the couch, where I put my keys and wallet. T.J. looked over to acknowledge it then watched me run back to the kitchen to grab my phone and plop down on the couch on the side opposite where he sat. I didn't want to obstruct his view of the TV.

"Just give her a text to let her know you have her purse," said Ron. "It'll just take a minute."

"I guess I have to. Unless you want to do it for me. Tell her you're with the force and she should stop by the station when I'm not working to pick it up."

"I'm not going to do that," he said, flatly.

"Yeah, I didn't think so."

"Was she that bad?"

"I don't know," I said. "I wasn't paying attention to most of the date."

"Yikes," Ron said with pseudo-surprise.

"I mean, I'm sure she's a nice person, once you get to know her."

"Just not a nice person for you."

"Not really," I said and stroked T.J. along his back.

"Well, it can take a while to find the one," he said.

"Man, finding the one is a lot of effort. Can't I just be envious of other people's ones?"

Ron snort-laughed "Hey, I think Sue might know—"

"Ron, don't you dare." I cut him off.

"I don't dare, what?" he asked.

"Please don't set me up. Last time was… Awkward."

"She still talks about you, you know."

"Ron."

"Alright, alright," he said. "Hey, I'm coming over. Don't fall asleep by the time I get there."

"You know, most people ask permission to come over to their friend's houses and watch TV. I'd really like to sulk, right now. I'm not in the mood for company."

"Sean," he said with a sigh. "After what you did, the only reason you're not unemployed is because of how short-staffed we are."

I didn't respond.

Ron continued. "Martinez is the one that should be sulking for having to deal with you. Now grow up and take some accountability."

"Ron…"

"You're a detective. Detect or whatever it is you do."

I shook my head and let that hang in the air for a moment. "Hope you like old sci-fi serials. I have more on the watchlist."

"Love 'em," he said. "See you in a bit."

"See ya." I disconnected the call and put the phone on the coffee table.

I turned to T.J., still lying on the back of the couch, and asked, "Did your last owner's friends treat him like that?"

He studied me with giant green eyes. I could swear he understood what I just said but was choosing not to answer. He was very wise. I stroked him on his head, and he leaned into it.

"You're right. I should." I dug the remote out from between the couch cushions and started the next title on the watchlist.

The screen went black for a moment then a bright picture quickly emerged of young, costumed people running around as if something very exciting was happening. A booming male voice announced, "Detective Ian: Space Detective!" as the title card flashed on the screen. I was already hooked. No wonder Allister watches this stuff.

"Last time on Detective Ian: Space Detective, we left him, and

Commander Darling lost, deep in the catacombs of Mars," said the booming male voice.

"Damn it. You've got to be kidding me," I said under my breath. I grabbed my laptop from the other side of the coffee table and started it up. "Detective Ian, why can't I be as smart as you?" It took a while for everything to load. They really need to get me a new one.

"Ian, sometimes I don't understand you," said Commander Darling, walking over to look at a piece of cloth like it was in a museum. "How could this possibly be important?"

"All in good time, Darling," he said as if lost in thought.

T.J. stood up and stretched a very long stretch, first with his front end down and his back end up in the downward dog position, then the other way around in no rush about any of it. He sat on his butt with his front paws together, facing the coffee table, and looked at me.

I spent the rest of the episode of Detective Ian: Space Detective in police databases, county records, hospital records, and old newspaper articles from half a lifetime ago. I scoured the internet, verifying timetables and testimonies of eyewitnesses then confirming hypotheses, and disproving potential leads. Then compared it all with everything everyone had told me since the beginning and eliminated the impossible. Just like a good detective is supposed to do. Once I was done, I did it all over again because I started to get that feeling when you know you're about to fall off the side of your house. The one where you can see what's about to happen and you try to reason your way out of it, but you can't because the laws of physics absolutely prevent things from happening any other way. Then I did it again. My stomach turned a little.

The victims weren't random at all. Why did it take me this long? I really suck at this job.

"I know who the killer is, T.J. It was staring me right in the face. It has been staring at me, the whole time and I just didn't want to see it."

T.J. looked back at me like he'd figured it out a long time ago and was just waiting for me to catch up. Or wondering if I've cleaned his litter box, today. It could've gone either way. I think it was the first one, though.

J.S. Johnston

"You'll never get away with this, Baron von Virsnickle," said Detective Ian, as he and Commander Darling lay strapped side by side to the tail end of a large and imposing missile. The missile stood propped up on an incline, pointing out of a huge rectangular open window, aiming at Washington D.C. on Earth. At least it was supposed to be aimed at D.C. from what the Baron said, ten minutes earlier as he gloated in the way that only space villains can do. Earth, of course, clearly showed in the upper-right of the room-sized opening at the top of the screen with North and South America at its center and not a cloud in the sky. I'm not sure you'd be able to see Earth that clearly, but he also has his window open on Mars so whatever.

I sat frozen on the couch while the drama played on the TV for a minute. My shoulder ached, and my stomach gurgled and twisted. I pinched the bridge of my nose and ran my fingers through the hair on the top of my head from front to back. I inhaled deeply and let it out in shaky breaths. My heart pounded inside of my chest like a convict in a cell, demanding to be let out.

"Oh, I think I will get away with it, Detective Ian. In fact, there's nothing anyone can do to stop me," said Baron von Virsnickle as he dramatically waltzed over to a lever sticking out of the wall, probably a yard long and topped with a round knob the size of my fist. His sparkly cloak flowed behind him. He stopped at the lever, raised his arm, and grabbed it, just below the knob.

"Hell with it," I said out loud. I grabbed the remote and turned off the show. I jumped up and grabbed my keys and phone then made for the door. Just as I got there, a knock came from the other side. I vigorously swung it open to reveal a very startled Ron standing on my porch. He stood with his eyes wide and his mouth hanging open, a little. He looked at me like he was waiting for me to say something. So, I did. "I have to go. Sorry." I stepped past him and shut the door, behind me.

"Wait, let me—"

"Not a real cop, Ron!" I shouted as I ran out.

Chapter 22

Why don't these things ever happen in the daytime? I put the red and blue flashing bar up on the dashboard as I drove my Chrysler 300 under the downtown Tampa streetlights. It was stuffed in my glove box under a lot of fast food napkins. I never had to use it before and wasn't sure if it actually worked. Lucky for me, it did. I couldn't remember what the rules for using it were, but I also didn't know how long I had before someone found another victim on a sidewalk somewhere or when the killer would be gone for good. So, I threw the flashing red and blue lights up on my dash and drove like I was already too late. Which it probably was. People started to pull over to the side of the road like they were about to get a ticket, getting out of my way. I sent a mental thank you to all of them as I drove a little faster.

The voice of Sargent Martinez came over the car speakers that surrounded me as I drove to the murderer's house. Papers shuffled, and the people chattered in the distant office background. Like it was another day at work. "Sean. Thanks for calling me back. I—"

"Sarge. I need you to send me an arrest warrant and have a team of uniformed cops meet me at the address that I just texted you. Whoever's available. I'm on my way there, now." The traffic light in front of me changed to red, and I went right through it, my own flashing lights clearing a path for me. Someone leaned on their horn in protest. There's always someone.

More ruffling of office papers. She put down whatever she was reading. "You figured out who the murderer is." Her voice immediately became attentive and louder as if she'd turned her head to face her cell phone.

"I have. Been kicking myself for not figuring it out sooner. I'm on my way to the residence, now." The Oldsmobile in front of me wasn't getting over. I passed him on the left, into the oncoming lane where headlights, a blaring horn, and screeching tires rose to meet me all at once. Then hit the gas, and came back into the right-hand lane, in front of the Olds. I couldn't slow down. I was probably already too late. Damn, I'm getting old.

"What was that?" she asked, noticeably concerned.

"Just traffic this time of night. Can you have them meet me there?"

"Sure. I'll get the warrant filed and have backup there, shortly. And good work."

I reached up a finger to hit the little red phone icon on the screen of my cell, attached to the dashboard.

"And Sean."

"Yeah?" I took a left, cutting someone off in the middle of the intersection. I took it so fast that my tires squealed on the pavement. More horns blaring. Maybe they didn't see my lights.

"Three people have died, already. I hope you're right about this," Martinez said.

"Don't worry. I'm right. Just have those uniformed cops meet me there. Whoever. As many as you can get. And tell them not to park right in front of the place this time."

She paused. "I just got your text. That name." Another pause. "Wait, don't you know—"

"Yeah. I do," I said.

"Sean, if this is personal… If you need me to send someone else to do this, I promise I won't judge you. There are lots of other cops."

"No," I said forcefully. When I caught myself, I lowered my voice and added. "I'll do it. Just send backup."

"Alright," she said, more concerned than I wanted her to be. "If you—Never mind. Good luck."

"Thanks." I tapped the little red phone on the cell and then merged onto the freeway.

* * *

A green Volvo rested under a tall standing light in the Paradise Arms parking lot in the silent peace of the night air. It practically bathed in the warm artificial glow, just next to a grassy median a few yards away from the stairway entrance of Building 3. The front and back seats were as clean as the day it rolled out of the factory, except for a few paperback detective novels, carelessly discarded on the front passenger seat. The engine was cool. I ran the plate to be sure. It was the right car. They were home.

Baker stood at the ready with this back along the building's wall, just out of sight of the sliding glass door of the screened-in porch. Sweat ran down his cheek. He held his weapon out, just like they teach you at the academy. And he wore his bulletproof vest over his uniform shirt with creases sharp enough to shave with. He crouched slightly, poised to spring into action. He looked awake with the wide-eyed face of someone ready to take part in something important. Rookies. The door's long vertical blinds were closed, anyway. You never know.

Goldstein waited beside the bedroom window on the far side of the apartment. He wiped his sweaty palms on his dark blue uniform pants then rested his right on his weapon, still in its belt holster. His stern glare was that of someone who wouldn't hesitate to do what needed to be done. He wasn't wearing his vest. I don't know if he'll need it. That's on him. But I think his wife would have kittens if she knew.

Those were the only two exits out of the apartment. We covered them, but I'd feel better with more coverage of the area, to be sure. Ron isn't a real cop, so he couldn't help. Two guys were all I got. In all of Tampa, I get two guys. You'd think I was knocking on the door of someone with a handful of unpaid parking tickets, not a serial killer. Two guys.

Anyway, both squad cars sat parked around the corner, like I asked. Baker and Goldstein had to hike for a bit but at least there wasn't a blaring sign in the parking lot that said RUN with flashing lights on top.

As I walked up to the door, I met their eyes and nodded to each of them. I mentally rehearsed what I was going to say once or twice to get the tone of my voice right. And paused for a moment to regret not bringing my vest.

I knocked on the door. The hollow wooden sound carried along the cement walkway that ran in front of the row of apartments and into the empty night. The music of a Disney movie played on the TV, behind it. Bright and chipper. Uplifting. When no answer came, turned my head to Goldstein as if asking his opinion. He shifted his weight and looked back at me in agreement. I knocked again.

A man in khaki shorts and a loose-fitting white t-shirt walked his little black terrier along the footpath, between the buildings. He looked over at us and walked a little faster.

"Clara? Are you there?" I called into the closed door.

Happy music continued to play on the TV in her apartment, but no response came. The man with his dog stopped and turned around to watch us from down the path. Maybe I got his attention. Goldstein waved off the man with the dog, shaking his head. He kept walking.

I knocked on the door, again, a little louder. "It's me. Sean." I did my best to cover up any hint of stress in my voice.

I knocked again. "Clara, it's important."

Nothing but the music on the TV, trying to convince me that everything gets better.

"Shit." I took a step back and motioned to Baker with a shallow nod, who was watching me and not the sliding glass door on the porch like he should've been. He returned my nod. I drew my weapon. I leaned back and with one solid kick to the door at the knob I busted the frame. It swung open, slamming into the wall. Splinters flew into the apartment. "Hands where I can see them!" I shouted, with my weapon out. But it was empty. She wasn't there.

The TV was on, directly in front of the door. A young girl with impossibly long blonde hair sang to a green pocket-sized lizard with large round eyes about the world outside. The lizard watched her dance.

A small stack of paperback detective novels sat perched on the corner of the white coffee table. Half of a glass of sweet tea sat on the endstand beside the couch. Ice still floated in it and sweat still glistened on the side of the glass. An opened box of syringes lay on the kitchen counter, by the sink. A vial of something was just a few inches from it. Probably the lidocaine used on Sandra Miller.

"Clara," I called into the empty room, gun still drawn. "I don't want to hurt you. Just come out." I scanned the room. Checked the corners, beside the couch, below the kitchen counter, the door to the bathroom, just before the hallway—Something came from the bedroom, down the hall on the opposite side of the apartment. So, I stepped closer, aiming my weapon into my path.

"Clara," I called, as direct as I could manage without sounding like I was there to put her down. "If you come quietly, I'll do my best to get the judge to grant leniency."

No response.

"It's not too late. You still have control of the situation. If you—"

As soon as I walked past the couch, light footsteps came from behind me. I swung around just in time to catch Clara slipping out from behind the open door and bolt. I swear it slammed against the wall when I kicked it open. And how is she that fast?

"Clara, stop!"

She kept running straight for her car. Which happened to be parked directly in front of her apartment door, just a couple of rows out. She had a straight shot to it and a head start on all of us. She knew I'd eventually figure it out and set it all up.

I took off after her, shouting, "Stop, damn it!"

Baker and Goldstein ran out from their posts on the side of the building. Baker drew his weapon and fired at Clara, still running for her car. The gunshot echoed off the stucco-covered buildings of the complex. And the bullet chipped the pavement, a few feet in front of Clara.

"Hold your goddam fire! Do not shoot her!" I yelled at him. "What's wrong with you?"

"She's getting away!" he shouted back.

Clara jumped in her Volvo, started the engine, and drove off all while he was still talking. Damn, she's fast.

I stormed over to Baker, took his pistol from him, and connected my fist to his chin with a right cross. He stumbled backward and collapsed to the ground. Goldstein immediately knelt to help him and looked up at me with a sneer.

"Detective, you just let a serial killer get away," he spat at me.

"You normally go around shooting kids?" I retorted. "No one got away. I know where she's going." I dug out my phone and called Dr. Khatri on video chat.

"Detective?" she asked, registering my obvious look of concern.

"Doctor, meet me at USF. And stay out of Clara's way."

"Stay out of her way? Why? What's going on?" Now she looked concerned.

"You don't want to hear this over the phone. I'll explain everything when I see you in person. Do not go inside without me. Okay?"

"You're scaring me, Sean. Why can't you tell me now?"

"I just can't. I'm sorry. But it's very important. I'll explain everything when I get there."

She looked at me like I just told her that her dog might have cancer then ended the call. Hell.

* * *

When I got to USF, the whole parking lot was empty, lit by the bright lights on the side of the building. Up until then, I'd always come in the daytime when it was so full in the punishingly bright Tampa sun. It looked so unnatural this way. I was able to pull right up to the glass double doors at the front unfettered by the mass of cars that normally took up almost every available space.

Dr. Khatri stood on the sidewalk in front of the building as I pulled into the spot in front of her. I didn't recognize her at first, without her long white lab coat. She'd worn it so much that I got to think of it as part of her. Instead, she met me in a light blue tank top with the USF logo on the front, white denim shorts that showed off legs that my sixth-grade science teacher sure as hell didn't have, and a pair of wedge sandals. At least I think that's what they're called. I might've caught her when she was on her way to bed. It was pretty late.

As soon as I put it in park, she walked up to my door before I'd even shut off the engine. Her black opal-colored eyes showed a kind of pain. She didn't wait for me to get out of my car to ask, "What happened to Clara?"

I stood at the open driver's side door with a hand on it and tried to construct a sentence that would convey how her adopted daughter murdered three people without giving her a stroke.

"Well? What's wrong with her?"

"Doctor," I think my heart stopped for a second. "Clara is responsible for the murders."

Someone pulled the plug on Dr. Khatri's facial muscles and her expression dropped from her face. I didn't think she heard me, at first. She stood up straight and looked right past me. Then all at once, her eyes hardened and she slapped me hard across my cheek. Her brow creased as her bottom lip quivered. There isn't time for this.

"Don't you dare!" she said as if she just spat venom at me. At least it stung like she had. I'd never known her as anything other than warm and friendly. It was an entirely different woman that just assaulted me.

"The evidence fits," I said, nursing my tender cheek. "She knew we'd catch up to her. She was waiting for us. Now, she's on the run and probably terrified. I wanted you to wait out here, in case—"

She slapped me again on the same cheek. It hurt that much worse. You'd think I would've expected that one. Tears welled up in her eyes.

"Stop it!" she shouted, pointing an accusing finger at me. "She looked up to you! You were her hero, Sean! Don't you see that? You should've heard what she said about you when you weren't there. She'd never—"

"Doctor," I said gently.

"You can't just—"

"Doctor," I said with a little more effort and put a hand on her shoulder. "I like her, too. It took me this long because I didn't want to believe it, either. But all the evidence lines up. It was her." I did my best to deliver it with as little emotion as possible so she could absorb it the best she could. "We went to her place, and she ran. She knew we were coming, and she had it all planned out. Clara's a smart girl. She knows what that would look like if she were innocent."

She swatted my hand off her shoulder. "What evidence could you have? She's just a kid! Most of the time, she's with me in the lab. When she's not, she's at home reading books. She never goes out. She has maybe two friends and—"

"About twelve years ago, there was a problem with a traffic light that caused a multi-car pileup," I said. "Clara was in it with both of her parents. She was thirteen years old at the time. The three of them were rushed to the hospital. Clara recovered with minor injuries. Her parents were critically injured. The insurance agent that took the call refused to pay for the operations that would have saved their lives, saying their policies didn't cover the type of procedures that the doctors asked for. The hospital administrator at the time refused to let them have the procedures without the funding. Clara's parents died from their injuries, a few days later."

Dr. Khatri looked down at the pavement, lit by the pale glow of the building's lights, and shook her head. "You're lying. It's all lies. She couldn't do something like that. She couldn't. You don't know her like I do."

"William Horner was the traffic controller at the time, working the switchboard," I continued. "They blamed him for the accident until the investigation revealed the defect with the traffic light. Some people still blamed him for it, anyway. He was the first murder victim."

"Stop." A tear dropped from Dr. Khatri's left eye and disappeared into the asphalt at her feet.

"Timothy Sween was the insurance agent who took the call and denied the claim," I said. "He was the second victim."

Dr. Khatri balled her fist and pounded my chest. "It's not true." Her assaults sent waves of pain shooting out of my injured shoulder. I grabbed her hands and held them against my chest as I continued. She struggled, wanting to keep pounding at me. Or the thought of what I was telling her. The way I held her arms to my chest made her stand closer to me, wrapping me in the warmth of her body and the scent of her honeysuckle perfume.

"Sandra Miller was the hospital administrator who denied the procedure due to the lack of funding. And the third victim," I said. "Clara used the time suit to go into the future. She lied to me and told me that it couldn't do that, to keep me off the trail while she did her work. Clara found exactly when and where each of the victims would be vulnerable, and then she just made sure she was there for it. She already knew how not to leave any evidence from all the detective novels she reads. And she was the Morlock, trying to scare me away. Clara looked bigger from that time shadow illusion you told me about, so it didn't look like her."

Dr. Khatri didn't say anything.

"That's why I wanted to see you. This isn't something you tell people over the phone."

She wiped her tears away with the heels of her delicate hands and sniffled. She shook her head and looked at the trees at the end of the parking lot, lit by the yellow security lights. I can only imagine what would've been going through her head right then. After a moment I let go of her wrists. She slowly laid a hand flat on my chest, as gently as if it were a baby's forehead, then broke the silence. "What do you need me to do?" She didn't sound eager about it.

"Clara wants to use the time suit as an escape vehicle." I tried positioning my head to get into her line of vision.

She closed her eyes and stepped away from me.

"Doctor, whatever you need to get through to accept this, you have to do it right now," I said. "She's probably already gone. And I need your help to find out where she went, so I can follow her there and bring her back. *When* she went. Whatever."

Dr. Khatri snapped a look back at me like someone flipped her switch. "You have to stop her! She can't use it to escape anywhere. The law of conservation of matter and energy prevents it. She'd have to keep the suit on forever."

"Are you sure? She may have figured out a way."

She nodded. "That's the intention we had when we started this project. We wanted to be able to travel to and from other times. We could use it to stop tragedies from happening. Or get people away from them where they're inevitable. But the more we studied it, the more we confirmed that it's—impossible. Sending matter to a different point in time would effectively duplicate the particles of the object and the laws of the universe won't let that happen. It's one of the commandments that they teach every high school student. 'Thou shalt not duplicate matter or energy.' Everyone knows that."

"So, what would happen if she went back in time and took off her suit?" I asked.

"Her particles would return to our time, like a bubble of air returning to the surface," she said academically like it's something everyone knows.

"That doesn't sound so bad."

"You don't understand." Dr. Khatri put a hand on my chest. "They wouldn't return—assembled."

"Oh."

"And they might convert to energy as they return," she added.

"You mentioned that, before. That's bad, right?"

"Very bad. Nuclear explosion-bad. The blast would vaporize most of Tampa. Sean, you have to stop her!"

"Come on," I said tearing myself away from those damn eyes. "We're wasting time."

Chapter 23

Clara had already beaten us to the physics lab at USF and stolen the time suit by the time we got there. No surprise. This had been her plan the whole time. She knew I'd eventually catch up to her, and this was her out. I massaged my ego a little and told myself that I caught her off guard. And that if she really knew I was coming, then she wouldn't have even been at home when I got there. It sounded good in my head, anyway.

We found the lock on the lab door smashed, probably by the fire extinguisher on the floor, next to it. Wooden splinters were everywhere. The mannequin in the lab lay knocked over on the floor, stripped of its suit and with its right arm broken off at the elbow. It looked like a crime scene of its own, the way it lay on the floor like it did.

Thankfully, she was in such a hurry that she forgot about the second time suit. The new one. The one that Dr. Khatri added the improvements to, based on my feedback about the first one. They just finished a couple of days before and it's still hanging up in Dr. Khatri's office. Maybe I did catch her off guard, after all. Go me.

* * *

"Are you sure this is where she went?" I asked, parking the car behind Clara's dark green Volvo on the curb by the driveway. Even at night, the neighborhood looked like the backdrop to a Disney movie. A really bad one where they think the biggest concern a suburbanite has is how people don't pick up after their dogs. I hate those movies. "She's very smart. She could've ditched her car at the wrong place."

"This is where the logs show that she initiated a time portal," said Dr. Khatri, scrolling through them on her tablet. "They even show the date and time that she went to. We've been logging everything. But it's for peer review, not for—I should've looked through them to make sure no one was using the suit."

"Don't beat yourself up about it. I don't make a habit of expecting my friends to be serial killers, either. Are you sure we don't need the console in your van?"

She shook her head. "The console can initiate a portal but it's not necessary. We were using it to record detailed logs, stream and monitor the video feed from the suit, communicate with you, and—"

"Okay, okay. I got it." I unhooked my seatbelt and let it retract into the side of the cabin then turned my body to her slightly. It's not easy in those seats.

"Just tell Watson you want to open a portal, and he'll do the rest, just like the old suit. The new suit has better power management so you can create more now if you need to."

I nodded my head.

A very confused man, somewhere in his thirties, and wearing very expensive-looking clothes, paced around a toddler on the front lawn just in the light of their porch. He had his phone up to his ear, franticly talking to someone on the other end. I expected him to be trying to explain to a 9-1-1 operator that some crazy blue-haired girl in a spacesuit made his front door shimmer purple then walked through it and disappeared. I also expected the operator to think he was stoned.

"Must be the right place," I remarked, watching them. "If this is her childhood home, it's a nice place to be a kid. That's a big house. Can't blame her for wanting to go back to it." It was very much that. Two-story, Spanish tile roof, one-and-a-half-car garage.

She put a hand on my forearm and squeezed it. I met her eyes. "Just promise me that whatever happens, you won't hurt her."

"She may not let me. Desperate people do—"

"Promise me you won't hurt her!" Dr. Khatri looked up at me with eyes of black onyx from the passenger seat of my car and took a breath. I hate it when she does that. "Make sure she's okay." She had a pretty good grip.

"I will do my absolute best to bring her back safe and unharmed," I said slowly.

She nodded and looked at the floorboard in front of her. "That would be acceptable."

"Hey. I really mean that. She couldn't be safer if she was my own daughter."

Dr. Khatri swallowed and turned her head to look at me. "Are you ready?"

"No," I said plainly. "And I'm not sure I *can* be. But Clara needs us."

She nodded.

We got out of the car and walked up to the house. The rampaging father on the cell phone put up a hand as we stepped onto his lawn. I carried the folded suit under my arm in the sling and the helmet with my free hand. And I can only imagine what I looked like to him. He looked mad, though.

"Hey, hey, hey. You people can't just come up here," the angry father said, holding up his phone. "I have the police on the line and—"

"Sir, I am the police," I told him. I handed the helmet to Dr. Khatri so I could grab my badge from my belt and hold it up. "My name is Detective Sean Papadopoulos. This is my assistant, Dr. Khatri. You just had a woman in a spacesuit turn your front door into a purple shimmering soap bubble then walk through it and disappear. Right?"

"I can't get the damn woman on the phone to believe me!" He looked a little relieved, though still angry. He showed me the phone like it was cursed.

"Would *you* believe you?" asked Dr. Khatri, walking up to him.

I dropped the suit to the ground next to the toddler and started to put it on where I stood. He picked up one of my gloves and commenced his toddler investigation of the new object.

"Don't run off with that," I told him. "I'm going to need it back in a minute."

"What are you going to do about it?" demanded the father, pointing at me with his phone.

"I'm going to ask you to open your front door," I replied, stepping into the suit. "Then I'm going to go bring her back."

"I mean, are you going to let criminals run around doing their demonic magical things? This is a nice neighborhood. I have a family to think of!" he shouted.

"No one *lets* criminals run around, sir. That's why they're called *criminals*." I put on my left boot and fastened it to my pant leg.

He drew a breath to say something then Dr. Khatri stepped between us and held up her hands like she was holding back an enraged, slobbering, snorting man-shaped beast. There's a thought.

"You're not very good at talking to people, are you?" she asked me.

"Hey, I said I liked my job. Never said I was good at it," I said and put on the other boot. "I'm going to need help with some of this." Then I wiggled my bad arm in its sling.

Dr. Khatri turned back around to the enraged father. "If you can open your front door, we'll be out of your hair, in just a moment."

The man huffed. As he walked towards the door, he said, "Fine. But you people better keep those degenerates out of this neighborhood. I pay my taxes!" I wonder why people keep bringing that up. Huh.

Dr. Khatri bent down and said to the little boy, sitting in the grass and playing with my glove, "I'll need that, now. Thanks for keeping it safe." And she smiled at him.

The little boy smiled back, showing every one of his four teeth, and giggled a little as he drooled on his shirt. Why are some things adorable when you're two years old but so creepy when you're forty?

Dr. Khatri pulled the suit over my shoulders and let me put my good arm through its sleeve. The bad arm went in, held up by a sling made from the same material as the rest of the suit. (It only hurt a little.) She explained that if it was regular cloth, something bad would happen when I went through the portal, and we might all die in a fiery nuclear holocaust, reducing the surrounding area to a radioactive hellscape for a hundred years afterward. Or something like that. I remember it was bad, anyway.

She also said that Clara must've had her baseball bat wrapped in it, to use it as the Morlock. Always thinking ahead, that one.

As Dr. Khatri helped me with my gloves, she told me, "Remember, don't hurt her. She's just scared and confused."

"Every blue hair on her head is safe. Don't worry."

I winced when she fastened the glove on my bad arm and didn't mean to. It'd been a while since I'd taken pain meds.

"Oh my god, I'm sorry," she said, hovering her hands over my arm.

"It's okay. It can't be helped. You're doing fine."

"Let me do it," she said and started to take the glove back off before I stepped away.

"No," I said more forcefully than I meant to. "I'll do it. The suit won't fit you."

"Yes, it will. I've worn it before. It's just baggy." She reached for the glove again.

"I have to do this," I said pulling it away from her.

"Why? She trusts me. I can talk her down, I can—"

"I just do. It has to be me," I said to her.

The angry father waited impatiently by his open front door, under the porch light. "Well?" he asked.

"Men," said Dr. Khatri, shaking her head. She put my helmet on me and fastened it to my collar.

"Well?" asked the cranky man.

The kid giggled and looked up at Dr. Khatri.

"Peter," scolded the man. "Get your ass in this house, right now." As he came over and yanked the kid off of said ass, he added, "It's pitch black out here. You know that?"

"He has such a way with children," Dr. Khatri said to me in her soft voice.

I chuckled, cleared my throat, and announced, "Watson." In the time it took to say it, a heads-up display showing a temporal readout, a compass, and a bunch of other information that I'm sure would be useful if I took the time to read all of it, filled the inside of my helmet.

"Good evening, Detective Papadopoulos," said the helpful British-sounding male voice through the speakers of my helmet. "I have a predetermined set of time coordinates. Shall I initiate a temporal gate?"

"Yes, please."

"Do you have a preference for the location of the temporal gate?" he asked.

J.S. Johnston

"The doorway beside the cranky man would be ideal," I said.

"Acknowledged. Shall I warn the bystanders?"

I smiled and answered, "That won't be necessary. Just open the portal."

A thin sheen appeared, covering the space of the front door in swirling purples, reds, and blues, like the surface of a soap bubble. The angry man's eyes popped out as he fell off the porch in fright. The trappings of a decade ago replaced the modern interior of the house.

I turned to Dr. Khatri, nodded, then walked through the portal.

Chapter 24

A tsunami of events flowed around me, nearly bowling me over. Every moment in thirteen years happened all at once, blasting right through where I stood while I tried to hold on to anything real that might anchor me in place. I braced against the current, curling into a crouch with my head into the stream as it went past me, as unimpeded as the force of nature that it was.
Breathe, Sean. It's just another day at work.

Furniture from a generation ago replaced the surroundings of a modern living room. A small and boxy CRT replaced the large-screen LED TV. An overstuffed lime green sofa replaced the stylish, rectangular white couch. The short light beige carpet was now a dark brown wood floor.

The pictures of a loving family hanging on the wall were switched with impostors. It took me a moment to recognize her, but one of them was Clara as a little kid. She looked somewhere around twelve or thirteen with a tiny nose and a pointed chin. Her hair was a mundane blonde, instead of the normal shiny blue. It was straight and long, cascading over her shoulders like so many other tween girls her age. Her eyes showed the happiness of a carefree youth, provided by the loving parents that stood behind her.

I hadn't been that far back in time before. It wasn't the day or two that the investigations had allowed for; this was thirteen years in the past. I was thrown off the deep end when I barely learned how to swim.

On the other side of the time portal, Dr. Khatri stood on the front porch, wringing her hands. She looked at me expectantly and made me not want to let her down. I slowly raised my hand to chest height, in a half-wave gesture. Not sure why. She returned it.

"Shall I discontinue the temporal gate to conserve power?" asked

Watson from the helmet speakers.

It took me a moment to register what he asked. "Yeah. Shut down the portal."

The swirling purple sheen that covered the empty doorway disappeared while Dr. Khatri was still in mid-wave and the darkened back side of a closed door replaced it.

The young and chipper voices of a man and woman came from the side hallway that led into the living room. They walked in, continuing their conversation, oblivious to the time-traveling spaceman at the door.

"Okay. I'll pick up some hot dogs from the store and we'll have the cookout on Saturday." A Black man built like a tree stood dressed in a dark blue policeman's uniform, freshly pressed with sharp creases down the pant legs. His thick hair was cut short and well-sculpted, making him look a lot more professional than I've ever been. He walked into the kitchen and picked up an insulated lunchbox from the counter.

"Does that old grill even still work? It's been sitting in the backyard for years. There has to be a gas leak, somewhere," said the woman. She was tall and pretty. Her long blonde hair cascaded over her narrow shoulders and down her back. Thick eyelashes flashed bright blue eyes that lit up the room. She carried a red purse in her hand and dropped it on an endstand by a reclining chair. "It might explode if you try to use it."

"Well, then she'll have a very exciting birthday party." He smirked at the woman.

Her bright red high heels made knocking sounds on the hardwood floor as she walked up to him in the kitchen. She slid her fingers around his muscular arms, looked up at him, and smiled sweetly.

"What if you burned off your hair? You'd look terrible bald," she said.

"If you don't like bald guys, what are you going to do when I get older?"

"Buy you a toupee. Or date a twenty-year-old. I haven't decided yet," she said with a grin.

He bowed his head and kissed her gently on the lips. They did other mushy stuff that I didn't pay attention to. People really need to stop doing that when I'm time-traveling.

"Watson, are you able to detect if another person in a time suit is in the house?" I asked.

"I do have that capability, Detective Papadopoulos."

"So, is there another time suit here?"

"Affirmative," he said. "I have detected a chroniton disturbance indicative of the Mark III time suit in the vicinity of this structure."

"Awesome. Can you tell me where they're at?"

"That capability is currently slated to be rolled out in the Mark VI time suit," Watson said without even apologizing.

"Well, that's not helpful. I guess we just go look, then."

"Would you like me to begin a video recording?"

"That's a good idea. Thanks, Watson."

"You're welcome, Detective Papadopoulos. Beginning video record."

The amorous couple walked back into the living room, making goo-goo eyes at each other and I had to step around them to get out.

On the second story, down the hall from the stairs, a white-painted door stood on my right, decorated with incredibly fancy red capital letters, and covered in a layer of sparkles that read CLARA'S ROOM. Fluorescent pink flower stickers surrounded it in no particular pattern.

I put a hand on the knob to open it, which I couldn't do because I can't move anything in the past. I wasn't really there. The knob held fast as if someone had welded it in place.

A tiny and young-sounding female voice floated up from the stairs in a very frustrated tone. "I can't believe this!" she shouted, indignantly.

An adolescent Clara stormed up the steps with her face beat red in anger and her hands in the air in the universal 'I've had it' gesture.

"We're your parents, Clara. We want to be part of your thirteenth birthday," pleaded her mother, right behind her. "It's just a barbecue. It's not like we got you a clown."

Clara stopped in her tracks and turned around to face her mother. Her eyes widened, making a nice contrast to the red of her face. "A barbecue that'll take all day! Where I'll be forced to talk to aunts and cousins that I don't even like!"

"Clara, it's your special day. We want—"

"Yeah! *My* special day!" Clara yelled with balled-up fists.

"Clara—"

"Do you know what Cindy Holechek got to do for *her* thirteenth birthday?" Clara shouted with her face so near her mother's, still on the stairs, that she could probably smell what she had for lunch.

Clara's mother straightened to her full height and pointed her chin at her. "I don't care what Cindy Holechek got to do," she said in a voice sterner than my mother ever managed.

Adolescent Clara stabbed a finger into the air like she was pointing at an invisible Cindy Holechek. "She had a party at the skating rink," and she stressed this part. "With her own friends! And boys!"

"Clara—"

"Sugary soda! With Extra sugar!"

"Clara—"

"Cheesy, greasy pizza!" she shouted.

"Clara!"

"And lots and lots of boys, mother!"

"Clara Michelle Heartwell!" her mother yelled. "We are going to have a barbeque for your monumental thirteenth birthday."

"But!"

"You will converse with all of your relatives in attendance!" Clara's mother sounded like my old drill sergeant in boot camp.

"But!" Clara pleaded. The look on her face read as defeat.

"Even the ones you hate!"

"But!"

"You will eat your stepfather's horrible cooking and like it!" Clara's mother pointed down the steps as if her stepfather stood at the bottom.

"But!"

"And you will have fun!" Clara's mother demanded.

"You are the worst parents ever! I hate the both of you!"

Adolescent Clara spun around and stormed off to her room, behind me. As she opened her very sparkly door, I caught a glimpse of grownup Clara—the Morlock—behind her. Her stark black silhouette stood in front of a sun-filled window, looking down at a twin bed, and the small mountain of stuffed bears, elephants, and creatures previously unknown to science that lay on top of it. She didn't take any notice of the rampaging younger version of herself.

Before adolescent Clara could slam her bedroom door shut, I darted through it.

Chapter 25

I expected a computer, a huge microscope, and a copy of Steven Hawking's *Brief History of Time* strewn around Clara's childhood bedroom. Or maybe a chessboard or whatever it is that smart people do for fun. But there was none of that.

The room was almost wallpapered with posters of boy bands and pop stars. Frilly girl clothes hung out of half-open glossy hot pink dresser drawers. A lamp of a cartoon unicorn with a rainbow-colored mane and tail stood on a curvy white nightstand. Its gold trim made it look like a prop in a French movie about rich people.

There wasn't a microscope or particle collider in sight. I'm not sure what a particle collider looks like, but there was nothing in the room that might make me think it was one.

Morlock Clara had been looking down at the worn Disney's Alice in Wonderland comforter on the twin bed in the corner of the room. When adolescent Clara stormed in with me at her heels, she didn't look up. Maybe she couldn't hear the commotion or was just lost in thought. For whatever reason, she kept her attention firmly planted on that comforter.

Adolescent Clara made a beeline for the bed, hopped up on it, and buried her crying face in the pillow with a matching pillowcase. She screamed into it. At least, I think it was a scream. Even as muffled as it was, it still sounded like the locked metal wheels on a train screeching against steel railroad tracks as the whole thing grinds to a halt. Whatever you call that sound, it came out of a thirteen-year-old girl.

As if I tapped her on the shoulder, Morlock Clara snapped her head in my direction. I didn't have a plan for that part. After all that talk with Dr. Khatri, I assumed that once Clara knew that I knew she was just Clara and not some monster from my nightmares, she'd come along quietly. It sounded very plausible in my head. Sometimes, I could kick myself.

Morlock Clara pivoted on her heels to turn her body in my direction and barreled straight at me. As I stood there like an idiot wondering what she was doing, she plowed into my stomach like a linebacker. The wind in my lungs blew all over the inside of my helmet and I crashed to the ground.

I lay flat on my back and looked up at her black form towering over me. She pulled a hand from behind her back, revealing the baseball bat that she'd been carrying. At least, I hoped that's what it was. She took it in both hands and raised it over her head.

"Clara!" I shouted. "Don't do it!"

She dropped down to one knee, taking a swing at me and I shot to the side, rolling out of the way. Clara's bat hit the floor so hard that I could swear I could feel it.

"Clara, please!"

She took another swing and came an inch away from the right sleeve of my time suit. I backed away, only to hit the wall behind me. She swung again, but this time I was able to block her with my forearm.

"Clara, for God's sake!"

She grabbed my throat with one hand and made for my stomach with the other. I instinctively grabbed each of her hands with both of mine just to be overwhelmed with a sharp pain from my shoulder and held her back with my good arm with all I could. She pushed against the floor with her boot, using all her strength to attack me.

"Watson! Can she hear me?" I barked into the helmet like I was about to be fed to a shark who skipped breakfast.

"Time suit occupants cannot affect the medium in which sound can propagate."

"Christ, just speak English!" Clara was getting really close. My one good arm wasn't doing much to stop her. "Can she hear me?"

"She cannot hear you, Detective Papadopoulos," Watson answered.

Clara gave up on my throat and used both her hands to try to push the bat into my stomach. But once she drove it into me, it was clear that it was not a bat. It was thin and sharp—like a knife. Hell.

And she was making progress. The tip of the blade inched closer as my strength vanished.

The voice of her mother came from behind the closed bedroom door. "Clara, it's time for dinner."

I fished a leg out from in front of Morlock Clara, planted it against her, and pushed hard. She tumbled backward, dropping the knife.

Adolescent Clara hopped up from her bed and stormed over to the door. As she threw it open, she screamed, "Dinner? Are you serious, right now? You're ruining my life and you're asking me about dinner?"

Her mother backed up from the doorway and Clara followed her.

Morlock Clara saw them and within a second, a portal appeared in the doorway. She sprinted over to it and passed through. I followed her as fast as I could, watching it close when I was barely through it.

Day had turned to night and the pastel wallpaper had changed to a deep blue. I tried to chase after her down the hallway but damn she was fast. In less time than it took to think it, another purple shimmer covered a side doorway, and she slipped through it. I bolted through after her, hoping the hell I didn't have to find out what happens when those things close when you're halfway through.

The blinding light of day burst through the window, and I wrapped my arm around the glass of my helmet to shield my eyes. When I lowered it, Clara was gone, and the fact that this was the house she grew up in smacked me in the face.

I was in the primary bedroom. The queen-sized bed stood to my right with its carved wood headboard against the wall. Its crumpled dark green comforter with a banana leaf pattern lay on top of it.

A time portal shimmered in the doorway to my left, showing a darkened room.

I stopped and turned around to the door that I had just come through. It was still open, but not fully against the wall. The trick wasn't original, and to be honest, a little insulting. I reached out to grab Clara's arm, who was hiding behind it. The Morlock Clara. She tried to pull back from me but had nowhere to go. And she didn't have a knife to threaten me with, anymore.

However, she put the toe of her boot to my shin harder than I'd expect for someone her size. A lot harder. So hard that a moment later, I was on my knees, screaming about it.

As she came out from behind the door, she put a hand on the side of my head and pushed me aside. I collapsed to the floor, fully enveloped with shooting pain. Then without even pausing for a moment, she created another time portal and hopped through it, closing it behind her.

Chapter 26

"Watson, can you tell where she went?" I asked, collecting myself as soon as I could. I knelt on one knee while I nursed my aching shin. The bright sun of the past flooded through the window and filled the empty primary bedroom with a pale light.

"Due to the nature of temporal—"

"Are you able to tell or not?"

"I am unable to determine the temporal destination of the previous gate," Watson said.

"See? Now, wasn't that so much easier?"

"The action of rephrasing the same statement into more colloquially simpler vocabulary required an equal amount of compute cycles to perform." And he said it like he was reading me my cable bill.

"Never mind."

The purple shimmer of Clara's escape portal was now just an ordinary doorway that led to an empty hall. You'd think there'd be at least a wisp of smoke as a telltale sign that it was actually there, but there wasn't. There was nothing but empty space.

I stood up to my full height and examined where I was. *When* I was. Whatever. I couldn't tell whether I was in the future or past from where I started. The pale-yellow flowers on the queen-sized bedspread and the faux-wood finish on the nightstands looked just as ugly as any you'd find anywhere else. And I wasn't sure what I'd learn if they didn't. It still wouldn't tell me where she went.

I stepped over to the window. The thick blackout curtains were thankfully already pulled open. It all faced the backyard of the house where a massive live oak tree sprawled its branches over a wooden swing set, giving it shade. The swing set was pretty substantial, made of thick, new-looking wooden beams. A corkscrew slide, monkey bars. Big enough for all the kids in the neighborhood to play on if they wanted to. I imagined little Clara's parents holding her so she could climb up the ladder for the slide; her pudgy, tiny little legs stretching to reach each step. A smile crept onto my face for a moment.

"We never really know who we are until something happens, do we?" I asked, floating in my imagination.

"I am Watson version 4.33, artificial intelligence for the Mark IV time suit and property of the University of South Florida, all rights reserved," he responded.

"—You certainly are."

He didn't say anything.

"You know, we're probably thinking about this too hard. Figuring out where she went shouldn't be that complicated."

No response.

"Dr. Khatri mentioned that you're able to create more time portals than the previous model. She did say that, right?"

"I do possess an improved battery capacity that lets me initiate additional temporal gates without a recharge than the previous model," he said.

"Now, based on what you know about the previous model, how many more can Clara make?" I asked.

"Based on the number of temporal gates that she created since arrival the other time suit is not able to create any additional gates. Shall I create a gate back to the present?"

"She didn't go to the present," I said, proudly figuring it out. Sometimes I'm good at my job.

"Without the ability to create another temporal gate, she would be trapped in a different time."

"Not Clara. She's too smart to get trapped like that."

"Detective?"

"Clara didn't go back to the present," I said. "Create a new time portal, Watson."

"Of course. Please provide coordinates to initiate the temporal gate."

"The same coordinates you used to get us here but advanced to just after we went through her first portal. That's where she went.

Can you do that?"

"Affirmative. One moment, detective."

The open bedroom doorway shimmered with purple, yellow, and red swirls, showing a different hallway, behind it. I walked through and ordered Watson to close it behind me. Clara's parents talked to each other, downstairs. And I made my way down.

"What if we did have it at the bowling alley?" asked her dad, arms folded and leaning against the kitchen counter. "It wouldn't be that hard to tell everyone to meet us there."

"We've already told her no," said her mother, standing in the middle of the kitchen.

"What's this '*we*'? You mean *you* already told her no." He backed it up with some raised eyebrows.

"Hey," she said, drawing out the word in a playful tone. "We have to be on a united front. Remember?"

"What's in it for me?" He looked at her with loving eyes.

I fought the urge to throw up in my helmet from all the mushy sweetness. When I walked into the kitchen to wait for Clara, someone kicked the side of my knee hard as soon as I passed the outside counter. Something in it snapped and things moved into new places that I didn't know were there. I screamed as I crumbled to the floor like a pile of wet laundry.

Morlock Clara lackadaisically rose from behind the counter and looked down at me while I frolicked in newfound agony. She cocked her head to one side like she was deciding what to do with me.

"Watson, can you open up a channel to her?" I asked through the wave of pain.

"I can, Detective Papadopoulos." A digital chirp played over the speakers. "The channel is open. You may speak to her, now."

"Clara! You can't do this!"

"I'm doing it. And you can't stop me," she said very calmly and just as assuredly as telling me she was in the checkout line at the grocery store. She lifted her black head and looked at the embracing couple. "How did you finally figure out it was me?"

"Besides all the detective novels you left lying around? Books that basically tell you what evidence to not leave behind so you can get away with murder? The butterfly was straight out of one of them."

She snorted a laugh. "*The Silence of the Lambs.* Every good killer needs a calling card. They should pass a law about those books. But that could've been anyone. There are those CSI shows, too. Everyone watches them."

"That's true. It was the crocodile tears that pointed to you."

"Crocodile tears?" she asked like she already knew the answer.

"The Julia butterfly lands on the head of an alligator and irritates its eye to produce tears so it can drink them. You left those things behind at the murder scenes to tell everyone that their tears were just for show; a display so that other people don't think that they're monsters. You were telling everyone that you could see right through their crocodile tears."

She gingerly stepped in front of her oblivious parents, still looking at each other with dreamy eyes.

"The rest fell right into place, after that," I added. "You delayed the video of the Timothy Sween murder. You said it took a while to download, but it was really because you had to remove your face digitally while no one else was in the lab.

"Sandra Miller died from an overdose of lidocaine. Something you could've easily gotten from the medical department at USF. You injected her with it at the Gasparilla parade as Jimmy Buffett. With the distortion of the time current, you just put on a Hawaiian shirt and hat, and I'd never be able to tell the difference from where I was. The crowd made sure I couldn't get any closer.

"William Horner's cause of death was obvious. You shot him with his own gun. You chose the day he was cleaning it so you wouldn't make him suspicious by looking in his house for it. It was right out in the open. You knew when that was because you'd been watching him in the time suit. You didn't leave any prints in the house because you used a pair of gloves. You didn't leave any glove powder residue anywhere because you knew enough to use hypoallergenic gloves that didn't have it. You came in posing as a cable repair tech. He made you coffee. You didn't sit down because you knew you might leave threads behind. He didn't think anything of it because repair techs don't sit down."

"That's pretty good," she said in a whisper of a voice, still looking at her parents.

"But how did you know his cable would be out on the exact day he was cleaning his gun?" I asked.

"Because I cut it," she said as a matter-of-fact.

"Oh. I guess I should've thought of that."

"They deserved to die for what they did. Look at them. Do you see the love they have for each other? This is what they took from the world."

"They were doing their jobs, Clara," I said. "Your parents got caught up in a system that just wants to get work done so they can go home at night. Pay their bills. That's all. They didn't deserve to die for—"

"Would your conscience let you do what they do? Could your incompetence lead people to critical injury and then deny people what they need to stay alive?"

"William Horner didn't cause that accident. He was just the guy who happened to be working when the electronics in the traffic light went bad. They did an investigation, Clara. He had nothing to do with it."

"Lies!" she shouted. "It's his fault they're dead! He's just as guilty as the others." She reached out a hand to touch the back of her mother's shoulder. She must've known she couldn't touch her. "None of that matters, now."

"Why, Clara? Why wouldn't it matter? Those people are dead. I'd say it matters a hell of a lot to them."

"It's my thirteenth birthday, today," she said like she wasn't talking to me.

"I got that part."

"Eventually, Mom and Dad caved and decided to have my party at the bowling alley. They were going to tell everyone else to meet us there. They were even going to call my friends' parents and invite them. I mean, who does that, right?"

"Good parents," I said.

She nodded and looked at the floor. "We were all on our way there when it happened. Dad was in the middle of saying something about the pizza that the place had when…" she trailed off.

"I'm sorry. That has to hurt like hell. But you can't change the past. You said so, yourself."

She snapped her head towards me. "Yes, I can. I've been staying up at night doing the calculations. All I have to do is tell them to have the barbecue. They don't have an accident. They don't die. And I don't have to murder anyone."

"But you can't." I propped myself up on my arm. "If you take the suit off, at best you'll just disintegrate into little particles. And at worst, you'll blow us all to Hell. Dr. Khatri said the blast would take out Most of Tampa. Do you know how many people that is? Do they all deserve to die, too?"

She tapped a finger in my direction. "That's what I figured out. Ever since I read Dr. Khatri was working on the time suit, I've been busting my ass to get onto the team so I could do this. I just had to keep you busy long enough to finish my work." She laughed. "I have about ten seconds after I take my helmet off to tell them. After that, it doesn't matter what happens to me. Because none of this will have happened, anyway."

"What if you're wrong? What if you were so desperate to find a way that you didn't see something obvious? Like you forgot to carry the one or something. Do you have any idea what you could end up doing?"

She shook her head and said, "I've been working on this way too long. I know I'm right." She started to fumble with the latch that sealed her helmet to the collar of her suit.

"Clara, stop!" I tried to stand despite the pain, but as soon as I put weight on my hurt knee, I dropped back to the floor.

She turned to look at me. "I really like you, Sean. I'm sorry to put you through all of this." The latch on her helmet snapped open.

"Please, Clara!"

"Goodbye, Sean. If this doesn't work, tell Dr. Khatri she's been like my second mother." She lifted her helmet off her head and her technicolor face appeared, planted on stark black shoulders.

Her parents stared at her with wide eyes and open mouths. She must've looked like a disembodied head, floating in midair to them. That disembodied head was the grownup version of the one having a teenage fit in her bedroom.

"Cl—Clara?" asked her dad. He reached out to touch her.

She opened her mouth to speak but looked like she was choking on something. Her eyes widened, and she clutched her throat. Tiny pieces evaporated from her skin, blown away like dust.

"Clara!" screamed her mother, horrified at the sight.

Clara's face scrunched up like she was in pain, and she tried to scream but nothing came out. More of her blew away. The air was full of the bright blue of her hair, the tan of her skin, and the brown of her eyes. She clawed at the collar of her suit as if it was choking her. She clamped her eyes shut as the pain of being taken apart a piece at a time consumed her.

Muscles and tendons along her cheek and jaw appeared and vanished as she evaporated. The bone of her skull. The front of her thumbprint of a nose. They were gone. One of her eyes looked like it was bitten in half.

Her parents watched on in astonished horror as the disembodied head of their grownup daughter writhed in agony as she disintegrated in front of them. There wasn't anything they could do to help. Even if there was, their shock wouldn't let them move.

Then Clara screamed. It was pain, rage, and despair. It was inhuman. She only had part of her mouth left and half of her tongue. The bone of her jaw lay open to the air with some of her teeth still in it. The blood that dripped down from her open wounds disappeared before it could land on the kitchen floor. But she could still scream. If you could call it that.

After the air left her lungs, she collapsed on the floor. Her father dropped to his knees, almost instinctively. He put out his hands as if he wanted to comfort her. Like she was just sick or something. But before he could touch her, the rest of her blew away like so much dust.

Epilogue

I adjusted myself, sitting in Dr. Striker's chair. I wasn't looking forward to this appointment, but here we were. There are only so many excuses I can come up with to get out of them and still sound believable.

He watched me with a blank face and laid a gentle hand on mine.

I paused the video on my phone. Clara had just taken off the helmet of her time suit. Her glistening eyes were full of hope and the drive to fix all the wrongs in the world. She looked at her parents like she had just come home from school and wanted to tell them all about it. As far as I was concerned, the rest didn't need to be seen. This—This was good. I could delete the rest.

I ran a thumb under my eye to wipe away an escaping tear. Then turned off the screen of my phone without looking at Dr. Striker.

"A Scooby-Doo ending," he said, calmly and evenly as he sat back in his chair and crossed his legs. He did that thing where he put his elbows on the armrests and made a teepee out of his arms.

"What?" I asked in a bit of a daze, pulled out of the memory.

"A Scooby-Doo ending. You know how every episode ended with them solving the case—well Velma would solve it—and the unmasking of the monster. And it usually turned out to be Old Man Jenkins who ran the haunted amusement park."

I snorted. "Yeah. I guess it was a little Scooby-Doo." I paused a moment and added. "Velma was the monster, this time."

"Imagine that."

"Yeah. Imagine that." I sat back in my chair and tucked my phone into my arm sling.

"You solved the case," he said in a calm, encouraging voice. He sat back in his chair and reached for the coffee on the table beside him. Concern showed on his face. His tie looked stupid. "The murders have stopped. Didn't you say it was unsolvable with no evidence to go on? No leads?"

I shook my head and counted the threads in the carpet. "This isn't what I wanted. She was my friend."

He sat forward in his chair and rested his elbows on his knees. He was close enough to reach out and pat my leg, but he didn't. "She's not still your friend?"

"She's dead, Doc! Weren't you paying attention? Or do you need me to play the rest of this damn video for you?"

He sighed, and said gingerly, "People don't really die in the hearts and minds of the ones they leave behind. Their bodies die, sure. But if I looked inside your head, I'd probably find your parents very much alive. For better or worse. Even the love and friendship we feel for others never really dies. She's still your friend, Sean. It wouldn't hurt so much if she wasn't." He probably got it from a cheap greeting card.

"No. That's dead, too. She was a murderer. Premeditated, cold-blooded murder. Three people. They had lives. Families. People who depended on them. She wasn't the person I made friends with. That person didn't exist."

"That's the thing, isn't it? People are never who we think they are. When we get to know them, we meet the person they want us to see. Or the person *we* want to see. Like when Superman becomes the mild-mannered reporter. He's still Superman, but all you see is the reporter. But real people aren't Superman. Finding out who they are when they leave their phone booth can hurt pretty bad, sometimes."

"People don't use phone booths, anymore."

"You know what I mean," he said.

"Yeah."

"You can still be friends with the person you thought she was. She's a real person to you. As real as anyone. You're allowed to miss her."

I stared into nothing, somewhere in the vicinity of the fake diplomas he had hanging on the wall. I wanted a drink. No, I wanted lots of drinks.

"Did she say how she knew the guy with the dog? The one that got you run over and gave you that arm sling?" he asked and pointed to it with his forehead.

"She didn't mention him. And I didn't think to ask when she was about to kill herself. But I looked it up, later."

"Oh?"

"It turns out she knew him from a foster home she lived in after her parents died," I said.

"She knew he was capable of it, back then?"

I nodded and pulled my phone out from my sling and turned it over and over in my good hand. "Guess so. Or she knew him well enough to know what it took to push his button."

"I know what you mean," Dr. Striker said. "We all have that button. Some of us, you have to really dig for it. Then some of us—"

"We walk it around on a leash and pick up its poop."

He stifled a laugh. I didn't mean for it to be funny.

"You know, I went to school with this kid that grew up to be The Florida Overpass Sniper? So far, he's the only guy I know that has his own Wikipedia page," I offered, unasked.

"Is that so? What was that like?"

"He was—weird," I said. "You know how people say serial killers are just like everyone else until one day they start piling bodies in their basement? It's all bullshit and I have no idea why people say that. There are clear signs. This kid was… broken. I had a few classes a day with him all through high school. Even sat right next to him for some of them. He didn't have any friends. He talked about doing terrible things to animals… Anyway, so when he grows up, he starts going to overpasses with his sniper rifle and takes potshots at the passing cars, underneath. At his trial, he said the voices in his head told him he was weak, and he wanted to prove them wrong."

"I remember the news stories. It's all anyone talked about for months," he said, crossing his legs.

"Yeah. I could've prevented it if I'd known what I was looking at. And knew what to do about it. But things were different back then."

"So, you feel responsible for the deaths of those people."

"Because I didn't see it. Yeah." I nodded. "There's something called the MacDonald Triad. It started back in the 1960s and a lot of people say it's bullshit, just people looking to explain the unexplainable. But it has three signs that they say allude to an increased risk of someone becoming a serial killer. A fascination with fire, bedwetting past the age of five, and excessive cruelty to animals."

"It sounds familiar. One of the officers around here might've mentioned it."

"This kid—who I sat right next to—exhibited two out of the three, a fascination with fire and cruelty to animals. He might've wet the bed too, but he wouldn't have talked about it if he did. If I had seen it, I could've done something. Maybe people wouldn't have had to die."

"What could you have done?" he asked.

"I don't know. Maybe told him things would be okay. Urged him to get help. Back then, there wasn't a playbook for it, but anything would've been better than nothing. But people died because I didn't see him. And I'll never know if I could've made any difference."

"Is that why you're so protective, now?"

"I think. Yeah," I said.

"So, what brought on this story?"

"Randal Jablonski." I shifted in my chair. "The pyromaniac I was assigned to, before."

"The same one you were suspended for decking," Dr. Striker said.

"Right. With these recent murders, I was looking for him. Psychopathic and terrible. Well—'him'—anyway. I wanted it to be someone completely despicable so I could feel justified in my righteous hatred for them. But I got Clara Heartwell. I didn't see her, and people died."

"Eventually you did," he said. "And you prevented more deaths."

"I guess."

"So, did she change the timeline?"

"What do you mean?"

"Clara," he said. "That sounded pretty dramatic when she took her helmet off. Her parents were probably traumatized. You'd think they'd have done something differently and changed the sequence of events."

"I have no idea how I could tell. Chetna says that—"

"Wait, who's Chetna?" Dr. Striker raised his eyebrows.

"Sorry, I mean Dr. Khatri. She says that—"

"You're on a first-name basis with her, now?" His eyebrows remained raised.

"Oh, don't start."

"I'm not starting anything. I just think it's interesting, is all." He reached over to the coffee on his table and took another sip. "Don't let me interrupt," he said with no shortage of eagerness and a slight grin. "What did Chetna say?"

"She said nosey psychiatrists should watch where they step."

He smirked at me.

"Actually, she said something about a different timeline splitting off at the quantum level and yadda, yadda, abraca-science. I didn't really pick up the rest. But it meant no."

He snorted a laugh. "Good to know the fabric of reality is safe." He took another drink of coffee. "So, you solved the case and brought a murderer to justice. And now you're on a first-name basis with Dr. Khatri. That sounds like a win, to me."

I shook my head. "It doesn't feel like it. I still lost a friend. Clara is gone." I grabbed my cane from the side of my chair and pulled myself up.

"Do you need some help?" He started to get up.

I put up a hand, "I'm fine. The doctor said I have to learn to do this, myself." Clara had kicked me pretty hard, back in the past. My knee was nothing but a pile of Legos, rubbing against each other as I stood up. Even with the leg brace, it hurt. A lot.

"Will it heal?"

I shrugged. "The doctor expects it to. Eventually. But he also said I'll never be in the Olympics. Now my dreams are shattered." I finished standing up and collected myself.

"How long is eventually?" he asked, sounding like he didn't really want the answer.

"They expect me to need the cane for the next year or so."

"Ouch."

"I said the same thing."

Dr. Striker chortled. "Well, let me get the door for you, at least. You make me feel bad, hobbling around like that."

I smiled and gestured to the door. He opened it and stood like the doorman at a fancy hotel.

"Oh, one more thing. How was Clara so strong? You said she knocked you around pretty good."

"The robotics department at USF reported their prototype exoskeleton missing," I answered in my matter-of-fact detective voice.

His eyebrows raised, again. And as I stepped to the threshold, he asked, "If we are living in an alternate timeline, could Clara be alive, somewhere?"

I shrugged. "I don't know. Maybe. If she is, I hope she's doing better than the other one. I'll see you around." I nodded to him and walked out.

As he shut the door behind me, Dr. Khatri—I mean Chetna—stood up from her waiting room chair. She came to her full height and straightened the blue and white striped sundress that showed off her shoulders and hugged her hips just right. And she flashed me a bright toothy smile that made me smile back.

She brushed some of her short salt and pepper hair behind her ear. "I thought you would be in there, forever. Were you boys smoking cigars and doing other men things?" she asked with an endearingly facetious tone.

I chuckled as I hobbled with my cane to the glass door at the entrance. "Yep. That's what all men do when women aren't looking. We swear a lot, too."

Chetna stepped outside and held the door open while I tried to get my crippled self through it. Negotiating the lip was more effort than I wanted it to be. It was maybe a foot drop between the door and the sidewalk. It doesn't sound like much, but I couldn't just walk out with my knee in the condition that it was in. I had to do a sort of sideways crabwalk to get out. She only laughed a little.

"Come on, old man. We're going to be late for the movie. You promised to take me to this one."

"Isn't it like, *Terminator 15* or something?"

"No," she said, laughing.

"I'm sure it's just like the other fourteen. How old is Arnold Schwarzenegger getting, anyway?"

"Stop." She backhand-slapped me on my bad shoulder.

I yelped.

"Oh my god, I'm so sorry," she said.

"Me too."

She tried rubbing it with her thin, cool hands. The wind caught her hair and short locks blew across her forehead. A little of her honeysuckle perfume wafted my way.

"I'll be alright." I took her hand in mine, removed it from my shoulder, and stepped onto the sidewalk with her. The sun covered me like a blanket, warm and bright. I kept her hand as we walked to the car. She didn't seem to mind.

"Come on or we won't have time to get any snacks before it starts," she said.

"You're really bossy for a temporal physicist."

"Yes. I am. Now let's go. We're late."

"Nah, we have time," I said. "We have all the time in the world."

She smiled, gripped my hand tight, and rested her head on my shoulder. "That was really corny. And we're still going to be late."

"Yeah, I know."

"Hey, did you ever call that girl back to tell her you have her purse?"

"Ah, dammit!"

J.S. Johnston

I hope you've enjoyed my musings. It would mean the world to me if you would leave an honest review on Amazon and Goodreads. Your feedback will help me write better books.

Leave me a review on Amazon and browse my other books:

www.amazon.com/stores/J.S.-Johnston/author/B094Q66GKH

Visit my website to sign up for my newsletter and follow me on social media:

www.jsjohnstonauthor.com

About the
Author

Photo © 2024

J.S. Johnston has been writing books since he was nine years old. His first was about Pacman and his friends, written in pen and ink on notebook paper and bound with yarn. He took it to every house in his neighborhood in the Ohio suburbs, but no one bought a single copy. Born and raised on Star Trek, he put a lot of its wonder and exploration in his writings. Now, you can find him still writing from his home in Tampa, Florida. (But his sales are better)

www.ingramcontent.com/pod-product-compliance
Lightning Source LLC
Chambersburg PA
CBHW072117300726
48975CB00003B/842